BREAK YOUR PUCKING HEART

USA TODAY BESTSELLING AUTHOR

RACHEL LEIGH

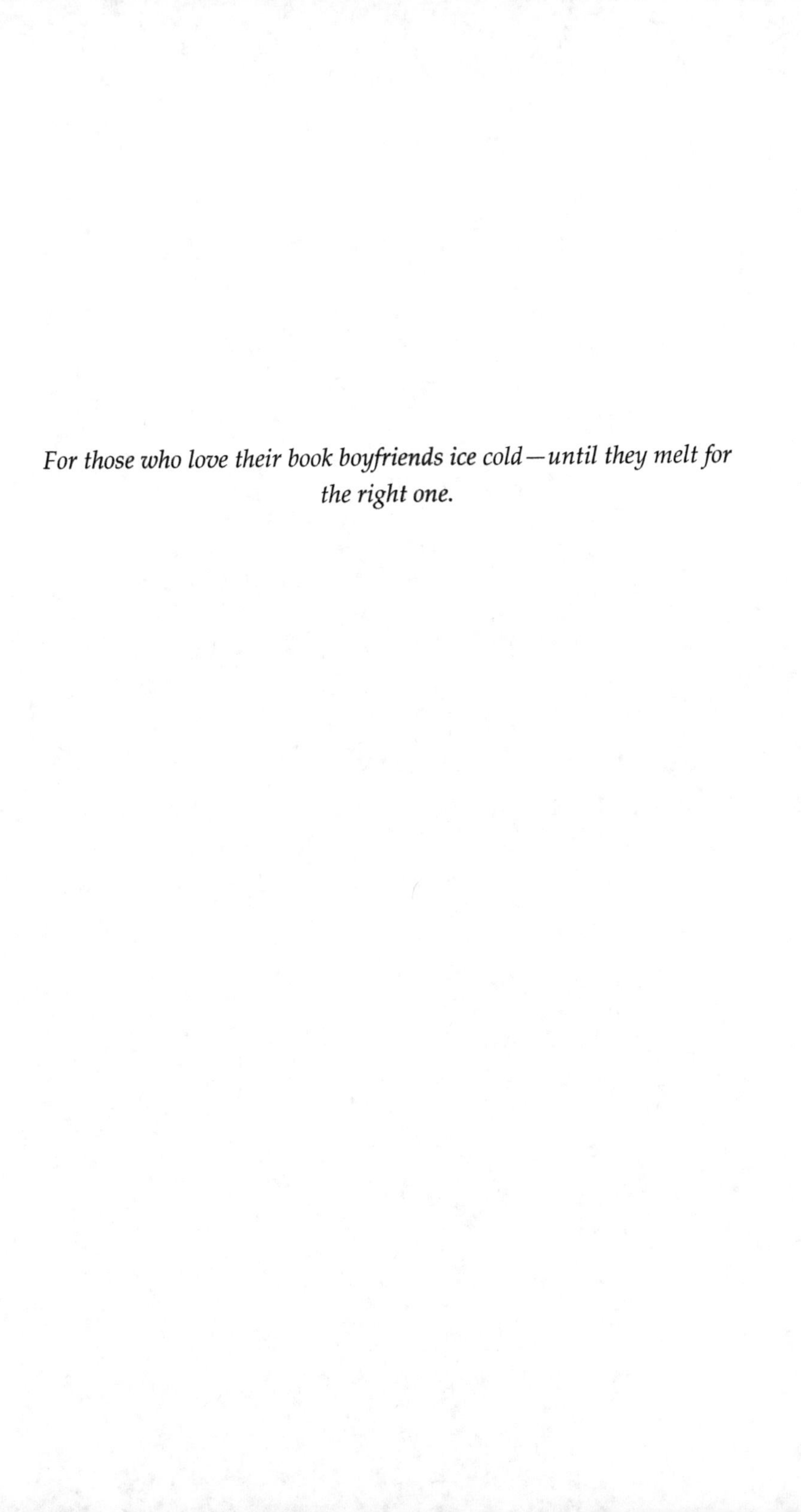

For those who love their book boyfriends ice cold—until they melt for the right one.

DEAR READER

BLURB

Break Your Pucking Heart **is an Enemies to Lovers, Why-Choose, Dark, College Hockey Romance.**

I've been captured by the Ice Lords, and I fear they'll never let me go.

What was supposed to be a fun night out at a hockey game is derailed when I accidentally find myself in the rival team's locker room.

Not only do I get an eye full of chiseled bodies, but I also overhear a secret that could destroy the reputation, and future, of every player on the team.

Before I can decide whether I should run or hide, the choice is quickly made for me when a pair of piercing green eyes meet mine.

Callan Cromwell—the brooding center of the Lords hockey team. Not only did I steal his virginity in high school, I shattered his heart when I insisted we never tell a soul.

To make matters worse, he's my best friend's brother.

As soon as the leader of Callan's pack discovers I'm onto their sinister plan, he makes a vow to ensure my silence. At *my* expense.

Now I'm caught in a web of secrets and my only chance of surviving is to do exactly what they say. What *he* says.

As I'm swept deeper into their savage world of power plays and fierce loyalty, I begin to realize that in this dangerous game—at the mercy of these men—I just might be the biggest casualty of them all.

PLAYLIST
CLICK HERE TO LISTEN
https://spoti.fi/3ThJtbr
Torn in Two by Breaking Benjamin
Hear Me Now by Bad Wolves
Limits by Bad Omens
Far Behind by Candlebox
How I'm Feeling Now by Lewis Capaldi
At The Risk Of Feeling Dumb by Twenty One Pilots
Wildflower by Billie Eilish
Nightmare by From Ashes To New
The Worst In Me by Bad Omens
Killing Me Slowly by Bad Wolves
I Can't Carry This Anymore by Anson Seabra
Throne by Bring Me The Horizon
Shame On Me by Catch Your Breath
Voices In My Head by Falling In Reverse
Words as Weapons by Seether
You Don't Know by Katelyn Tarver
Alone In A Room by Asking Alexandria
Echo by Trapt
Risk by Gracie Abrams
Push by Matchbox Twenty
So Good by Halsey
I Miss the Misery by Halestorm
Glass Heart by Caskets
Favorite Crime by Olivia Rodrigo
Without Me by Wind Walkers
Live Before I'm Dead by From Ashes To New
CHECK OUT THE: PINTEREST BOARD
https://pin.it/4H2EXO2u4

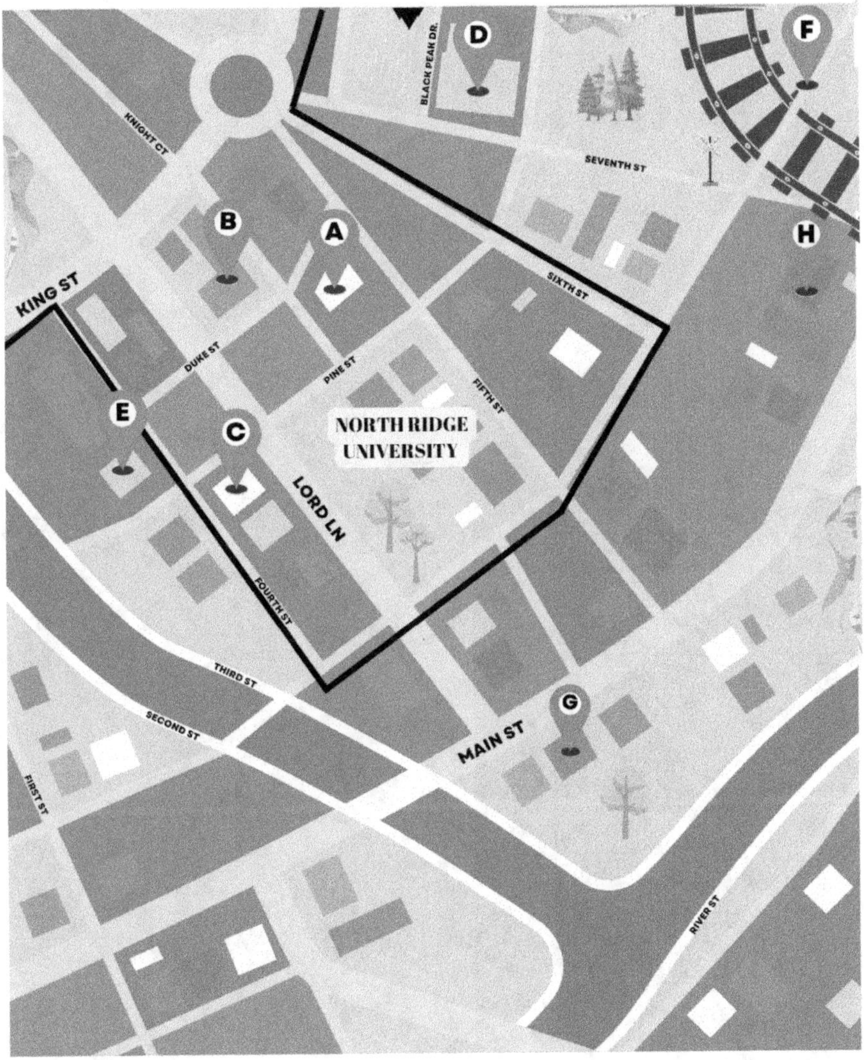

ICE LORDS

D
F
H
BLACK PEAK DR.
SEVENTH ST
KNIGHT CT
B
A
SIXTH ST
KING ST
DUKE ST
PINE ST
FIFTH ST
E
C
NORTH RIDGE UNIVERSITY
LORD LN
FOURTH ST
THIRD ST
SECOND ST
G
FIRST ST
MAIN ST
RIVER ST

A library
B fifth street student center
C athletic center
D hockey house

E e. einhorn arena
F rosewood-u campus
G hospital
H faraway archery range

PROLOGUE

CALLAN

BLOOD. *So much fucking blood.* It wasn't supposed to be like this. I wasn't supposed to enjoy this depraved shit. *But I do.* I crave the looks on the faces of all those who betray us. I'm thirsty for their pain.

What began in the late 1940s as a quest to win national titles has cultivated into a schism of tasks, pledges, and belonging. Our society is comprised of various chapters around the nation that sit under the umbrella of an organization that very few know the whole truth about. We are Ice Lords, and this is our way.

Within the chamber that rests beneath our living quarters, respect is not optional, it's earned and upheld. This is a room of honor, carved by the very first of our legacy, Edison Einhorn, and crafted into something of ominous beauty. In this room we bow to those chosen to guide our paths.

Authority belongs to those of rank:

Our leader—Aidric. Silence is his method of control, his presence alone commands obedience. He doesn't speak, and he doesn't have to.

The council advisor—formerly Julian. A mentor, a confidant, the bridge between leadership and the members. His role is to guide, to counsel, to ensure The Society's foundations remain unshaken.

And then there's our revered Ice Lord speaker—Sebastian. Aidric's left hand, his voice, his enforcer. Sebastian speaks where Aidric remains silent, delivering orders with authority.

Each holds power. Each plays their role. And in The Chamber, their word is absolute.

However, upstairs, all bets are off. In the hockey house, The Society doesn't exist. We don't speak of it, don't acknowledge it. We're just a band of brothers playing the sport we love.

With that comes the usual grapples, trash talk, the occasional bruised ego. In layman's terms, we give each other shit, and we do it well.

Julian, our *former* council advisor, thought he could double-cross us. Thought he could whisper our society's deepest secrets to our biggest rival and walk away unscathed.

Now, he gets to endure our wrath.

Suspended above the altar with his wrists shackled, chains groan under Julian's weight. The dim light overhead flickers, casting jagged shadows across his battered body. He's the star of this grim spectacle, a traitor laid bare for judgment.

A brother steps forward, the heavy rustle of his ceremonial cloak the only sound before the next strike lands. A sickening thud resounds as Julian's body jerks. He gasps, breaths ragged as the chains rattle in protest.

Another blow. Then another. Each one delivered with precision. Each one a lesson.

Our Lord speaker, Sebastian, sweeps his gaze over the remainder of us, his eyes glinting with something feral behind the symbolic hockey mask we all wear for our ceremonies. A silent reminder that this isn't just a game. *This is who we are.*

He lifts a hand, his voice a guttural roar. "Mark him. Feed him your pain. An eye for an eye! Show him what happens when you betray an Ice Lord!"

His command electrifies the room. One of our seasoned

members, Emmett, presses a branding iron to Julian's chest, leaving a blistering red X in its wake. The screams of the traitor reverberate off the walls around us. But beyond down here, no one will hear him. The Chamber is impenetrable, our fortress well-guarded. Only those granted an invitation may enter, but not all leave with their limbs still attached to their bodies.

The next brother steps forward, gripping a leather whip. A sharp crack splits the air as it lashes against Julian's flesh, leaving angry welts in its wake.

Slade goes for a handful of salt, rubbing it into the fresh wounds, drawing out a screeching howl from Julian. Just when we think he's finished, he unbuttons his pants and drops them to his ankles. Without hesitation, he aims a stream of piss at the traitor.

The room fills with a mixture of laughter and gasps, but I smile under my mask, always impressed with my friends' unique forms of torture. And trust me, he has many.

As Slade walks away, pulling his pants up, I move to the altar. Opting for the greatest weapon I've been blessed with—my hands. I grip Julian's chin and lift his head, so that I can peer into his regretful eyes. "You don't fuck with my family without consequences."

Fist clenched tightly, I feel my bones shift under the skin when I drive them into his bruised and swollen cheek. Each blow vibrates down my arm and into my chest, where a sick satisfaction builds within me. As my knuckles connect with his flesh, it reminds me of the power I was promised when I came here, and the severity of what betraying that power will cost me. Julian's face twists in pain, a low groan escaping his lips as I continue to strike him.

I have lived my life as a ghost in my family, always cast to the side and easily forgotten. It wasn't until I ended up in rehab that a member of The Ice Society said I have potential. He spoke of a brotherhood that breeds loyalty and comradery. It was then that I knew I wanted more. I craved to be a part of something worth fighting for, and this society is worth every bloodied fist.

This is my calling. These are my people. *That is my family.*

"Save some of him for the rest of us," the guy behind me shouts from below the altar.

I step back with an unhinged smile on my face, blood dripping from my hands as I gesture toward the man who thought he could get away with stabbing us in the back. "All yours, brother."

By the time we've all had our turn at Julian, I'm surprised he's still alive. His body is a crimson canvas. From his face, a mask of purple and blue, to his eyes that are barely visible through all the puffiness. Blood trickles from head to toe, mingling with the grime covering him. Deep cuts crisscross over his skin that sit by patches of raw, blistered flesh from the burns he endured.

"Let this be a warning," Sebastian says sternly while pointing at Julian. "Our secrets are in place for a reason. Not only did Julian endure the wrath of the Ice Lords, but he's also been expelled from North Ridge University. We're family in this society, and I'd hate to see any of you share Julian's fate."

What we just did was brutal but necessary. It's a lesson for all of us. I, personally, never intend to be in his position. Not only would my future as a hockey player cease to exist, but I would lose all of this. My family—my brotherhood. I look around The Chamber, taking in the scene before me like food for my soul. Each man-made mark on the brick stone that surrounds The Chamber leaves me captivated. Every intricate design in the structure that keeps the house above us afloat has me curious about the history of this house and the legacy of the Ice Lords.

Aidric, our leader, unclasps the cuffs on Julian's wrists and he drops like a sack of potatoes. The sound of bone meeting cement reverberates through the room.

With a tip of his chin, he calls over two of our newest members. I watch as they grab Julian by the ankles and drag him across the cold pavement, retreating into the shadows in the dimly lit room to the heavy metal door that leads to the catacombs. It groans on its hinges as it opens.

I lean forward, peering down the dark entrance. Cold air rushes out and a chill runs down my spine as the scent of death seems to seep out from the unlit room.

When they brought Julian out of the catacombs and up to the altar, he was only wearing a pair of boxers. He looked like he'd been dragged through hell and back already. His face was caked with mud and filth, and his hair was slick with dampness.

This explains why he hasn't been at practices this week. I knew something was up, but I never would have guessed the reason behind his absence.

As we're preparing to go upstairs where our living quarters are, I'm halted by the gruff call of my name.

"Cromwell." Sebastian's voice cuts through the bustle of shuffling footsteps. "A word."

I suck in a deep breath, preparing myself for whatever comes next. Being part of this society has its perks, but the tasks they ask of us can be brutal. I'll do it, though; I'll do anything for this brotherhood.

Long strides lead me to him and I refuse to so much as flinch when he lifts the X-shaped branding iron Julian was stamped with. He rubs a wet cloth over it, creating a puff of white steam before wiping it clean. With his mask pushed up on his head like a makeshift hat, his eyebrows cut low, creasing his forehead as he and Aidric assess me. Likely searching for any sign of trepidation, which they will not find.

"We have a job for you," Sebastian says, tone stoic.

"A job?" I question, standing taller.

He nods. "Assuming you're willing to prove you're the man we think you are." Aidric pats a strong hand down on my shoulder.

"Tell me what you need me to do, and consider it done," I say without a bite of hesitation. I rub my bloody fists together, ready for something new. I can do this. *Where there is a Lord, there is power. And I am a Lord.*

"Now that Julian is gone, we need to fill his position." Sebastian looks at Aidric, tilting his head toward me as they engage in a silent conversation. All the while, my heart is ready to flee my damn chest.

I've been chosen?

A mix of emotions ripples through me—uncertainty, unease—but more than anything, I'm fucking elated.

Sebastian's gaze saunters back to mine. "I must warn you, the position comes with a hefty price tag. You'll never be the same again."

The logical part of my brain tells me to turn it down, but the fucked-up part of it speaks for me. For the first time in my life, *I've* been chosen. "I'm in."

I don't even need to think twice. I'm. Fucking. In.

Sebastian's mouth draws up in a wide grin. "Wonderful. Your instructions will be delivered shortly. Until then, I suggest you mentally prepare. You'll soon learn what it feels like to lose who you are, before rebuilding yourself into someone better—someone *powerful.*"

Aidric tips his head at me, a devious glint in his eye. They walk toward the stairs and I take a look around the empty space. A rush of courage floods through me as I stand down here in The Chamber, alone in the silence. There is strength in this room, a humming energy that draws me in. It's as if our ancestors are calling out to me, encouraging me forward on this path. I take it all in. This is the only place I've ever been accepted. This is where I belong. This is my calling.

Whatever comes next, I'm ready. I'm an Ice Lord, and it'll be my honor to serve our members.

CHAPTER 1
THREE MONTHS LATER

AVERY

THE CLOCK WINDS DOWN. One minute left, and the Devils are trailing by two. The odds aren't great, but truth be told, I don't really care. Yeah, it's my school's team, and yeah, I should probably want them to win, but hockey isn't exactly my thing.

I only come to these games for Brogan—my best friend, my roommate, my ride or die since high school. When she asks me to freeze my ass off in an arena while a bunch of dudes chase an Oreo across the ice, I show up. Not because I care about the game, but because I care about her, and she loves this shit. The energy, the fights, the sheer brutality of it all. Sure, she's here to watch her boyfriend, Hayes, but let's be real, Brogan lives for the violence.

Not me, though. Give me a compound bow, an arrow, and a target in the middle of nowhere. That's where I find my thrill.

Archery was never supposed to be more than a box to check. It was an elective I picked up my freshman year that unexpectedly sank its hooks into me. Now, I'm a member of a collegiate club, slinging arrows like I belong there.

All that to say, I stumbled upon something I like to do with my free time that doesn't involve swiping a credit card. In doing so, I've mastered a weapon with sharp edges that would bring anyone to their knees if I wanted it to.

I'm pretty damn good at it, too. In fact, I took second place in the women's compound competition last semester, and at the end of this month, I plan to take first.

Brogan jumps to her feet, eyes pinned to the brute force unfolding on the ice. "Come on, Hayes," she hollers as her boyfriend drives the puck toward the net. He swings and shoots, sending it straight to the Lords' goalie who blocks it and sends it right back.

Damn. That was embarrassing.

Hayes is a damn good center, but the Devils are down a man tonight. One of our second-string centers, Evan, had a brutal accident two nights ago that left him in the hospital, fighting for his life. Before the game, they announced they were playing in his honor.

I know Evan. Maybe not as well as I once did, but well enough for my heart to ache for him and his family.

I'm not a hockey fan, but back in freshman year, I actually enjoyed watching Evan play. Feels like a lifetime ago, though it's only been two years. We weren't exactly dating, but we were talking.

That's a lie. We didn't talk—we fucked, and I showed up to his games. Evan wanted more, but I had nothing else to give. I have nothing to give *anyone*. On the outside, I'm polished and put together. On the inside? I'm fractured beyond repair. That's why I keep my heart locked up. Vulnerability feels more like a death sentence than a connection, so when Evan reached for more, I pulled away.

A win in his honor would be cool, but the Lords seem hell-bent on making sure that doesn't happen.

As if the stakes weren't high enough, Brogan's caught in the middle of this war. Her stepbrother, Callan, plays for the opposing team. The Lords and the Devils have been bitter rivals for years. Only thirteen miles and a railroad track separate our two campuses, but on the ice, it might as well be a battlefield.

I actually considered North Ridge University at one point because of their reputable psychiatry program. But when Brogan committed to Rosewood University to cheer for their football team, I followed.

Suddenly, one of the Lords' players slams into Hayes, driving him hard into the glass barrier right in front of us. The boards rattle, the impact echoing through the arena.

Brogan shoots to her feet, hands flying. "What the hell, Callan!"

Damn. Her brother just leveled her boyfriend.

Callan is an asshole. I'd never say that to Brogan's face because she coddles the fuck out of him, but it's the truth.

At one point, I thought he might be different from the usual jock stereotype. Back in high school, he was a ghost, always lingering on the outskirts. Smart. Athletic. Silent. He never said much, never showed much either. At first, I figured he was just shy. But then, little by little, his walls started to crack. Piece by piece, he let me in.

I'd bump into him in the hallway at Brogan's house, half asleep in my pajamas, and he'd poke my side, smirk, toss out some offhanded comment about how I didn't need makeup because I was naturally beautiful. The kind of thing any girl would kill to hear from someone as devilishly sexy as Callan Cromwell.

Then everything changed.

After one too many bottles of hard lemonade, I took a walk down the hall with him into his room. Before I could talk myself out of it, we were having sex. The second it was over, regret sank its claws into me. He was my best friend's brother. Stepbrother, technically, but Brogan loves him like he's blood. I couldn't do that to her. Not when I knew it would end with me walking away.

Callan and I agreed it could never happen again and that nothing between us would change.

But everything changed.

The easy hallway flirtation twisted into sharp-edged insults and lingering glares. He got weird. Then, just like that, I became the most despicable person on the planet in his eyes.

He fell in with the wrong crowd. His grades tanked. Trouble followed him like a damn shadow. He was breaking and entering into houses and getting in fights. There was even a grand theft auto charge that miraculously disappeared.

I went out of my way to avoid him, knowing full well he'd jump at any chance to cut me down. He became my own personal bully, a constant reminder of the mistake I wished I could erase. If I could go back and un-fuck him, I would.

I told him that once when he cornered me. It didn't end well.

I went home that weekend, told Brogan I was sick, and locked myself in my room to cry. To this day, I have no idea how he found out about one of my most carefully guarded secrets, but he did. And the following week, he spiraled into drugs and drinking. Before long, he was someone I no longer recognized.

Callan's dad forced him into rehab his senior year of high school. He might have cleaned up, but let's be real, Callan Cromwell is anything but saved.

I never told Brogan, and I never will. She'd spin a hundred and one excuses for him, each one more desperate than the last. But none of them explain how someone's heart can turn so completely ice cold.

Yes, he lost his mom before his dad married Brogan's mom. But so did his brothers, and they don't walk around acting like everyone is indebted to them.

Just as Callan lets up on Hayes, giving him an out from where he's pinned, his eyes lock on to mine. A wave of unease rolls through me.

He looks away, but only for a second before his gaze snaps back, darker this time.

My brows knit together, head tilting slightly as I try to decipher whatever storm is brewing behind his sultry green eyes. But his scowl only deepens, like he's daring me to look away first.

I get it, our team is his rival, and we had a meaningless one-night stand years ago, but I'm still his sister's best friend. A little respect wouldn't kill him.

As fast as his glare landed on me, he snaps his focus back to the game, controlling the puck with calculated precision. But before he sends it soaring across the ice, he looks at me one last time, dead in the eye.

Brogan blows out a sharp breath as she sits back down. "He's such a little shit."

"He's more than that," I grumble, while holding back any elaboration.

I've made up my mind about her brother. Not only because of the way he treats me, but also because of all the shady shit he did when he had his asshole awakening in rehab. Brogan has no clue that he once threatened to spill my secret if I didn't play nice —partly because she doesn't know my secret. So I've learned to keep my mouth shut when it comes to him.

She insists he's doing better, that hockey has given him purpose. But the look in his eyes just now? That wasn't the gaze of a reformed man. That was something darker. Something far from the saint she believes he is.

Four seconds left…and we lose. *Damn.* I can practically hear the sarcasm dripping from my own thoughts.

Brogan groans, dragging a hand down her face before perking up and adjusting her ponytail like she didn't just spend the last minute sulking. "That was depressing, but at least Callan's team won. Ready to get out of here?"

I slap the arms of my seat and push myself up. "I thought you'd never ask. I need to pee."

Brogan slings her purse across her chest, slipping her phone into the front pocket. "I'm gonna try to catch Callan before he leaves so I can see how he's been. I know he was struggling during preseason." She shifts on her feet. "Meet me by the guest locker room when you're done?"

I sigh, but only after she turns away. If I never had to talk to her brother again, it'd still be too soon.

We weave through the maze of seats, and at the top of the stands, we split up. Brogan heads left and I go in the opposite direction toward the glowing blue sign above the restrooms.

CHAPTER 2

AVERY

I wash my hands and look up at my reflection, my honey brown eyes staring back at me. Dragging the tip of my peach-colored, almond-shaped nail down the center of my hairline, I set my middle part just right. My wavy curls fall, framing my face, and I smack my glossy lips together.

Maybe if I take my time in here, I won't have to talk to Callan at all. I adjust my jeans and fluff my shirt, just keeping busy before staring at myself again, trying not to think about my purpose in life. It's depressing to feel like I'm going nowhere, but part of me isn't ready to let go of my past.

Shaking that thought off, I carefully reconstruct my smile and head out in search of the opposing team's locker room. Now that I think about it, I have no idea where it is.

I scan the space, searching for another glowing sign like the one above the restrooms. This place is massive. *Too massive*. Every hallway looks the same, stretching endlessly in every direction.

Before I know it, I've covered at least a quarter mile, and the damn locker room is still nowhere in sight.

Just as frustration takes root, it vanishes when I spot a group of guys in Lords jerseys stepping out of a door to the left. *About damn time.*

I scour the area, searching for Brogan, but I don't see her anywhere. With a sigh, I pull my phone out of my purse, hoping for a message from her. The screen lights up, but the only notification is a two-day-old text message from my dad.

I round the corner, pacing down the hall as my mind runs through possibilities. Maybe she already left. Maybe she's *in* the locker room.

I check my phone again. Still nothing.

She has to be inside.

A thought strikes me as I backtrack to the locker room entrance—what if the guys are naked in there?

Oooh—what *if* the guys are naked in there?

Well, aside from Callan. Been there, fucked that.

Okay, fine. Seeing Callan naked wouldn't be the worst thing in the world. The guy is a menace; his ego could use a good beating, and his attitude makes me want to throw punches, but damn he's hot.

That dark brown hair, always unkempt like he just rolled out of bed and let the wind style it. Those green—almost teal—eyes, eerily close to the Lords' team colors. Not that I've noticed. And I sure as hell wouldn't admit it. He'd take the compliments and twist them into something he can use as a weapon against me.

Throwing caution to the wind, I crack open the door and peek inside.

A narrow, dimly lit hall stretches ahead, leading to a brick wall that curves around an open entryway.

My gut twists with nerves as I ease the door shut behind me, careful not to make a sound. Moving like a mouse, I creep toward the brick entryway, pressing my back against the wall before peeking around the corner.

"Brogan," I whisper-yell. "Are you in there?"

Silence.

Frowning, I pull out my phone and call her. Straight to voicemail. *Great.* Either her signal is shit, or she's ignoring me.

I slip my phone back into my purse, my mind spinning. Do I wait? Do I leave? Or do I take my chances and go in?

Distant voices ring in my ears, which I take to be a good sign. At least, that's what I tell myself as I step farther inside, hoping to hear Brogan.

Dammit. Why couldn't she just wait and call Callan when we got to the bar? A blackberry mojito sounds a hell of a lot better than sneaking around a locker room full of our rival team's players.

After every home game, the team heads to Legends, a local sports bar. Since Brogan's dating one of the star players, she and I usually tag along, blending into the crowd of puck bunnies who fight for the players' attention.

I move in closer, tuning in to the voices drifting through the space. There's a mix of gruff, but low murmurs. None of which belong to Brogan.

Regardless, I need to find Callan and figure out where Brogan is. I'm exhausted, starving, and more than ready to leave this damn arena. He's the last person I want to deal with, but it seems I don't have a choice.

I round the next corner, but immediately step back, pressing myself against the wall. Four guys stand in a tight circle, their voices hushed but stern. Tension crackles between them and whatever they're discussing seems serious.

They're probably giving each other shit over a bad play. You'd think they'd be a little more cheerful after their big win.

But damnnnn. The Lords look good.

One is sweat-slicked, still in uniform. Another stands in nothing but black briefs that cling to his scrumptious thighs. I'm forced to press mine together just from looking at him. The last two are fully dressed with their backs to me. All of them are the full package with broad shoulders and raw strength.

They huddle close and the air around them is heavy with something I can't quite place. Then, I see him.

Callan.

For a split second, relief washes over me. That is until I notice his hard, serious expression. I've been acquainted with that look more times than I can count. At least this time it's not directed at me.

I tuck back around the wall a little bit, hiding my body while keeping my gaze set on him.

"I want out," I hear the guy in uniform say in a low, but gravelly tone. "I didn't sign up for murder."

A sharp gasp escapes me before I can stop it, and I slap a hand over my mouth. *Murder?* No. I must have misheard. This is a college hockey team, not the damn mafia.

"Fuck the pledge," the guy mutters, his voice tight with panic. "I'll quit the team. I'll give up my seat as an Ice Lord."

Seat? What seat? And since when did players have to pledge?

"That's not an option," the sexy underwear guy, with jet-black hair and the bluest eyes I have ever seen in my life, says sternly. I'm ashamed of myself for even noticing how mysteriously gorgeous he is at a time like this.

"You knew the stakes," he grinds out. "You're one of us now. But this is not the time or the place. A meeting will be arranged later today in The Chamber."

The Chamber? Jesus. The NHA doesn't mess around when it comes to securing players.

I've heard enough. I need to get the hell out of here. *Now!*

"Go lock the door," Underwear Guy snaps.

My heart plummets straight to my gut.

Think fast, Avery.

My gaze darts around the room, searching for somewhere to hide. My only option is a locker within arm's reach. No door, so it's not ideal, but it's better than standing here in plain sight.

As the footsteps close in, I lunge forward, taking two long

strides before diving into the locker. My head smacks against a coat hook with a dull thud and I bite back a curse.

Crouching, I press myself into the shadows. my breaths are shallow, and my pulse is racing so hard I can hear it echoing in my ears. I rub the sore spot on my head, but the sting is a small sacrifice I'm willing to make, considering I'm trapped in a room with four men much larger than me who are talking about murder. It really isn't on my bingo card to die this year.

My mind races as I struggle to process what I just overheard. Maybe they're talking about a video game. *Yeah, right. Who am I kidding thinking I'm lucky enough to not be in deep shit right now?*

I have a bad feeling that the Lords' hockey team is up to something…something dark. And to my absolute horror, I think I've just stumbled upon information I was never meant to know.

Callan steps into view, and I drop my chin, squeezing my eyes shut. I can't bear to see the look on his face when he realizes I'm here.

Seconds seem like an eternity. Then, footsteps move past me.

I crack my eyes open just enough to catch the faintest blur of his silhouette disappearing from view. A slow, measured breath slips from my lips, my chest finally deflating. *I think I'm safe.*

"I can't do it," I hear the fearful, timid guy say. "I won't do it." His tone is firm, but the quiver beneath his words betrays him. He's fucking terrified. And that same terror races through my veins knowing I'm stuck here.

What could they possibly be forcing him into? And why do the other three hold so much power over him?

My entire body trembles, every nerve on edge as I inch forward, just enough to peek around the corner. The guys stand, oblivious to my presence, their attention locked on their prey. I know I'm playing a dangerous game, but I can't look away. I have to know what they're making him do.

Underwear Guy leans in, his jaw tight, fingers twisting into the fabric of the other guy's jersey as he yanks him close. His voice is almost lethal. "You can, and you will. Need I remind you of the consequences for failure? If Evan Sanders comes to, it's all of our asses on the line. You will take care of him."

A chill slithers down my spine. My stomach churns. *Did I hear that right?* Are they responsible for Evan's fall from the mountain?

I've heard enough. I should've run the second murder entered the conversation. This isn't just a power play. It's a cover-up. And if they ever find out I was here, that I heard this. *No!* I won't even think about what might happen.

Suddenly, the room goes dead silent. I swallow hard and it's as if the sound echoes across the room, making my fear triple and my adrenaline sky rocket. It feels like I can't breathe. My mind races, but every escape route feels like a gamble.

These are the kinds of conversations no one wants to overhear because once they do, there's no undoing it.

Just step out of this locker, tiptoe to the door, unlock it, and run like hell.

This never happened. You heard nothing.

But I did.

I heard Brogan's brother talking about murder, and a chamber. Callan changed after his father forced him into rehab. He pulled away from everyone except Brogan, but this? This is something worse. Even for him.

I don't know who those words were meant for, but it doesn't matter. Someone on the Lords' team is responsible for what happened to Evan. I'm certain of it.

My pulse pounds out a frantic tempo, loud enough that I swear they'll hear it if I don't get out of here.

Run. Move. Do something.

But I'm frozen—replaying their conversation like a scene ripped straight from a horror movie.

Then, my phone buzzes.

Oh shit.

It's on vibrate, but wedged against the wall inside this coffin of a locker, the sound might as well be a gunshot.

Panic surges through me as I fumble with my purse, hands trembling so violently I can't grasp the zipper.

The next thing I know, Callan's eyes are meeting mine. My heart slams into my throat. Wide-eyed, I shake my head with a firm finger pressed against my lips.

For a split second, I think Callan might let this slide. Then he crushes that hope beneath his boot. With a small lazy nod, he nudges Underwear Guy and jerks his chin in my direction.

Shit.

I cower deeper into the locker like it'll somehow swallow me whole and make me disappear. But it's useless. I can't run. And now, I can't even hide.

"Get him out of here. We'll deal with him later." Underwear Guy barks the order at one of his teammates. A tall, muscular-framed guy with sandy brown hair grabs hold of the one they were arguing with and drags him down a row of lockers until they disappear from sight.

Underwear Guy crosses the room in three long strides, his hand latching onto my arm in a bruising grip. With one yank, I'm out of the locker like a discarded rag doll.

"Who the fuck are you?" His voice is sharp, edged with suspicion.

"I...I, um—" My mouth is dry, words scrambling over themselves. I shoot my thumb toward the door. "I was just leaving."

His eyes darken, his grip tightening. "Not so fast." He leans in, voice low but lethal. "How long have you been here?"

"Not...not long."

Terror coils around my lungs, squeezing until I can't breathe. *Oh my God. I can't fucking breathe.*

Every inhale sticks to my throat, unable to make it to my lungs.

"*What* did you hear?" he asks sharply.

He's closer now. Closer than I can handle. The scent of sweat and cedar rolls off him, mingling with the heat of his body pressing against me like a second skin. I lift my chin, trapped by his angry gaze.

"Answer me!" he grits out. I flinch at the bite in his voice, instinctively jerking back, only for his fingers to snap around my wrist like a vise. "What. Did. You. Hear." He says each word like it's its own sentence, forcing me to process them one by one, even as my mind scrambles for an escape.

I whip my gaze to Callan, silently begging him. But he's already sold me out. There's no saving grace here. No lifeline.

Callan averts his gaze and I'm not surprised. A little disappointed, maybe, but not surprised.

Their other teammate returns, a bottle of water in his hand. He takes a seat on one of the benches, watching as the situation unfolds.

I suck in a breath, forcing the air deep into my lungs. I can't let any of them see my fear. They'll feed off it—twist it and use it against me, just like Callan would do when he knew he could hurt me.

These guys don't know what I heard. For all they know, I just walked in.

So I steel my voice and meet Underwear Guy's glare head-on. "Let. Me. Go."

His grip tightens, fingers biting into my arm as his hot breath fans my cheek. Then, I feel it. Something hard nudges my hip bone.

Oh, God. Is he turned on right now? Revulsion coils in my stomach as the realization slams into me.

He is!

His growing erection presses against me like this is some sort of sick game.

Even worse, a shiver runs through me. Not entirely from fear.

What the hell is wrong with me?

"Who sent you?" he grits out, completely ignoring the fact that he's hard as a rock right now. "Why are you here?"

No matter what I say, I'm doomed. I stumbled onto a secret

these guys would kill to keep buried. So, I do the only thing that makes sense. I throw the one person who could've protected me straight under the bus.

I jab a finger at Callan, a smirk curling my lips. "I came for him."

Silence snaps through the room like a live wire. Every pair of eyes locks on to Callan. His face burns crimson, his mouth parting, but his words never make it past his lips.

"Come on, Callan," I taunt, my voice dripping venom. "Tell them. Tell them I'm your sister's best friend. Tell them *you're* the reason I walked in here."

Callan lifts his head, squaring his shoulders like he's preparing for a fight. "It's true, Aidric," he says, voice tight. "I know her, but she sure as fuck isn't here for me. Can't stand the girl."

Underwear Guy has a name.

I snort, rolling my eyes. "Can't stand you more." The words slip out before I can stop them—petty, yet satisfying.

Aidric clicks his tongue, amusement flickering in his gaze. "Ahh," he drawls, tilting his head. "So that's it. You're a Devils fan. Snooping for your boys, are you?"

I almost laugh at the absurdity, but Aidric's grip tightens, his fingers digging into my arm like he's trying to squeeze the truth right out of me.

I tilt my chin up, refusing to show weakness. "I don't give a damn about your rivalry. I don't even like hockey," I snap. "I was looking for Callan's sister who happens to be my best friend, and I walked into the wrong place at the wrong time. That's it."

Aidric's lips curl into a smirk, but his eyes stay cold. "That so?"

"That *is* so," I say with a bite of sarcasm.

Aidric doesn't budge, his stance unwavering. "Well, regardless of what you came for, you're a problem now."

A slow, devious smirk tugs at his lips as his menacing blue

eyes flick down at me, savoring the moment. "You walked into the wrong room, Little Devil." His gaze sweeps lazily over the space, meeting the eyes of his teammates, who watch in eerie silence. Then, with a sinister grin spread across his face, he looks back at me. "In fact," he muses, letting the words hang like a death sentence, "I think we'll keep you."

I sputter a laugh, downplaying the situation while hoping a sign of humor masks my fear. "Keep me?" I chuckle again. "You can't keep me. I'm not an object."

In a slow, deliberate motion, Aidric shifts his gaze to Callan. "I think we should leave that up to our boy, Callan. What do you think? Have a little fun with our new toy?"

"Callan," I choke out, yanking against Aidric's iron grip. "Tell him to let me go."

Callan storms toward us with heavy, intentful steps. The moment I jerk back, Aidric's hold slips, but my freedom is short-lived. Before I can bolt, Callan's hand clamps around my arm, pulling me hard against his chest. His breath is hot against my ear, his voice a low, seething growl. "What the fuck are you doing?" His fingers tighten. "Have you lost your damn mind coming in here like this?"

"I really was looking for Brogan," I murmur. "How the hell was I supposed to know your teammates are psychopaths?"

He doesn't respond right away. Instead, he drags me aside, away from the others. His grip is firm, but not as rough as Aidric's.

He leans in, his voice dropping to a dangerous whisper. "I can't let you go until you tell me the truth, Avery." His fingers flex around my arm. "This is serious. What the hell did you hear?"

God, I despise his stupid, sexy, raspy voice. I hate the way he smells—like sweat and sweet pine, an infuriating mix that shouldn't be appealing but somehow is. And more than anything, I loathe that he's fucking gorgeous. A guy like him shouldn't be allowed to possess those qualities.

"Nothing," I sputter. "I heard nothing. I was literally standing there for a nanosecond."

His gaze sharpens, his lips pressed into a thin line as he scrutinizes me for any sign of deceit. Maybe, just maybe, he'll surprise me and prove there's a shred of humanity buried under that hardened exterior. With any luck, he'll convince Aidric to let me go. If not, I'm ready to scream until my lungs give out. Someone will hear me. Someone has to.

Just then, my phone rings.

My breath catches, eyes wide as I fumble to reach for it. But before I can even grasp the strap of my purse, Callan clamps onto it and yanks it from my grasp like it belongs to him.

"Hey," I stammer. "What the hell are you doing?"

Ignoring me, he digs out my phone, brows lifting as he glances at the screen. He looks at Aidric. "It's my sister," he says as he hands Aidric my phone. "She's probably looking for her." He rubs a hand down his face like he's already exhausted by this exchange.

"She *is* looking for me. And she said she was coming to talk to Callan, so she'll probably walk in here any second."

Aidric looks amused, twirling my phone between his fingers. "Oh, Little Devil," he muses. "Smart people don't just walk into the players' locker rooms."

My jaw clenches. "Are you calling me stupid?"

He grins, all teeth and arrogance. "I'm certainly not calling you smart."

A subtle growl climbs up my throat as I jerk against Callan's ironclad hold. It's no use—he's not letting up. But damn do I want to give this asshole a piece of my mind.

Aidric tips his chin at Callan. "What's it gonna be, Cromwell?" he asks with an edge to his tone. "Do we trust your little friend wasn't eavesdropping? Or do we bring her with us and get the truth out of her the fun way?"

A sharp swallow burns down my throat. Pleading eyes snap to Callan. "Please," I whisper.

He studies me, a dark look in his eyes. Finally, he exhales, shaking his head. "You know you're a shit liar, right? Your bottom lip quivers and your eyes don't stop dancing around."

"I'm not lying," I cry out. "Just tell him we're good, and I swear, none of you will ever have to see me again."

Aidric clicks his tongue again, stepping closer. His thumb brushes my lower lip, sending a sick shiver down my spine. "Hmm. He's right, you know. Your lip is trembling." His fingers trail to my chin in a firm but teasing hold. "Lucky for you, I've got bigger things to deal with tonight. So, I think we'll cut you loose."

Relief floods through me. "Thank you," I blurt out, hating how desperate I sound.

"Don't thank me yet," Aidric smirks. "I'll let you go under one condition."

My stomach knots. "What do you want?"

He leans in just enough to make my skin prickle. "Practice. Tomorrow at ten a.m. You'll be there cheering us on like a good little fan."

I glare. "That's your condition? I don't even like hockey."

"Yeah, well," he chuckles, stepping back, "you do now. You're our new biggest fan, Little Devil. And if I find out you heard something you shouldn't have..." His smile drops to something dark, almost dangerous. "I'll fucking *ruin* you."

Then, with a casual shove and my phone slapped to my palm, he says, "Run while you can."

I don't waste a second of time. I bolt.

CHAPTER 3

AVERY

I'M NOT GOING...OR should I?

An hour late isn't *that* bad. Show up, linger just long enough to keep the assholes off my back, then slip out before anyone cares.

My bare feet thud against the hardwood, each step a steady rhythm as I pace in front of my twin-size bed. I've walked this same path so many times this morning that the heels of my feet are starting to crack.

I told Aidric I'd watch their stupid practice, but I was under a lot of pressure and I wanted out of that locker room in one piece. And at the time, I meant it. I really did.

Now, I'm second-guessing the whole deal.

I mean, what are they going to do if I don't show? Kill me over a missed practice? Doubtful. They act like they hold all the cards, but they only had power over me when I was trapped in that room with them. There was no place for me to go then, but now that I'm not in their demanding presence, they have no leverage.

It's settled, I'm not going.

Still, I keep pacing, overthinking until a migraine feels inevitable.

Our dorm room is a cluttered mess. Clothes strewn all over, textbooks stacked on each desk, and the faint scent of coffee hanging in the air. Our first month here, we kept our small space tidy, but it's since turned into a pigsty with us rushing in and out so frequently.

Brogan spends most nights with Hayes, so I'm usually here alone. I hate it. It's too quiet. I get so wrapped up in my own thoughts, probing every life choice—every next step. I like noise. Even if I did escape it last night only to come back here and send myself into full-blown panic mode.

After the events in the Lords' locker room last night, I put on a brave face and went to Legends like I planned. I knew Brogan would be suspicious if I didn't go, considering I live for the nightlife. I had half of a mojito and faked cramps then caught an Uber back to our dorm. She slept at Hayes's and, well, I didn't sleep at all.

I got a text from Brogan five minutes ago that she was coming back to grab a change of clothes and she wanted to talk real quick. I could hide, but she has my location on her phone. So I'll force a smile and act like everything is fine. I've gotten pretty good at that over the years.

I stop in front of my vanity and lean forward, drawing my fingers under my mascara-stained eyes. Probably should have left it in place so it could hide the redness from my tearstains.

I resume pacing, ready to just get this over with. She'll either be unsuspecting, or she'll see right through the act I'm about to put on.

The door swings open without warning, slamming against the wall. I jolt back, a sharp breath catching in my throat as my hand flies to my chest.

Brogan steps inside, dropping a laundry bag by the door before nudging it shut with her foot. "Jesus. What's got you all jumpy?"

Your brother and his teammates—that's what. They're fucking psychos.

Instead of saying the thought out loud, I exhale slowly and force a shrug. "Nothing. Just thinking about the competition next month. Nerves, that's all."

My mind churns. I've been struggling with whether to tell Brogan the truth or not. Maybe she could talk some sense into Callan. But if I pull her into this, they could assume I told her what they think I heard.

Damn, I've really got myself into a mess here.

"Since when do you get nervous over a competition? You're a natural with the bow. You've got this."

I force a smile, but it barely touches my eyes.

She steps closer, gently taking my hands in hers. *Fuck.* She sees right through my facade.

"Ave," she murmurs, her voice even softer now. "Ever since the game, you've been off. And I know you didn't have cramps last night. Our cycles are synced and we're not due for another two weeks. If this is about Evan, you can talk to me."

If only she knew.

This *is* about Evan—just not in the way she thinks. It's not about feelings or some messy breakup. It's about the truth I can't unhear. The Lords' hockey team, or at least four of them, had something to do with his fall. I'm stuck between getting close to them so I can find out the truth, and insisting I know nothing while never breathing a word to another soul.

Too bad I know myself and my curiosity won't let it go. It makes sense why it kills the cat, because I have a feeling murder isn't off the table after what I heard last night.

Gentle fingers glide over the back of my hand, slow and reassuring. Brogan tilts her head slightly, eyes searching mine. "Whatever you say stays between us. You know that, right?"

I nod, playing on her assumption that I'm shook up over what happened to Evan. "It's just so sad, ya know? I can't help but wonder if this could have all been prevented if I hadn't ended things with him." My gaze drifts past her, settling on a photo collage above her bed. I can't look her in the eye when I lie. Callan was right—I am a terrible liar.

"Avery Castle. Do not do that to yourself. Come here." She pulls me into a hug, and for a moment, I just let myself sink into it. It's been a while since anyone's held me like this, and that realization plays on my emotions. Brogan is all I have right now. I keep my heart guarded, walls up, never letting anyone in, but with her, it's harder to pretend I don't need this.

"You did what was best for you, Ave. Besides, it's been over a year since you ended things with him. There is no part of you that should feel any guilt over what happened." She takes a step back so she can see my face. With downcast eyes, I blink away the tears threatening to fall. "Would it make you feel better if we went to see him later today?"

"No." I immediately shake my head. "Not yet."

I'm not ready to stand in that cold spot beside his bed and look down at his unconscious body, knowing what I know. Or what I think I know, anyways. I keep telling myself I had to have misunderstood, but those words play on repeat in my head.

If Evan Sanders comes to, it's all of our asses on the line. You will take care of him.

My heart drops to my stomach, yet again. It's not only what they may have done, but, more importantly, what they plan to do next.

"You sure?" Brogan asks again.

I nod. "I'm sure. I don't think I can handle seeing him like that."

I don't tell her it's also because I hate hospitals and going in one will only make me feel sicker than I already do. Brogan's my best friend, and I tell her damn near everything, but some things are mine to keep. Even if someone else already knows my secret and has used it against me more times than I can count.

Someone like Callan fucking Cromwell.

He won't tell me how he found out about my mom's illness, but he knows.

Aside from him, everyone assumes I come from stuck-up, rich parents who are too busy working to check in on their daughter. And for one of them, that's true. What they don't know is that the other one barely recognizes me anymore.

Or maybe it's the other way around. Maybe I'm the one who doesn't recognize her.

I still remember the vivid smell of the hospital when my mom was first admitted. I can still hear the shrill sound of her screams.

"It's okay, Mom." I run my fingers through her thinning hair, my touch usually enough to bring her back, but not this time.

Her eyes dart past me as if I'm a stranger. "You're not my daughter," she cries, her voice frantic. "Give me back my daughter!"

Tears spill down my cheeks, soft drops hitting the white sheet draped over her fragile body. "Mom, it's me. It's Avery. Your daughter."

"Liar!" Her scream ricochets off the hospital walls. "You're not my daughter. You're him!"

I swallow the knot in my throat. "Who, Mom? Who do you think I am?"

Her eyes blaze with fury, locking on to mine with a hatred that doesn't belong to her. "You're Satan!" she shrieks.

Before I can react, she snatches a plastic food tray from the bedside table. It all happens so fast, I don't see it coming until she slams it against the metal bed rail, causing it to splinter into two jagged pieces.

"Mom, stop!" I lunge forward, reaching for the broken piece, but I'm too slow.

The sharp edge plunges into my arm, pain igniting as she drags it downward, tearing through my skin like paper.

I can still feel the warmth of my own blood trickling down my arm. I rub my scar, feeling the raised skin—a painful reminder of who she is now.

Only a few people know my mom has spent the last six years in a psychiatric facility after suffering a psychotic break she has yet to overcome. We were told she had one of the most severe forms of paranoia they'd ever seen. We knew her mental health was on the decline, but we never could have guessed how bad it really was.

I didn't blame her then, and I don't today. I try to see her as much as they'll allow, even if she is heavily sedated. I like to think she knows who I am and comprehends what I'm saying to her.

As for my dad, he hasn't been to the facility in over a year. I'm not sure if it's because it's inconvenient, or if it's because in his mind, he has better things to do with his time. I think we've both just been pretending for far too long. We've convinced ourselves she'll get better one day and everything will go back to normal. But as more time passes, I'm beginning to realize this is who she is now.

If only I had a sibling to share this pain with, maybe life wouldn't feel so lonely. I always held on to the hope that once I left for college, I could finally experience a normal life. For a while, it was nice pretending, but my heart is still heavy as I grieve the loss of my parents who are still very much alive. They're just not the same anymore. None of us are.

"Earth to Avery." Brogan snaps her fingers in front of my face, pulling me out of my thoughts. "You just let me know when you're ready, and I'll go with you."

"Of course," I tell her. "And thank you." I hug her again, unsure what I would do without her. This friendship literally saved my life. One minute I was walking down the hall, plotting my own death, and the next, I was heading to class with a new best friend.

"Shit," Brogan huffs as she steals a glance at her watch. "I need to go. I told Hayes I'd meet him in the student center for coffee."

"Go, go." I give her a gentle nudge. "I'll be fine."

Skepticism flickers in her eyes. "Promise?"

"Of course." I force a smile. "I promise."

Standing with my arms crossed tightly over my chest, I watch her turn the knob and push the door open. As she steps aside, my heart skips a beat, and my face hardens. Framed by the doorway stands none other than Callan Cromwell.

CHAPTER 4

AVERY

With his fist raised as if he was just about to knock, Callan's shadowy figure blocks the view to the hallway. The room thickens with tension as our eyes lock and the warmth in my gaze is quickly replaced with a cold, steely glare.

"Callan! It's so good to see you." Brogan's voice bubbles with enthusiasm and a wide smile parts her lips. All the while, I stand here miles away from matching her eagerness. "What are you doing here?"

It's an appropriate question for her dear stepbrother. He never comes to our dorm, let alone the Rosewood U campus in general. I already know the answer, though. Callan is here for me. He must have cut out of practice early to hunt me down and drag me there.

"Don't act so surprised, sis." He throws an arm over her shoulders while his icy stare pins to mine. He walks her back into the room, eyes flickering back and forth between the two of us. "I came to see you. Wanted to apologize for roughing up your man in the game last night."

I call bullshit.

"Bullshit." Brogan cackles, reading my mind. She slaps a

hand to his chest and pushes him back teasingly. "There isn't an ounce of remorse in that stone-cold heart of yours."

She might seem like she's joking, and I doubt she truly means what she's saying. However, I'm convinced. Callan isn't the brother she once knew. High school changed him—the Lords' hockey team changed him.

I should use this as my chance to escape. Grab my things and get out of the room before he has a chance to tell her why he's really here. The deal was, I'd go watch their stupid practice. There was never any mention of *them* coming here.

Snatching my purse hastily from my dresser, my eyes deliberately skim over Callan, whose presence feels like a thorn in my side. "I'm leaving," I say with a rushed breath as I make my way to the door. The last thing I want is for Brogan to get caught in the crossfire of what's going on.

"Actually," I hear Callan say. "I need to talk to your roommate."

His confession sends my heart into my throat. Pretending I didn't hear him, I keep walking. It isn't until I'm halfway out the door that Brogan stops me.

"Avery," she calls out. "Callan said he came to talk to you. Though I can't imagine why. Since when do you two *talk*?"

I spin around cautiously while trying to expel any apprehension. "Sure. I've got somewhere to be, though. Can we make this quick?"

Callan takes three deliberate steps toward me. Unfortunately, our room is small so that's all it takes for him to stand directly in front of me. "And where might you be running off to?"

I lift my chin, portraying a confident persona. This is Callan. Regardless of what those other guys did, or threatened to do, Callan won't hurt me.

"I don't think that's any of your business," I tell him with conviction in my tone.

"Sort of is," he quips. "After all, we had plans."

I gulp, surprised he brought it up in front of Brogan. I glower at him in warning. He better not say anything. His sister doesn't need to be brought into this mess.

Brogan steps between us, waving her hand. "You two had plans and didn't tell me?"

"No," I blurt out, while Callan spits an affirmative, "Yes."

Brogan studies us. "What's going on with you two?"

I shrug. "Got me. I don't have a clue what he's talking about." My hand presses firmly to my hip as I snarl at Callan. "Am I missing something?"

Scratching the back of his head, he chuckles dryly. "Come on now, Avery. Best friends don't keep secrets. Tell Brogan how we bumped into each other after the game last night and you offered to help me and my teammates study for that big test we have coming up. Can't risk our grades dipping in the middle of the season."

"You offered to help the Lords' hockey team?" Brogan asks, surprised.

All the blood in my body rushes to my cheeks and I'm certain they can both see it. This motherfucker. "Right," I grit out. "I did offer to help them. Must have slipped my mind with the sudden cramps and all." A smug grin creeps across my face. "I offered to help them in exchange for access to their archery club. They just had the winning international team revamp their fields and targets and Callan said he would get me time there.

Callan mouths the words, "You bitch," and I just keep the smile pinned to my face. Two can play this game, asshole.

"Can't say I'm thrilled you're helping our rival team," Brogan says. "I don't think Hayes will be too keen on the idea either. I do appreciate you helping my brother, though. You're a good friend." She rubs my shoulder gently before stepping around me. "I have to go. I'll let you two figure this out."

The minute Brogan is out the door, I shove my palms to Callan's chest, pushing him back a few steps. "What the hell was that?"

He quickly eats up the space between us, nose to nose. "Are

you trying to get us both killed? Why the hell didn't you show up today?"

"I didn't think that guy was serious. It's just practice. Big fucking whoop." I take a step back, retreating from his intoxicating scent. Damn him for lacking any physical flaws. I need to find one soon so that I'm as repulsed by his appearance as I am his character.

"Well, it was a big mistake." He snares me by the wrist and attempts to pull me to the door. "We have to go."

"Over my dead body." I jerk away, freeing myself. "I'm not going anywhere with you after what I heard last night. For all I know, you're a murderer."

He studies me. "So you did hear something"?

"I heard enough to know I don't want anything to do with you. You're lucky I'm not telling Brogan. It would break her heart if she knew you and your stupid teammates hurt Evan."

Callan throws his arms in the air as if I'm the unreasonable one here. "It'll break her heart even more if her best friend goes missing because she doesn't know how to follow the goddamn rules."

"Rules?" I laugh, trying to brush off my nerves because no one tells me what to do. "I'm twenty-one years old, Callan. I make my own rules."

He steps forward, a menacing scowl on his face. "Not anymore, you don't. And if that's all you gathered from what I just said, you're in for a rude awakening."

I cross my arms, refusing to let him intimidate me. We're on my turf. "Oh, I heard you. But I'm not biting. You see, I wrote down everything I heard last night, word for word, and made plenty of copies. If I go down, you all go down, too."

It's a lie. I didn't write anything down, but now that I've thought about it, I need to. I have to protect myself and make sure that if something happens to me, the world knows there are monsters playing on the Lords' hockey team.

I hear the grinding of his molars as his fist tightens. "You better pray you're lying, Avery. Because if you screw this up for me, I swear to fucking God, I'll—"

"You'll what, Callan?" I step into him. Despite the lingering fear from what I heard last night, I'm not afraid of Callan. Do I despise him? Yes. But fear him? Absolutely not.

"I'll fucking break you, Avery." His voice is low and venomous. "Limb by limb. I will *destroy* you."

I tilt my head, a smirk playing on my lips. "I'm not a tree you can just snap. So go ahead and give it your best shot."

"I beg to differ. You see..." His voice drops as he glides a strand of hair behind my ear. "You might think you know what me and my boys are capable of," he murmurs, his breath warm against my cheek. "But you have no idea."

That pulls a laugh from me. "Callan, I once watched your stepmom fill a sandwich baggie with ice because you tripped over your own shoelaces in the kitchen and bumped your knee. Forgive me if I'm not shaking in my boots."

His jaw tightens, but his expression stays composed. "Don't say I didn't warn you."

Cold, deliberate fingers trail along my cheek. To anyone else, it might look like a tender touch, but I know better. With Callan, it's not affection, it's dominance—a reminder of who holds all the power.

"You might wanna watch your back, Avery." His voice drops to a quiet threat. "You never know when a Lord might be lurking."

His thumb presses against my lips, prying them open. Then, without hesitation, he slides it into my mouth.

Defiance ignites in my chest. *You wanna play?*

I bite down, hard. The roughness of his skin scrapes against my teeth, and I don't let up. Let's see how tough this asshole really is.

"You bitch," he seethes, yanking back. But my teeth follow, sinking in deeper and refusing to let go.

Something almost inhumane awakens inside me. The look of

desperation in his eyes only fuels my desire to bring him pain. At this moment, I have the power.

His free hand clamps around my throat, fingers pressing into my skin as I hold his thumb hostage. The harder he squeezes, the harder I bite. *Can't play hockey with a missing thumb.*

"Don't test me, Avery. I'll leave you lifeless on this floor if you don't let go of me, right fucking now!" He shoves me back and my mouth opens on instinct.

Before I can react, we hit the floor, the impact jolting through me as he grabs my wrists and pins my arms above my head. His weight presses down, caging me beneath him. "That was a bad move, Little Devil."

"Oh, for the love of God," I spit out as I thrash against his iron grip. "Not you, too. Enough with this Little Devil shit. I don't call you Little Lord."

"Ya know…" He pinches my chin with his fingers and I lift it with all of the spite I feel for him shining in my gaze. "I was gonna cut you some slack. Maybe tell the guys to take it easy on you. But now, I think I'll let them eat you alive."

I relax, knowing his muscle is too much for me to take on, but I'm not without power even as I lie here on my back at his mercy. My words are my weapon. "I'm not scared of you, Callan. In case you've forgotten, I broke you first."

His grip loosens slightly, confusion flickering across his face. "Broke me?"

"You heard me." I tilt my chin up, meeting his gaze head-on. "You wanted more from me after we had sex. But for me? It was just sex. Not even good sex, I might add." That's a total lie, but I'll never tell him that the one night I had with him is what I imagine when I touch myself.

Silence stretches between us, his cheeks darkening with rage. Raising both of my wrists, he slams them back down on the hard floor. A sharp jolt of pain ripples through me. I wince, but I don't look away.

"The only thing I ever wanted from you were your tears," he

growls. "I think I made that abundantly clear when I dug up every secret I could use to break you."

"Yet, you've never told a soul. Why is that, Callan?"

His jaw tics. "Your secrets are my ammunition. If I share it, it's no longer mine."

I let out a quiet laugh, shaking my head. "Then I guess I've got nothing to worry about. You need them to hold over me. Without them, you have nothing at all."

He chuckles, and it reverberates right into my chest. "That's what you think. I have more than you could ever imagine. Your future is in my hands now—*our* hands. One phone call and your whole world will crash down."

"Enough with the empty threats." I sigh, bored with this conversation. "Now, get off me. I have better things to do than lie here and listen to you try and play God over me."

"Not God. A Lord. *Your Lord.* And you're nothing but a sinful little devil. Whether you realize it or not, you will serve us, Avery, or you will pay for the secrets you eavesdropped on."

When he talks like this, it only solidifies my suspicion that he's in some sort of cult. He wouldn't come all the way to my dorm and seek me out like this if there wasn't a damn good reason. They're all scared. Shaking in their skates because I know their secret.

Maybe Callan does have leverage on me, but I have something bigger on him.

A smirk stretches across my lips. "An eye for an eye, old friend. You take me down, you're all going with me."

His jaw clenches. "Where's the damn letter, Avery?"

I shrug, feeling my shoulder blades grate against the hardwood. "Somewhere safe."

Suddenly, Callan jerks me upright, lifting me to my feet. I look at my wrist, noticing a smear of blood, but it's not mine. The skin on his thumb is peeled back, proof of just how hard I bit him. He doesn't seem fazed in the slightest. Meanwhile, my stomach churns at the realization that his blood was in my mouth.

Without hesitation, he hauls me toward the door, fingers tightening around my arm as he reaches for the handle.

"What the hell are you doing?" I huff, twisting against his grip.

"What I came here to do. Taking you to my leader."

"Like hell you are. I'm not going anywhere with you." I firmly plant my feet on the ground, yet Callan effortlessly drags me along. My protests fall on deaf ears as he shoves me out of my dorm and slams the door behind us.

"I'm serious, Callan. I have to be at the field in an hour. I don't have time for this."

"Your little bow and arrow hobby can wait," he says, steering me forward without a second glance. "We have more important things to do right now."

"Hobby?" I spit. "It's much more than a hobby. A hobby is lacing up skates and slapping a puck around. This…" I jab a finger at his shoulder. "This is a life skill. And if you don't quit shoving me down this damn hall, I'll show you just how useful it can be."

After I'm shoved into the elevator, we go down to the first floor. As I'm stepping out, I stumble over my feet, barely catching myself before I crash to the floor. My pulse spikes with irritation. "Quit that," I snap, yanking my arm. "I'm not a damn toy you can push around."

Callan smirks, unbothered. "Sure you are. Now get your stubborn ass out the door."

I stop in front of the main doors to the parking lot and cross my arms over my chest. "Not happening. I told you I have somewhere to be."

He exhales an exasperated breath. "I'll tell you what. You come with me and talk to the guys, and maybe I'll give you a ride."

A dry chuckle escapes me. "I'd rather hitchhike with an unhinged serial killer than be trapped in a car with you."

He shoves the door open and drags me forward. "Be careful what you wish for."

A black SUV parked in front of the dorm catches my eye. The windows are so dark I can't see who might be inside. A shiver runs down my spine. Something feels off.

"Whose ride is that? I know it's not yours. Is there someone else in there?"

My nerves spike. I may have put on a brave face for the last twenty minutes, but I'm beginning to crack. Callan doesn't scare me, but Aidric does. He might be the unhinged serial killer I never actually wished for.

As I'm being steered to the SUV, I dig my heels into the pavement, turning to face Callan as I walk backward. In a last-ditch effort, I plead with him. "Callan, please." I clutch at his waist, trying to stop him from moving any farther. "We've known each other since I transferred to Willow Creek in eighth grade. Please don't do this. You can trust me. I won't tell anyone what I heard."

It's true. If they'll just let this all go, I'd take what I know to the grave.

Callan's gaze darkens. "You should've never hidden in that locker. Now you have to earn our trust."

Reaching around me, he pulls open the back door and I'm shoved inside like a useless piece of trash. I barely catch myself before colliding with the leather seats. The second I regain my bearings, my stomach drops. One of the guys from last night sits beside me, his expression unreadable. Worst of all is the driver in the front seat.

Aidric.

CHAPTER 5

AVERY

"WE MISSED YOU TODAY, LITTLE DEVIL," Aidric chimes from behind the wheel. "Thought we had a deal."

I snarl, "This might come as a surprise, but I have better things to do than watch a bunch of boys slap a puck around for an hour."

The front passenger door swings open, and Callan slides into the seat in a swift motion. Once he's settled, he pulls the door shut with a firm tug.

It's strange that I feel a sense of ease knowing Callan is here. I loathe him from the depths of my soul, but familiarity can be comforting when you're in a powerless position. Besides, I don't think he would do anything that would hurt his sister, which gives me a sense of safety. He might let me get hurt, but I don't think he would let me go missing like he said earlier.

I still can't believe he's doing this, though.

"Ya know," Aidric begins while shifting the car into drive. "You say we can trust you, but today you proved otherwise. Your first mistake was putting your nose in our business. Your second was not showing up at our practice like you promised."

I sink into the seat, feeling the vibration beneath me as we cruise over the train tracks—out of Rosewood and into North

Ridge. My eyes drift sideways, catching sight of the guy beside me. With his hoodie pulled up, he bows his head, a curtain of disheveled sandy brown hair slipping from the hood, concealing his face as his fingers dance across his phone screen.

Feeling the heat of my stare, his eyes slide to mine. They're a soft brown, like honey. Sort of like mine but lighter. Without lifting his head, or pushing his hair out of his face, he watches me. He comes off as a typical guy, wearing a pair of gym shorts, a Lords hockey hoodie, and a pair of spotless white high-top sneakers. Oddly enough, I don't feel threatened or intimidated. I can't help but wonder if he was dragged into Callan and Adric's chaos, or if he made the choice himself.

"Who are you?" I whisper, hoping he might be someone open to persuasion. If I can get in his good graces, maybe we can help each other out.

Instead of responding, he simply sweeps his unruly hair out of his face. It's then that I see his perfect side profile—his jawline sharp enough to cut glass, pronounced cheekbones that look like they were sculpted by an artist, and a rice-sized scar just above the right side of his lip. His eyes flicker to the rearview mirror in the front in an almost calculating gaze. When I follow his line of sight, I see Aidric's stone blue eyes glowering back at him.

A flicker of thought crosses over his features, and he looks back down at his phone as if he was commanded to do so. I don't let up, though.

"So what are you studying at North Ridge?" I ask, my voice low and measured.

I watch him, searching for any sort of reaction, a twitch of an eyebrow, a shift in posture—anything. But he gives me nothing.

"I'm a junior at Rosewood University, studying neuropsychiatry. And did you know that good or bad, everyone has the potential to turn evil?" I let the thought dangle between us before saying, "You could be the sweetest, most innocent person, and under the right circumstances you'd be capable of things you never—"

"Would you shut the fuck up!" Aidric slams his hand to the steering wheel, the sharp crack cutting through the air. My spine pins to the seat and my lips seal. "You talk too damn much."

Callan swivels in his seat, his eyes glinting with mischief as he flashes me a smug grin. I glare back at him, my lips pressed into a tight line while the heat of frustration rises to my cheeks. It's obvious he gets some sort of sick thrill over me being put in my place by Aidric. I wouldn't doubt it if Aidric has put him in his place a time or two. Hell, I'd actually pay to see it.

We continue the dreadful ride in silence, but my thoughts are screaming. I've determined that the guy next to me is going to become my new friend. Like a snake, I'm going to slither my way into his good graces and convince him to tell these asshats to leave me alone. After all, the one I've known for seven years sure as hell isn't doing me any favors.

Fifteen minutes later, we turn onto a long, paved driveway. The house looms ahead—instantly recognizable. No need to guess where we are. I already know.

The Lords' hockey house.

CHAPTER 6

AVERY

THE HOCKEY HOUSE is practically a legend in North Ridge. Some say Edison Einhorn's ghost still lingers inside. Last year, a freshman from Rosewood U took a dare to go into the basement on Devil's Night and prove it with a selfie or a picture of one of the demons they say lives down there. Five hours passed before he finally emerged, pale and silent. The picture never surfaced and the next day, he dropped out of school. No one's seen him since.

I, however, don't believe in that shit. The only demons people need to worry about are the ones in their own heads. Or, the three of them I'm sitting in a car with, in my case.

"What now?" I ask the enigma sitting next to me.

His eyes stay fixed on his phone, thumb flicking the screen in mindless swipes like I'm nothing more than empty space. This new friendship thing might prove to be harder than I thought.

Frustrated that no one will tell me what the hell is going on, I take matters into my own hands and yank the door handle only to hit resistance. *Stuck. Damn child locks.*

Then, I see my back seat neighbor reach up and tug an earbud from his ear. *Of course.* I almost laugh, but there's nothing funny about this situation. No wonder he was ignoring me. He didn't hear a damn word I said.

I glance toward the front just in time to see Aidric tip his chin at Callan. Without hesitation, Callan nods and pushes open his door. The thunderous sound of his black boots hit the pavement before he slams the door shut.

"Will one of you please tell me what I'm doing here?" I ask anyone who will listen. "I wasn't lying when I said I had things…"

My words trail off as my door finally swings open. A cool gust of air rushes in, whipping my hair into my face. I barely have time to brush it away before a hand clamps around my arm and yanks me out of the car. "Dude, would you chill with the grabbing? Keep it up and I'll have a permanent imprint from your fingers."

"Maybe if you'd just listen and go where I say, I wouldn't have to manhandle you."

I wrench my arm free, and to my surprise, he doesn't stop me. But before I can take a full step back, his hand finds the small of my back—firm, possessive, and guiding.

The car peels out, tires spitting gravel while the scent of burnt rubber lingers in the air. I watch as the taillights shrink into the five-stall garage. I'd question how they can afford such luxurious accommodations, but I'm sure it's all funded by sponsors and alumni boosters.

I tug my sleeves down, the fabric swallowing my fingers as I fold my arms against my chest. "Thanks for letting me grab a jacket before you kidnapped me."

"Kidnapped?" Callan chuckles, low and amused. "I'd hardly call it that."

His hand drops, fingers gliding over the keypad beside the door. After a sharp beep, the door comes unlocked. He shoves it open like he owns the world before he leans into the frame.

"Taking someone against their will is kidnapping, Callan."

Palm splayed against the door, he holds it open while his

heavy gaze settles on me. "Fair enough. So I kidnapped you. You gonna run now?" A knowing smirk twitches his lips. I bet he'd love for me to run just so he can chase me down.

I grit my teeth, shaking my head in deliberate, measured beats. I don't say a word as I step past him and into the massive house. For a second, I freeze, my mouth dropping open as I take in my surroundings.

The place is *gorgeous*. All stark contrasts, it's a gothic dream in black and white. Like Beetlejuice's suit—chaotic, but elegant. The vaulted ceilings stretch so high they could kiss the mountaintops behind the house. And somehow, despite over a dozen guys living here, it's surprisingly spotless. Must have a housekeeper…or magical powers.

Shaking myself out of the shocked state, I turn to face Callan who's staring at me.

"Well," I grumble, crossing my arms. "I'm here. What now?"

Before Callan can answer, Aidric and the other back seat rider step out from around a corner. Aidric barely glances at Callan before his glare slices straight to me. "Take her to The Chamber," he hisses.

My stomach knots. *The Chamber.* I remember someone mentioning it in the locker room. It was just a passing remark, but it was enough to leave me wondering.

Callan's fingers clamp firmly around my upper arm like I'm some prisoner being marched to my fate.

"Wait." The word barely scrapes out. "What's The Chamber? Is that, like…an inferno?"

No answer.

"Stop!" I thrash against Callan's grip. When that doesn't work, I drop all of my weight on him in refusal. My body goes limp and my knees hit the floor.

If he wants me in that chamber, he'll have to drag me there.

Callan exhales sharply, and his grip tightens. "This is exactly what I mean, Avery. You don't fucking listen."

Laughter and scattered voices drift through the air, along with footsteps shuffling somewhere nearby. *We aren't alone.*

My pulse spikes and I look up, wondering where the sounds are coming from. Does the rest of the hockey team have any idea what's happening? If not, they will now.

"Help!" I scream. "Someone help me!"

A sharp gasp leaves my lips as I'm hoisted off the ground, my world flipping upside down as I'm flung over Callan's shoulder.

"You're wasting your breath. No one is coming to help you, Avery."

"Please," I beg. "Don't do this."

My hand shoots out, scrambling for any kind of anchor. My fingertips graze the wall, and I drag my nails down hard, peeling away strips of paint and leaving a jagged trail of scratches. It won't stop him, but it's evidence if I go missing. That, paired with the camera footage outside my dorm, is enough to prove these guys are responsible.

"Would you chill the fuck out?" Callan snaps, jabbing another code into yet another keypad. A click echoes through the air just before he pushes the door open. "We're not gonna kill you. At least, not yet."

Well, that's comforting. Not!

Each step takes us deeper underground. The air thickens and the scent of damp cement wafts around me, causing my stomach to tighten.

Dim orange lights flicker in glass sconces along the walls, illuminating the path just enough to keep me from being swallowed by the darkness.

By the time we reach the final step, the space unfolds around me. A cavernous, dimly lit room with a larger sconce flaming at the far end. A row of chairs sits in perfect formation, all facing a raised platform. On top of it is a wood podium, like the ones you'd see in a church. But something tells me no prayers are being answered here.

This is definitely a cult.

My eyes immediately land on a pair of chains dangling from the ceiling. Attached to them are cuffs that look like they are used to lock around someone's wrists. My breath hitches, and it feels like the room is tilting.

Fear is something I have experienced plenty, but I have always held my head high. But right now, I'm afraid if I hold it too high, someone might try to chop it off.

I like to think I'm tough. I don't take shit from people. I fight back. But this? This is something else. This is a line I never thought I'd be standing on the edge of. And right now, it feels like I'm about to be shoved off.

"Callan," I say in a desperate plea, my pulse slamming against my rib cage. "Please don't do this to me."

The moment my feet touch the ground, I feel relief. That is, until Callan steps in front of me. He watches me like a cat would a wounded mouse, his eyes dark, but there's also something else. Something unreadable. I want to think it's pity, but part of me believes he could never feel such an empathetic emotion after all he has done to torture me.

"Listen to me, Avery." His voice drops to a whisper. "Just do what they say and you'll be fine."

His gaze flicks past me. A muscle in his jaw tics as he bites down on his bottom lip, hands burying deep in his pockets like he's holding something back. "You really fucked yourself when you walked into that locker room."

Hot tears spill from my eyes and my chest tightens. "Don't let them hurt me." My words are a breath more than a sound.

"Physically, you'll be fine." For the first time, his voice is stripped of its usual edge. No intimidation, no threat. It's almost…normal.

I swallow down the hard lump forming in my throat. "What does that mean?"

He pulls in a sharp breath, his gaze looking ahead. "You'll soon find out." And just like that, the moment of softness vanishes. His mask snaps back into place and the hardness returns to his eyes. With a firm shove, he forces me down into one of the chairs in the back row. "Don't. Fucking. Move."

Disappearing into the shadows of the room, he quickly reappears with a shiny skeleton key dangling from his fingers. My pulse hammers as he slides it into the keyhole of a heavy metal door. Just as it creaks open, footsteps echo down the staircase.

A chill runs down my spine. Even if I can't see him, I know it's Aidric. There's something about that guy that terrifies me in ways I can't explain.

I can't let him see my fear, though. He'll only feel more powerful than he already does. If there's one thing I know about men in charge, it's that they get off on putting others beneath them. While my height can't help me much in that department, my attitude sure as fuck can.

I spring to my feet, ready to demand answers. "What do you want from me?" My voice cracks, but I recover quickly, refusing to let him see me cower. "Why am I here?"

Silence.

Aidric just watches me. His unwanted stare slicing through the air like a sharp knife.

"Sebastian." Callan's voice drifts from behind the door. "Gimme a hand."

So that's his name.

Sebastian flicks a glance at Aidric, who gives the smallest nod. This silent talk between them is really getting old.

Still, Aidric says nothing. Just stands there, scrutinizing every breath I take like he's waiting for me to shatter.

My eyebrows knit into a tight V. "Whatever you're about to do, you won't get away with it."

Aidric's head tilts, a slow, sinister smile creeping across his face.

I swallow hard but stand my ground. "If something happens to me, my blood will be on your hands. You'll never get away with it, asshole."

This gets his attention. His back straightens, shoulders taut like a predator getting a whiff of a scent. He steps into me, a low growl rumbling out of him. His fingers spread as he reaches out for my throat. I jump back, but I'm not quick enough as he latches onto my neck.

His grip tightens the second his warm skin presses to mine. Not enough to crush my windpipe, but enough to cut off my airways. My pulse hammers beneath his palm as I claw at his hand, nails digging into his skin, desperate for him to let me go so I can take a breath.

"Whoa, whoa," Sebastian cuts in, his words laced with urgency. He plants a firm hand on Aidric's shoulder, guiding him back until he releases me.

"What the hell is the matter with you?" I cough out, rubbing the spot on my throat where he gripped me. "You're insane!"

Sebastian throws me a quick, almost apologetic glance before turning to Aidric. "Relax," he mutters. "Stick to the plan."

Plan? A cold wave of unease crashes over me knowing they've been plotting against me, especially in a place as sinister as this.

Callan reemerges, locking the door behind him. In his other hand, he clutches a small, rectangular box.

My box. Wait a damn minute.

My mom gave me that music box on my eleventh birthday. When it's opened, a ballerina twirls around to the melody of "You Are My Sunshine"—a song she sang to me as a baby.

My stomach twists. "Why the hell does he have that? Why did he take it?"

Their response is only blank stares and smug indifference. All this silence has my patience hanging by a thread. I might as well be talking to a damn wall.

"Did one of you break into my room?" I shove Sebastian hard, fingers digging into his chest. "Answer me, dammit! Were you in my room?" His lips curl into a slow, wicked smirk. "You assholes!"

"That box holds the key to your freedom," Sebastian finally says, his first words to me.

I let out a bitter laugh. "That box holds a dancing ballerina and a folded-up picture of my mom and me. My freedom is hardly in there."

Callan steps in, shoving the box against my chest. I barely catch it before it slips from my hands. As my fingers move to unclasp the lock, his sharp exhale stops me cold.

"I wouldn't open that if I were you," he warns.

My gaze snaps to him, searching for answers I'm not sure I want. My voice is quieter now, a bite of hesitation to my tone. "Why?"

"Listen," Sebastian says sternly. "Had you shown up to our practice today, we wouldn't be standing here right now. But since you broke our trust, you need to earn it back. Therefore, you're going to do exactly what I say. And if you don't..." He flicks a glance at Aidric and Callan, something unspoken passing between them, *again*. "Let's just say, it won't turn out well for you."

My fingers tighten around the music box as a sorrow I don't want to acknowledge pulls at me. But I repress it, shoving it as far down as it can go because I have no business mourning someone who is still alive. Especially not right now.

Lifting my eyes back to his, I compose myself. "What exactly do you want me to do?"

Sebastian's gaze darkens. "You're gonna burn that box and bury the ashes."

My breath catches, my heart slamming against my ribs. They want me to burn it? For fuck's sake... *What am I holding right now?*

"Wha...what's in it?" My voice barely rises above a whisper.

For all I know, it holds proof of what they did to Evan. His phone wouldn't fit, but maybe it's something else. Something they had in their possession that could tie them to his fall.

Callan shifts, his jaw tight as if he's waiting for my reaction.

Sebastian simply smirks. "You'll find out soon enough."

I tap the box with my fingers, my mind racing. *What am I about to agree to?*

"If I do this, you guys better leave me alone. No more showing up at my dorm. No more breaking in and stealing my things." My stance is firm, but my shaking hands betray me.

Callan steps closer, his eyes steady on mine. "As long as we know we can trust you, we'll leave you alone."

His tone is softer than I expected, his features less rigid. For a second I almost believe him. But Callan has always been good at deception.

"Fine," I snap, shoving past them. "I'll burn it and get rid of the ashes."

I don't look back. I can't. If I think too hard about what I'm about to do, I might hesitate. And that will lead to me asking questions I don't want answers to. Curiosity really did kill the damn cat.

This will end soon. *It has to.*

"Not so fast," Sebastian calls, his footsteps heavy behind me. At the bottom of the stairs, he cuts me off, slipping a folded piece of paper into my hand. "There are further instructions."

I flip it open, my stomach tightening at the sight of a map of Rosewood. In the center, there's a bold circle around a location pin.

I wave the paper in the air. "What the hell is this?"

Sebastian jabs a finger at the center of the circle. "Pay attention. This is important." His voice is low and measured. "Take the two-track on the right and drive until it ends. You'll see a wooden post with a red ribbon tied around it. Stand to the right of it, take six steps forward, and you'll find a black river rock with the number eight on it. That's where you'll burn and bury the box. Bring us the rock when it's done. You have three days."

I exhale sharply, rolling my eyes. "Do you guys really have to be so damn dramatic?"

Spinning on my heel, I take the stairs two at a time. Once I reach the top, I grab the handle, but it's locked.

My head drops back, frustration burning my insides. "Will someone let me out of this damn hellhole and take me back to my dorm?"

Aidric appears at the bottom of the staircase. With a tap to his phone, the door unlocks. *Fancy.*

Callan strides past Aidric, heading up the stairs, but I don't wait. I haul ass out of there. My feet don't stop until I'm out the front door. My lungs pull in the air like it's the first breath I've taken in hours.

I look down at the box in my hand, curious, but not stupid. I run my fingers over the painted yellow sunflower on the top, a ghost of a smile on my face as I think back to the day it was gifted to me.

It was a simpler time in my life—a softer world. Now those moments are few and far between.

"What is it?" I ask, my fingers carefully peeling back the tape on the metallic pink wrapping paper. My heart thrums with excitement, anxious to see what's inside. There's something so special about getting a gift, knowing someone put thought into picking out something just for you. It's not about the contents; it's about the gesture and the heart behind the gift.

Mom's grin stretches from ear to ear. "Open it and see."

The wrapping paper falls away, revealing a wooden box with hand-painted sunflowers on top. My breath catches. It's beautiful.

Impatient as ever, Mom reaches over, flicks open the tiny latch, and lifts the lid.

"It's so pretty," I whisper as I watch a ballerina twirl around to a familiar melody. I set it down gently on the table and throw my arms around her. "I love it, Mom. I'll keep it forever."

She pulls me close, fingers threading through my hair. Her voice is warm and so full of love. "You truly are my sunshine, Avery May."

The black SUV rolls to a stop in front of the house, yanking me out of the memory I wish I could live in for forever. Callan steps around the vehicle, and to my surprise, he opens the front passenger door for me. It's a polite gesture for someone so self-serving.

Still, I won't question my luck. At least it's him driving me and not Aidric or Sebastian.

Turns out, I won't need to play nice with Sebastian after all. Once this box is buried, I'm free.

"Get in," Callan gripes. "I've got shit to do."

"Like what? Pushing more guys off bridges?" The sarcasm slips out under my breath, but not quietly enough.

"It wasn't a bridge. It was a mountain ledge, if you must know. And I didn't push anyone."

"Well, someone did." I drop into the seat, and before I can say anything else, Callan slams the door shut.

Once he's behind the wheel, he mutters, "Seems you've already made up your mind about what happened to Evan. So go ahead and think what you want. Just don't let those accusations leave those pretty lips, or you'll have bigger problems than that box in your hands."

I drop my gaze to my lap, tracing the intricate details of the painted sunflower—losing myself in my thoughts. *How did this become my life? How did this become his?*

"Callan," I say softly, hesitating before glancing his way. "Why did you let yourself get tangled up with those guys?"

His fingers flex around the steering wheel, his shoulders pressing into the seat. "They're not as brutal as they seem. They're actually really good guys."

"Good guys?" I laugh, though the sound is devoid of any humor. "Sebastian and Aidric are anything but good, and you're right in line with them."

Callan's jaw tightens, his gaze fixed on the road ahead. "There's a lot you don't know," he says, tone low. "A lot you never will."

I shrug. "Fair enough. Not like I want the details anyway. Just one question…" A tightness coils in my chest. "Are you happy, Callan?"

His knuckles pale against the steering wheel. "Happier than ever."

As his heavy words settle between us, something about them doesn't sit right with me. I've seen Callan happy, truly happy before, and this isn't it. I study his profile, the sharp cut of his jaw, the tension in his shoulders. Callan comes from a good home. His dad might be tough on him, but he's not a bad man. And from what I heard, his mom was very involved in her boys' lives and she was so attentive to their needs.

I don't wish anything bad on Callan. Even though he's made my life hell, I know there's a heart buried beneath all that anger and indifference. I truly hope he finds peace, purpose, and maybe even happiness. But judging by the look on his face, he doesn't believe what he says.

"I hope that's true," I whisper softly.

His gaze flicks to mine. "No, you don't. You hate me, Avery. Almost as much as I hate you."

"True," I admit. "But I'm not cruel. I wouldn't wish a miserable life on anyone. Except maybe Aidric."

He lets out a small laugh. "Like I said, he's not as bad as you think. No one's ever had my back the way those guys do."

I scoff. "What about Brogan and your other sisters—Elodie and Lake? Or your brothers—Rome, Wilder, and Sayer? They've always been in your corner."

"The hell they have." His jaw tightens, but not before I catch the flicker of pain in his eyes. "The girls live in their own worlds. Rome and Wilder are the golden twins—perfect and untouchable. Sayer's all right, but he spends his life trailing in their shadow. And me?" He huffs out a bitter laugh. "I'm the fuckup. The one who was never going anywhere. That is, until I landed a spot on the Lords' hockey team."

The tires crunch over gravel as the car slows to a stop. I

glance out the window and realize we're at Faraway Archery Range.

My first thought is, this isn't over. He brought me here—to the only place I can truly be myself—and he plans to degrade and humiliate me in front of my fellow archers.

My fingers tighten around the box. "Why are we here?"

Callan leans against the steering wheel, smirking. "Told you I'd give you a ride if you came with me earlier. I always keep my word."

A short laugh escapes me. "Highly debatable. But thanks."

"At least you didn't have to hitch a ride from some unhinged serial killer."

My lips twitch with a smile. "Also debatable."

He nods toward the range. "You have everything you need to try and shoot your target?"

"Try and shoot my target?" I scoff, swinging the door open. "Please. I don't try. I hit every time. And yeah, I keep everything in my locker." I step out, feeling the cool breeze against my cheeks, but I pause before closing the door. Something heavy settles in my chest. Maybe it's pointless, maybe he won't hear me, but I say it anyway. "Your family loves you, Callan. And whether you admit it or not, you love them too."

He snorts, shaking his head. "You don't know a damn thing about me, Avery."

"Maybe not," I say, glancing at the clubhouse before my eyes meet his. "But I know when someone's lying to me, and to themselves."

His jaw tightens, but I don't wait for a response. I let him chew on that and without another word, I shut the door and walk away.

CHAPTER 7

CALLAN

As soon as Avery disappears into the clubhouse, I jerk the wheel and back into a tight space between a Corvette and a rusted-out minivan.

My grip stays firm on the steering wheel, eyes locked on the door she just slipped through. I should leave, but something keeps me here. Curiosity tugs at me, refusing to let go. She said she never misses the target and I wanna see for myself. No one is *that* good.

The field in front of me is nearly empty with only three archers, one of whom just sent her arrow skidding into the grass ten feet past the target. *Amateur.*

Not that I could do any better, but still.

After watching arrows go everywhere but the target at the other end of the field for what feels like twenty minutes or so, Avery steps outside, her long brunette hair now pulled into a high ponytail. Her outfit has changed. She's now sporting a pair of black knee-high boots, formfitting jeans that have me shifting in my seat, and a black track vest layered over her long-sleeved white t-shirt.

There's never been a doubt in my mind that Avery is hot as fuck. Any guy would kill for a chance to get with her. The thing is, once they get that chance, she'll rip them to shreds and toss them aside without a second thought.

Just like she did to me.

I sit up straighter, watching as she walks onto the field with all that confidence and sass that once had me willing to kneel at her feet. A hard bow case hangs from her hand like it weighs nothing. She's got a black belt cinched around her waist with a quiver clipped at her hip and three sharp-tipped arrows sticking out from inside it.

Maybe I've underestimated her. Avery has always had the bite to back up her bark. However, I never imagined that could extend outside of social situations. But right now she looks like a badass who belongs out there.

She strides to an open lane, stopping fifty meters from a black foam target with a yellow bullseye. The guy next to her turns and says something that makes her smile. A real smile. Not one of the shit-eating grins she's always throwing my way.

I shift in my seat, leaning forward as if it will bridge the gap between us. The guy moves closer. Almost too close. Crouching down beside her, his fingers brush over her bow like he's got any right to touch her gear. And when his hand lifts and grazes her cheek, something feral curls in my gut. My fingers tighten around the wheel, hot blood coursing through my veins.

I make a note to break those fingers if they ever land on her again. I may despise Avery, but she's mine to deal with and I don't share.

Raising her bow into position, she sets her stance. The guy makes a smart move and retreats while Avery squares her shoulders.

She nocks an arrow, and sets her sights on the bullseye. The moment stretches thin. My pulse drumming to the beat of her concentration. Then, in a single breath, she cuts the arrow loose. It slices through the air, sinking in the dead center of the target.

I catch myself smiling, feeling pretty damn proud. Maybe she was right. Maybe she really doesn't miss. Avery might be the kind of weapon we need in The Ice Society.

Her lips curve into a satisfied grin, and, of course, the guy beside her notices. He steps in again, palm pressing against her lower back. It lingers there for far too long. When I notice the tension in her shoulders and the look of apprehension on her face, I almost intervene. Lucky for him, Avery sidesteps away from him and his hand falls to his side.

She resumes shooting and I watch as she hits bullseye after bullseye. When the sun dips beneath the mountaintops, she packs up and disappears back inside the clubhouse.

That's my cue to leave. If she catches me out here, she might get the impression I'm still hung up on her. Which is the furthest thing from the truth. Sure, I once caught feelings I never meant to. But those died the night she ripped out my heart and wrung it dry with her dirty little fingers. What she doesn't know is, I was falling long before we ever slept together. I fought it hard, but when she started flirting back, I let myself believe, just for a second, that it meant something.

Then everything changed.

My chest heaves, breaths ragged and desperate as I push my body past its limits. Headlights slash through the darkness, illuminating the path ahead, while the car behind me barrels closer, determined to run me down.

My legs scream, muscles burning, but adrenaline surges through my veins, drowning out the pain. My heart pounds so violently I think it might burst, but I can't stop. Not now. Not when stopping means the end.

I reach the top of the clearing, my gut plummeting as reality crashes down. There's nowhere left to run. The brush is too thick, the cliff too daunting. One look at the drop sends a wave of fear tearing through me, my pulse roaring in my ears.

I have no choice. I put myself here, and there's no undoing my fate.

The glow of headlights sweeps over me again, cutting off my hesitation.

I make my decision, and with a sharp inhale, I throw myself forward, praying like hell I'll live to see another day. My body turns weightless—air rushing past me, the world blurring—as I accept my demise.

"Fuck," I grumble, hands planted firmly to the mattress on either side of me as I jerk awake.

Same terror, different night.

The nightmare clings until I look around my room and reality slams into me. My room, my bed, four walls. It's familiar and safe—yet nothing feels safe.

I take a deep breath, filling my lungs with the cool air blowing through my open window. Exhaling, I let my head sink back onto the pillow, but sleep feels miles away.

I stare at the ceiling, the faint glow of the moon casting shadows across the room. My mind drifts to our upcoming game on Wednesday. If Vermont doesn't get his shit together, he could cost us everything. He's a beast on the ice, but this weight on his shoulders is dragging him down. Aidric's pushing hard, expecting him to handle Evan. And we all know what that means.

Evan can't wake up. Not with his memory intact. If he does, it's over. Everything I've bled for, every inch I've clawed my way up, will all be for nothing.

Then there's Avery.

A storm I never saw coming. I should have. Hell, I should've braced for impact the second she crashed into my world. She's always been a thorn in my side, but now she's a knife, and every time she gets closer, it twists deeper and deeper.

I shut it down. I shut *her* down. I refuse to let myself fall into that trap again.

Kicking off the sheet, I swing my legs over the side of the bed and stand. The room feels like it's shrinking, threatening to swallow me whole. I need to walk off this restless energy.

I jerk open my bedroom door and step into the dark hallway, moving on autopilot as I head downstairs for a glass of water. The second I hit the bottom step, the scent of burgers floods my senses.

I don't even have to guess who's behind the grill at this hour.

Aidric is no stranger to sleepless nights. While I usually manage a few solid hours before my nightmare drags me under, he barely sleeps at all.

He swears the witching hours were made just for him, says he feels most alive when the rest of the world is asleep. He hardly touches food during the day and prefers to eat in the quiet of the night. Occasionally, he'll steal a catnap between classes, but five hours of sleep is more than enough for him. Yet, somehow, he's still healthier than any of us and built like a damn ox.

I round the corner into our massive kitchen to see a streak of ketchup smeared across the white granite countertop. Almost everything in here is white, except for the stainless steel appliances. It's a miracle it stays that way, considering the messes we leave behind. Not that we worry about it. Someone comes in four times a week to clean up after us. It's one of the perks of being who we are. Not just players, or students, but members of The Ice Society.

The sliding doors to the back deck stand wide open and a gust of cool night air rushes in the room.

"Smells good," I say, eyeing the freshly grilled burger Aidric is assembling at the counter.

I pull open one of the glass cabinets, grab a cup, and press it against the refrigerator's water spout before downing it in one go.

"Nightmare again?" He doesn't even look up—he already knows. Aidric sees me down here at least three times a week, chasing sleep that never sticks.

"Yep." I turn, leaning against the fridge. The cold steel feels nice as it clings to my hot skin.

Slathering mayo onto a bun, Aidric finally lifts his head, his eyes sharp and knowing. "You sure that's all it is? I can tell this girl's been stirring some shit inside you."

My hand cuts through the air. "I don't give a fuck about that girl."

Aidric smirks, as if he's seeing through a lie.

I don't know where he's getting this idea that Avery's gotten under my skin. While it's clear I can't stand her, I made a choice when accepting my invitation to play for the Lords. Everything in my past was left behind, The Ice Society my only way forward. Avery is no one. Nothing.

At least, that's what I keep telling myself.

"You sure about that?" he probes. "Sure she isn't getting under your skin?"

I shake my head, lying to him—lying to myself. "Not a chance."

Truth is, she *is* getting under my skin. But not in the way he thinks. That fucking girl clawed her way back into my life, dug her nails in deep, but I'll be damned if I let her break me like she did the last time. Not a fucking chance.

Aidric smirks, leaning back like he's testing me, waiting to see if I'll bite. "I wouldn't blame you if she was. The girl's hot as hell." He looks past me, gaze distant as if he's stripping her down in his head. "Wouldn't mind seeing those pretty little lips wrapped around my cock. Bet she's tight as fuck, too."

My jaw tics. He's baiting me, and *fuck*…it's working.

I step past him, unwilling to meet his eyes like somehow, if I do, he'll see something that isn't even there. No lust. No sorrow. Just pure unrelenting hate.

Turning on the faucet, I rinse my cup a few times before setting it in the strainer beside the sink.

"Avery Castle means nothing to me." I say each word sharply. "And I'll do whatever it takes to ensure her silence."

He hums in approval. "Glad to hear it. Seb and I knew we made the right choice with you." He slaps the top bun onto his burger, glancing my way. "What do you think we should do with her when we head to Cloverville for the game Wednesday."

His words catch me off guard. As far as I know, she's been dealt with.

"We gave her instructions," I say, keeping my tone even. "She'll obey, and then it's done."

His eyes narrow. "Why do I get the feeling there's something you're not telling me, Cromwell?"

I shrug, keeping my expression unreadable. "No fucking idea what you're talking about."

"We're brothers, you know that, right? There's no secrets between us. So, if there is anything you've left out. Anything we should know, now is the time to tell me. We'll deal with it together."

Dragging my fingers through my hair, I pull up something I've pushed far down. Avery's words climb their way back into my head.

I wrote it all down. If something happens to me, everyone will know who did it. I made copies.

Part of me wants to believe she's bluffing, but trust doesn't come easy for me unless it's with these guys—my family.

At the risk of her telling the truth, I spill.

"All right." I nod, rubbing a hand over my jaw. "There is something."

He pauses, setting his burger down slowly. Both hands press against the counter, his full attention locked on to me.

"She said she wrote everything down," I admit. "That if something happens to her, everyone will know exactly who did it. And…" I brace myself, knowing this next part will set him off. "…she claims she made copies."

His hand slams down on the counter, rattling the plate beside it. "That bitch!" he roars.

I shrug lazily, downplaying the situation. "I can't even be

sure she was telling the truth, to be honest. It's hard to read that girl."

"But the fact that she even said it means she thinks she's the one in charge here." His expression darkens, anger flickering beneath the surface. "I'm gonna fucking bury her!"

"I don't think she sees it that way," I tell him truthfully. "Avery talks a big game, but she doesn't throw any punches. I just can't see her making any bold moves."

He doesn't respond right away. Then slowly, the devious glint in his eye sharpens, telling me her fate is no longer settled. Doesn't matter what I say, he's made up his mind.

"Well," he drawls, amusement in his tone. "She actually thought she could sway us. Thought we'd believe she could be trusted. Our little devil has no idea who she's fucking with."

Part of me wants to revel in the power we have over her, to celebrate the way she's trapped in our world now. But another part of me wants that power all to myself.

"So, what are we gonna do about Cloverville?" he asks as he tosses a butter knife into the sink.

I exhale, shaking my head. "We can't bring her with us. It would raise suspicion."

More than that, Brogan would be on me in a second. She might not know the full depth of my history with Avery, but she does know we can't stand each other. If Avery suddenly became part of our world, Brogan would smell the bullshit from a mile away. I'm actually surprised she didn't dig deeper when I showed up at their dorm.

"Fine. But I'll have eyes on her while we're away. And if she fucks up, you'll be the one digging her grave." Slowly, he drags the pad of his thumb through the streak of ketchup on the counter, then pops it into his mouth, tasting it like he's savoring something far more twisted. "Oh, this is gonna be fun," he muses. "She wants to play, we can fucking play."

I should've known Aidric wouldn't let her get away so easily.

He thrives on control, on bending people to his will, and right now, Avery is just another piece in his game. In *our* game.

"What exactly did you have in mind?" I ask him—half curious, half ready to prepare myself.

His teeth sink into his rare burger, a smear of blood on his lips. Mischief glints in his eyes and I almost regret asking. "Guess we'll just have to wait and see," he says through a mouthful of food, chewing on whatever fucked-up plan is already brewing in his head. "One thing's for certain, our little devil won't even whisper our names by the time we're through with her."

This was supposed to be simple. She swore we could trust her. And for once, I sort of believed her. I saw the fear in her eyes. I felt the fire of her fury. She's not telling anyone. Regardless, something in my gut tells me this is far from over.

CHAPTER 8

AVERY

As I STEP onto the field, a knot tightens in my stomach. Callan stands in *my* lane, right in front of the target I pay good money to practice on.

My fingers tighten around the handle of my case before I let it drop to the ground. Picking up my pace, I rush to him with fire in my veins.

The second I reach him, I grab the back of his shirt and jerk him backward. "What the hell are you doing here?" I grit out, heat crawling up my neck.

"About damn time," he hums, glancing at his smartwatch before tipping his chin toward Benson, the archer in the lane beside mine. "Your friend over there says you're never late. So what gives?"

"That's none of your business," I snap, eyes scanning the area. There are no obvious eavesdroppers, but Benson keeps glancing our way, clearly trying to read the situation.

I take a step closer. "Answer my damn question. Why the hell are you here?"

Callan straightens, shoulders taut, and his hands shoved deep into the pockets of his stone-washed jeans. "It's Monday, Avery. Day three. Why don't we have our rock yet?"

My pulse spikes. I glance toward the clubhouse before lowering my voice. "It's in my bag. I'm taking care of it tonight."

"The clock is ticking. The sooner you get it done, the sooner this is over."

"Good," I say sharply. "Does that mean you'll stop showing up everywhere I go?"

A smirk tugs at his lips. "Maybe." He shrugs. "Guess we'll just have to see how this all plays out."

"No!" I stammer. "We had a deal. I bury that box…" Callan tenses, and I glance around before lowering my voice again. "I bury that box, and you guys leave me the hell alone."

"And bring us the rock," he adds smoothly.

"I know, Callan," I say, deliberately stressing his name. "What's so special about that rock anyway? Why does it matter so much to you?"

"It's symbolic. Something you wouldn't understand."

"Does it have anything to do with…Evan?"

His expression hardens. "You really need to quit bringing him up, Avery. It doesn't do anyone any good."

"He fell from a cliff, Callan. And rumor has it, he might not make it."

That gets his attention. His posture stiffens, and his expression turns serious. "Where'd you hear that? Someone actually said he might not survive?"

I nod, watching him carefully as I respond. "That's what everyone's saying. This wasn't just a fall down a hill. I heard they think someone pushed him."

For a split second, I think I see elation etched on his face. He doesn't want Evan to wake up, just like they said in the locker room.

"Well, it wasn't me," he says firmly, just like each time it's brought up.

Oddly enough, I think I'm starting to believe him. But there is clearly something going on here.

"For your family's sake," I murmur, "I sure hope not."

His fingers trace around his mouth as he stares past me, lost in thought. Then, after a sharp breath, his gaze snaps back to me. "Let me know if you hear anything else."

I scoff. "Umm, no. Why would I do that? Just because you say you didn't push him doesn't mean you don't know who did. I'm not protecting you assholes, or getting involved."

"Like it or not, you already are."

My head shakes, my pulse kicking into high gear. They better not try to pin this shit on me.

"The hell I am. I told you I'd keep quiet about what I heard and burn that damn box to prove it. But that's where it ends. If someone hurt Evan on purpose, I want justice for him. I won't say anything, but I sure as hell won't stand in the way of an investigation."

Callan chews his bottom lip, his expression darkening. "Go get your shit," he orders. "We're leaving."

"What?" I huff. "No. I have a competition coming up. I need to practice."

His gaze flicks to my target, scanning the bullseye covered in holes. Then, he looks back at me, unimpressed. "You don't need practice. Now, go get your shit. We're leaving."

I shake my head. "You've lost your mind," I mumble, turning toward my case, determined to do what I came here to do.

This is getting ridiculous. Ever since I went into that locker room, Callan continues to drag me away from my responsibilities.

I barely take two steps before he moves in front of me, blocking my path. A firm grip clamps around my wrist. "Unless you want me to make a scene," he grits out, "I'd strongly suggest you get your ass in that clubhouse and grab your bag. Right *fucking* now."

Something evil simmers in his eyes, sending a chill racing down my spine. But I'm not going. I call his bluff and jerk my wrist free from his grip, just as I spot Benson approaching.

Callan follows my gaze, his head turning toward Benson,

who slows his steps. "Is there a problem here?" His eyes flick to my wrist that Callan has back in his grip.

I quickly yank it away again, forcing a tight smile. "No problem here. We're good."

Benson doesn't look convinced, but before he can press further, Callan seethes, "Why don't you mind your own fucking business?" He steps toward Benson, tension radiating from him.

I reach out, trying to pull him back, but I miss by an inch.

Benson isn't a cowardly guy. In fact, he's got almost the same muscle and build as Callan, which says a lot. So it doesn't surprise me when he steps up, squaring his shoulders.

"Avery's a good friend of mine," he growls. "So when I see a guy getting rough with her, it becomes my business."

Callan smirks, tilting his head. "Oh yeah? And what the hell are you gonna do about it?"

"Put your hands on her again," he warns, "and you'll find out."

They're practically nose to nose, tension crackling, so I don't hesitate to jump between them with my arms stretched out to create space.

"Both of you, stop it." I turn to Benson first. "I'm fine, really. Callan and I have known each other since high school. He's an asshole, but he really is harmless."

It's a lie I'm willing to tell to stop them from throwing down right here. Still, it's comforting knowing Benson has my back.

Callan exhales sharply and takes a step back, cooling off. "I'd never put my hands on a girl, and she knows that," he says. "In fact, she was just leaving with me. Weren't you, Avery?"

I want this to end. I want out of this moment. But I really don't want to go with Callan. If he tries to force me, I know Benson will take him on without hesitation. And I don't want that.

No one should get hurt because of *me*.

So I force the words out, choking back every ounce of resistance. "That's right."

The second I say it, Callan's lips curl into a smug smile and I fucking hate it.

Benson studies me, searching for any sign of hesitation, but I give him nothing. "You're sure?"

I force a nod. "I'm sure."

He exhales, reluctant but unwilling to push further. "All right then. I'm around if you need me. Otherwise, I guess I'll see you Thursday night when I pick you up." He turns to leave, but not before the two of them share one last scathing glance.

Satisfied, Callan smirks and reaches down to grab my case. He flings it over his shoulder as we head toward the clubhouse.

"What's happening Thursday night?" he asks like it's any of his damn business.

"That's not your concern. I do have a life, you know?"

I reach for the door, but Callan beats me to it, pulling it open before I can. In a normal situation, I might take it as an act of kindness. But I know better with him. He's not being polite; he's just displaying an act of dominance.

I don't even thank him. I just step inside, still fuming that I have to leave with him at all.

"Meet me in the parking lot," he calls as I walk away.

I flip him the middle finger over my shoulder because, *fuck him.*

By the time I make it outside, he's waiting by the passenger side of a sleek black SUV with the door open. As I approach, he closes the space between us, slipping my bag off my back before I can react. My instinct is to snap at him for touching my things, but when he simply sets it on the floorboard inside, I let it go.

Getting into the car, I try to breathe and calm that storm within me that has me wanting to take another bite out of Callan's flesh. He starts driving, but the urge doesn't go away, in fact, I think it gets even worse because I really needed to practice today.

"What's with the pissy attitude?" he asks, as if I should be happy right now.

"Seriously?" I scoff. "You just pulled me away from my practice, and for what?"

Callan shrugs. "You said it yourself, you never miss. So practice is a waste of time. Besides, we have more important things to do."

"Like what?" I huff, annoyance seeping into my tone. "We don't hang out, Callan. We're not friends."

He claps a hand to his chest, mock-wounded. "Ouch."

"Stop pretending you feel pain," I mutter as I sink deeper into my seat. I look out the window and realize we're driving into the city. My stomach knots with unease. "Where the hell are we going?"

He glances over, lips curling into a smug grin. "We're going to the hospital to get an update on Evan."

"What?" My breath catches. "No! I don't wanna go there. I don't wanna see him, Callan. I can't go to the hospital."

"You are," he says smoothly. "We're gonna walk into that hospital hand in hand like a happy couple checking in on their good friend. And you're not gonna make it look suspicious at all."

Panic claws at my chest. Callan doesn't know I hate hospitals, and I'm not about to tell him. Instead, I force myself to breathe and not spiral.

But suddenly, it feels like all the air has been sucked from my lungs. Panic grips me as I shoot upright, my spine rigid. A wave of dizziness crashes over me, leaving me lightheaded and disoriented.

"Callan," I gasp, swallowing thickly, my throat tightening like a vise. "I can't breathe."

Suddenly, he whips the steering wheel left, and my body slams into the door with a jolt. Before I can recover, the car jerks to a stop, tires howling against the pavement.

He slams it into park and rips off his seat belt, the metal buckle smashing into the door with a loud thud. Then, before I can even process what's happening, his hands are on me. Both palms grip my shoulders, and I'm being shaken.

"Jesus Christ, Avery," he snaps. "Get it the fuck together."

I gasp, tears at the edges of my vision threatening to spill. But I won't let them. Instead, I force them back, swallowing the lump in my throat as I meet his gaze head-on.

My voice rises, matching his intensity, shaking with adrenaline. "Why the hell are you yelling at me when I'm over here panicking and barely able to breathe?"

"Because," he roars, his grip like iron. "This is happening, whether you fucking like it or not. You need to wrap your head around one thing, right now...*we* call the shots. *We* are in control. And the sooner you accept that, the better off you'll be."

Finally, his grip loosens, and he shoves me away as he drops back into his seat. His head falls against the headrest, eyes squeezing shut as he drags in slow breaths.

I don't say anything else. There's nothing left to say.

CHAPTER 9

CALLAN

She's breathing just fine.

Sometimes, all we need is a slap of reality to ground us and remind us where we stand.

I know damn well she doesn't want to go to the hospital. She made it abundantly clear. What I don't know is why she's so nervous about seeing Evan. Maybe it's their history and the fact that he's in bad shape, but something tells me it's deeper than that. Perhaps she still has lingering feelings for the guy. Even if she does, those feelings won't be reciprocated anytime soon.

The same can be said for Benson. Whatever he and Avery have going on has come to a sudden halt.

Something manic shifted inside me the first time I saw Benson walk up to Avery. The way she tossed her head back, laughing at something he said, sent fire surging through my veins. Then today, he had the audacity to approach us like he had any damn business doing so.

I've known Avery for damn near seven years. He's known her for, what? A year, maybe? And yet, he acts like he has some kind of claim to her. As if he even could.

The thought ignites an urgency inside me. A dire need to

make sure everyone knows she's off-limits. She belongs to the Ice Lords now.

She needs to stay far away from anyone who might corrupt her mind. *Anyone except me.*

"What's up with you and that nosey dipshit, Benson?" I ask her, my tone deliberately careless.

I steal a glance at her, catching the way her eyes narrow in suspicion. "Why do you care?"

Yeah. She's fine. Not only is she breathing, but that sarcastic tongue of hers is back in full force.

I shrug. "Don't care. Just curious why you'd waste your time on a guy like that. He seems violent."

A sharp laugh escapes her lips. "Benson? Violent? If that's what you took away from him trying to protect me, you're even more delusional than I thought."

My grip on the steering wheel tightens, curiosity thrumming through me. "I'm just saying, he came at me like he was ready to throw down. Maybe you shouldn't be hanging around someone whose temper is so short."

She shifts in her seat before leveling me with a scathing glare. "You showed up at my practice, threatened me, and forced me to leave with you. And let's not forget all the other bullshit you've pulled in the last four days since the locker room incident. If anyone's violent and short-tempered, it's you and your savage friends."

"Those guys are more than friends," I correct her. "They're family."

Her head shakes in disbelief. "What the hell have they done to you, Callan? Have you been brainwashed? Are you okay?"

Her patronizing tone unnerves me. She really doesn't get it. Not that I'd expect her to because she doesn't know a damn thing about us.

"What you're seeing aren't just random brutal acts. It's loyalty—unity to one another while protecting our own."

"Sure. Okay," she grumbles, sarcasm dripping from her tone.

I shake my head. Her little attitude gets under my skin in ways I can't explain. Her defiance is a challenge I crave, and her resistance turns me the fuck on. But the other night in The Chamber, when she cried, something stilled inside me. Maybe it's old feelings clawing their way to the surface. I refuse to let them breathe, though.

Avery made it crystal clear that what happened between us all those years ago was a mistake. In return, I made it just as clear that her words planted deep seeds of hate inside me. Not pain, or longing—just *hate*.

I should probably thank her. That night was a wake-up call. It was proof that I let people walk all over me for far too long. After that, my priorities shifted. I stopped living for everyone else and I started living for myself.

Now, I always get what I want. And it's time to make that clear.

"I don't want you hanging out with Benson anymore." I let my words hang for a moment before saying, "Therefore, I'm gonna need you to cancel your plans for Thursday night. We're throwing a party that night to celebrate our impending win against Cloverville, and you're coming."

"The hell I am," she scoffs.

"Oh, you are," I say, point-blank, leaving no room for argument.

There's no party—at least, not yet. But she doesn't know that. I'll throw something together last minute and leave her no choice.

I'm glad Aidric couldn't let her go now, because something dark and depraved inside me doesn't want to let her go either.

Her head shakes. "You sure are confident in thinking the Lords will win."

"We *always* win. And we *always* celebrate." I meet her smoldering gaze. "This time, you're celebrating with us."

That defiance that begs for a challenge is flashing in her eyes right now.

Fight me on this, baby. I dare you.

She crosses her arms over her chest, lips pressing into a stubborn pout. "I'm not going to your stupid party, and you can't make me."

I don't respond because arguing with her is a waste of breath. We both know she'll come if she knows what's good for her. And if she doesn't, I'll drag her there by her hair while she kicks and screams about it.

After backing into an empty space in the hospital parking lot, Avery goes dead silent. No begging, no sass, she's just... there. It's like a switch flipped inside her.

My hand grips the door handle, but I pause when I catch her staring down at her lap, making no move to get out.

With an exasperated sigh, I round the car and yank her door open, shoving down any intrusive thoughts that might suggest I care. "Would you just get out so we can get this over with?"

She doesn't argue. It's like her body is on autopilot as she swings her legs out of the door and steps down. Her lips part as if she might say something, then they close as I watch her visibly swallow. The way her neck tenses, the narrow column of her throat looking so squeezable, I get distracted watching her.

Without a word, she takes a breath and turns for the building, her body visibly shaking. *What the fuck is her problem?*

In two long strides, I'm at her side. Without hesitation, I reach over and grab her hand, locking my fingers around hers.

That gets a reaction.

She tries to yank away, but I tighten my grip. "Happy couple, remember?"

"There's no way I'm pretending to be in a relationship with you." The shaking in her limbs seems to stop as she puts up a fight and I have to assume this is better than whatever she was in her head about. I don't really care for silent Avery. I want the girl who bites back so I can show her my savage side too.

This time, I pull her close to my side as I drag her along, all the while a smile is on my face like this is the best trip of my life.

In a way, I guess it is. The girl who broke my heart is at my mercy in a place she feels uncomfortable. Now she can know what every damn day felt like at school when I would see her face in the halls. It was distracting, so much so my grades started to drop because that wound she left behind was reopened every time I had to watch her laughing or chatting with my sister.

"We'll see about that."

A low growl rumbles from her throat, snapping me back to the present as she stares straight ahead. "I *fucking* hate you, Callan."

"I know you do," I quip.

The entrance to the hospital is buzzing with people. A man pushes a woman in a wheelchair, a newborn cradled in her arms. The mother's smile stretches from ear to ear.

My heart splinters. But I tear my eyes away from her, shoving down the memories of my own mom that threaten to creep in. Not now. Not here.

"This way," I say firmly, leading her toward the elevator.

The day after Evan was brought in, I was here with Noah— the dipshit responsible for this mess in the first place. He had one job. One fucking job. And he failed miserably.

We step onto the elevator and I can feel Avery go rigid. Her breath hitches and her fingers twitch in my hand.

Just as the doors begin to slide closed, a woman joins us, the scent of vanilla and garlic wafting off her. She smiles tightly and I keep my expression neutral with a simple nod.

"I don't like this," Avery mutters under her breath, jerking her hand free from mine.

Just as she moves to cross her arms over her chest, slipping into that tough girl facade she wears like armor, I snatch her body so she can't go far. Wrapping my arm around her collarbone, I lock her back against me. My forearm presses against her throat in a partial headlock, just tight enough to remind her who's in control.

Leaning down, my lips graze the shell of her ear, and my

voice drops to a dangerous whisper. "Don't you dare fuck this up."

Then, I school my expression, forcing a smile as I slip back into our act. Louder now, for the lady listening. "I'm sure we'll get good news, baby. Evan's gonna be just fine."

She stiffens in my hold, and I'm certain I made my point because the rest of the ride to the fourth floor is dead silent.

As soon as we're out, Avery yanks her body away from me. This time, I let her have her way. Maybe it's best if there's a little bit of distance between us so we don't kill each other today.

I approach the nurses' station—Avery dragging her feet behind me—and my eyes land on the blonde sitting behind it. She's probably early twenties with a heart-shaped face and baby blue eyes.

"Good evening," I say smoothly, leaning into the counter.

She picks up a stainless steel cup with kittens on it and takes a small sip. Her mouth barely clings to the straw as her gaze meets mine. "How can I help you?" she asks, her tone holding a hint of flirtation.

I smirk at her, biting my lip when Avery suddenly smacks her hand against my chest, shoving me back with more force than I would expect. "Now who's fucking around?" she mutters under her breath before raising her voice. "You're seriously going to flirt with that chick right in front of me?"

My eyebrows shoot to my forehead. *Damn.*

Before I can react, she wedges herself between me and the desk. Then, with a no-nonsense tone, she says, "We're here to see Evan Sanders."

I chuckle, taking a step back. The cute blonde sighs heavily, clearly unimpressed. "Room four-twenty."

Without a word, Avery spins on her heel and strides down the hall, her posture rigid with annoyance.

I shake my head, following behind her because as much as she hates it, she's stuck with me.

Avery grumbles, irritation radiating from her.

"What the hell is your problem?" I scoff.

She suddenly stops, planting her hands firmly on her hips. "What's my problem?" she mocks. "You manhandled me, threatened me if I didn't play along with this happy couple bullshit, and then the second you spot a cute girl, you…" She jabs a stern finger into my rib cage. "…risk fucking it up."

I shrug, a smug grin on my face. "Thought you didn't wanna pretend?"

"Whatever," she huffs in annoyance, before drawing in a deep breath. We reach Evan's door, and Avery comes to a halt just outside. Her shoulders lift, another panic attack probably about to ensue. I don't have time for that. And I certainly don't need her out here drawing attention to the fact that Evan has visitors.

I reach for the handle, but before I can do anything, she shouts, "Wait!"

"For fuck's sake," I seethe as I shove the door open, yanking her by the arm and forcing her inside. "We're not doing this shit, Avery. All eyes are going to be on us if you can't keep it together."

Before the door even closes, I jerk the curtain shut, cutting off the unobstructed view of the nurses' station. The last thing we need is watchful eyes on us.

With her arm still locked in my grip, I spin her around and jerk her back flush against my chest. My hand clamps around her waist, holding her in place, while my other hand pinches her chin between my fingers, forcing her head up.

"Look at him," I growl, low and hot against her ear.

She flinches, her chin angling down in defiance, but I tighten my grip. "Go on, Little Devil. Take a nice, long look. This is what happens when you stop listening. When my boys think they can't trust you."

The sharp scent of antiseptic lingers in the room—I can almost taste it. The closed blinds cast thin slats of shadow across the room. Evan lies motionless, the bed cranked up just enough to give a view of his battered face. His eyelids are swollen shut, lips cracked, and skin the color of old bruises.

In the corner, a crumpled paper towel lies near the sink, still damp. I can only assume it means someone's been here recently.

Avery says nothing. Not a single fucking word. Her silence presses heavier than any scream, as she locks her gaze on Evan. I can see it working through her. From the tape on his arms, to the gauze tangled in what's left of his golden hair, all the way to the tube running from his mouth like a leash.

She trembles just before her head snaps down.

A white-hot bolt of pain slices through my arm. *She fucking bit me!*

"Fuck!"

I loosen my grip, just enough for her to rip herself free.

"That's what you fucking get!" she growls, her chest rising and falling rapidly.

Disobedience sparks in her eyes and she drags her tongue across her teeth, tasting *me*.

"Oh, you wanna fucking play, Little Devil?"

Game on.

In two seconds flat, I have her again. Face to face this time so she can't take any more cheap shots. Her breath hitches, and I see the fire in her gaze as she fights against the hot tears threatening to spill.

When one breaks free, I slam both hands against the wall on either side of her head, caging her in. Then, I slowly drag the tip of my tongue up her cheek, tasting *her*.

"You're disgusting," she groans, turning her head away.

"And you're a feisty little thing. Much feistier than I've given you credit for." My voice stays low, knowing there is a thin barrier between us and the hall. It's intoxicating knowing no matter how much she fights, there is nothing she can do to get me off of her unless I allow it.

Avery glares up at me with a tight jaw, some of her hair displaced across her face. "You haven't seen anything yet," she spits, twisting against my grip. "If you don't let go of my hands, I'll show you just how feisty I can get."

My cock twitches in response. *Fuck.* I sure do love when she challenges me like this. There's something about the way she forces me to go feral just to prove I hold more power than she does.

So, I do the one thing I know she'll hate to love. Maybe she'll fight me, or maybe she'll surrender to those dark, hidden desires she pretends no longer exist.

In one fell swoop, I drop one of her wrists, just fast enough to let my free hand dive down the waistband of her leggings, sliding beneath her panties.

Her reaction is instant. "What the fuck, Callan!" She shoves her hand against my shoulder, pushing me back with all the strength she can muster. Which is exactly what I expected.

What I didn't expect was to find her panties slick with arousal. *Well, well, well.* Seems my little devil is turned on right now, whether she wants to admit it or not.

I drag my fingers up her slick folds, savoring the way she bites down on the corner of her lip like she's masking a reaction.

Reaching her clit, I press the pad of my thumb against it, applying just enough pressure to make her breath hitch.

"Don't even pretend you don't want this," I say, daring her to deny it.

"The hell I do!" she growls as she claws at my bare arm, digging her nails right into her teeth marks.

"Tell me to stop, and I'll stop."

Let's see who really holds all the power.

If she truly asked me to stop, which she hasn't, I would— *maybe.*

With the tips of my fingers curled, I tease her entrance just enough to make her beg for more. And when the word doesn't spill from her mouth, I take what I already know to be true.

I shove two fingers deep inside her, filling her in one forceful, claiming motion. A sharp gasp rips from her lips, her body betraying her before she can even think to fight it.

What a little liar. She's fucking drenched.

"I hate you," she spits, her nails sinking into my arm, dragging down, leaving a trail of scratches in their wake.

I welcome the sting. Because in return, I punish her with pleasure, knowing damn well it kills her that I'm the one making her feel this good.

In response, her walls clench around my fingers, squeezing tight, and my eyes snap to hers, waiting for the moment that first moan slips past her lips. I can't wait to see the flicker of humiliation in her eyes when she acknowledges how good *I'm* making her feel.

"That's right, Avery," I rasp, my tone laced with control and need. "Don't fight it. Come around my fingers."

It's almost there. Moan for me, Little Devil.

Then it happens.

"Oh God," she cries, forcing me to drop her other wrist so I can put my hand over her mouth. For a second, I brace myself, half expecting her to bite me again. Then again, maybe I want her to so I can punish her harder while reminding her exactly who holds all the power.

I work faster, fingers plunging deeper as I chase her breaking point. I can't wait for her to fall apart, and all because of me.

Grinding against her, I seek pressure—needing something to ease the tension pulsing through me. My erection strains against the fabric of my jeans, threatening to break free. It's taking everything in me not to bend her over Evan's hospital bed and fuck her until she forgets why she ever pushed me away.

Her body tells me everything I need to know. Her muscles pulse around my fingers, her breath coming in short, ragged gasps. She's teetering on the edge, about to come.

Then, just as I think I have her, she shocks the hell out of me. Her hand cuts through the air before cracking against my cheek. The impact snaps my head to the side.

"Oh, you wanna play?" I seethe, jaw tight and my pulse fucking pounding.

I slam her harder against the wall, pinning her in place as my fingers drive into her so forcefully she has no choice but to let her body ride the wall with every thrust.

Her breath stutters, her hands gripping at nothing, caught between pushing me away and giving in.

I smirk against her ear, voice low and taunting. "You can slap me all you want, Little Devil, but we both know how this ends."

Fuck her for being so cold and calloused. Fuck her for playing games with my already broken heart all those years ago, twisting the knife and walking away like it meant nothing.

Fuck. Her.

Before I even realize it, I've got three fingers buried deep in her pussy and the sounds of her raw pleasure spit into my palm.

Only I can hear her, and only I know. She might hate me, but she's gonna hate herself even more when I'm done with her.

I don't even let her ride out her orgasm. The second it crashes through her, I rip my hand out of her pants like her cum is poison I refuse to touch. She glares daggers at me, knowing exactly what I've done as her pussy pulses around nothing, leaving her feeling even more like shit. I watch as she shudders, her body still trembling. Cruel? *Maybe.*

But she deserves it.

CHAPTER 10

AVERY

I LIFT MY HEAD SLOWLY, the weight of regret pressing down on me. I don't dare look at him. I can't stand to see the self-satisfied smirk on his face.

He won.

"Look at me," he says, his voice drenched with surety.

"Fuck you." I flip him my middle finger with my head down as I step around him.

I don't make it far before he throws an arm out, pulling me right back to his side.

Two wet fingers press against my chin, tilting my face up until my eyes are forced to meet his.

Shame coils inside me as his fingers trail upward, brushing across my bottom lip and smearing my own arousal like a brand.

"Taste yourself, Little Devil." He pops the same fingers into his mouth, his tongue flicking over them with a low hum of satisfaction. A wicked grin spreads across his face. "You taste so fucking good. Sweet...like sin."

"I truly hate you, Callan," I grit out through clenched teeth. "I'm not just saying it to hurt you or make a point. I mean it. I. Fucking. Hate. You."

He smirks. *He actually fucking smirks.*

"Sure as hell doesn't taste like it." He sucks on his fingers again, provoking me. "Is this when you tell me what a big mistake this was and you ignore me for four more years?"

"It *was* a mistake," I stammer, not holding back any of the anger and regret I feel.

"Why's that? Because your enemy just made you come while your comatose ex-boyfriend was listening?"

Shit.

My gaze snaps to Evan, my pulse hammering. Is he aware enough to know what's been happening around him?

No. Even if he can hear sounds and voices filtering through the fog of unconsciousness, there's no way he could fully comprehend what just happened. At least, that's what I'm telling myself.

I'm watching him, searching for any sign of life, when all of a sudden, his eyes flutter.

"Did you see that?" My breath catches as I rush to Evan's bedside, pushing away everything that just happened. "He blinked."

Callan is at my side in a sliver of a second. "Quit trying to distract me from the fact that you just came all over my fingers."

I don't even hear what he's saying, nor do I care. My eyes are trained on Evan. Then, his eyes flutter again. "See! He's waking up!" I turn my head to look at Callan, relishing the way the shit-eating grin he was wearing drops instantly.

His mouth falls open, disbelief flashing across his face. "No fucking way."

"What was that you were saying about having all the power?" With a slow, deliberate click of my tongue, I drive the blade deeper. "Oh yeah. You don't have any anymore."

Before he can respond with some bullshit excuse, the door creaks open. My heart kicks against my ribs and when I turn around, I see a guy who looks almost identical to Evan, but with a year or two on him.

Callan's hand presses against the small of my back, but I immediately sidestep away from him.

The guy who just entered wastes no time. In three long strides, he's in front of us, his angry glare locked on to Callan.

"What the fuck are you doing here?" he spits, eyes burning with something deeper than just irritation.

Unfazed, Callan smirks, casual and cocky. *Typical.* "Came with my girl to check on Evan," he says smoothly. "You got a problem with that?"

The tension thickens, pressing in from all sides. It's obvious these two have unresolved history. I'm just curious how much of it has to do with Evan.

"Actually, I do," he snaps, his voice razor sharp. "You have no fucking business being here. With your girl..." His eyes flick over me before cutting back to Callan. "...or without. Wouldn't surprise me one bit if you and your fucking Lords are the reason my brother's here in the first place."

His brother?

Callan steps up to him, his shoulders taut and his fists clenched at his sides. "Careful with your words, Liam. Wouldn't want your accusations hitting the wrong ears."

I open my mouth, ready to tell Liam that we saw Evan blink, but the air between them is too thick and the words die in my throat.

"Is that a threat?" Liam hisses. "Are you and your band of brothers gonna come for me now?" There is no terror in his words. If anything, he's challenging Callan.

"You're just sour because you didn't make the Lords' team, or any other team for that matter."

"Bullshit," Liam snaps. "I didn't join the team because I found out you're a bunch of snakes with your little secret society bullshit. You cheat for your wins. Wouldn't surprise me one bit if one of your pussy-ass teammates pushed my brother off that cliff because he was rising to the top."

Secret society? So that's what Callan is part of. I don't know much about those groups, but I know they're loyal to a fucking T. That explains his tight bond with Aidric and Sebastian. I wonder why the whole team isn't as close as they are. Or maybe, I just haven't seen them around anyone else.

"Once again, Liam," Callan stresses his name, "might wanna be careful with your words."

While these two argue over whatever it is they're arguing about, I step closer to Evan. It physically hurts as I look down, barely recognizing him.

The scene tugs at something deep—something buried. My chest tightens, and suddenly, I'm back in those hospital rooms with my mom. Visit after visit before they finally admitted her. She was usually sedated, lying still and unreachable, just like Evan is now.

The rooms always felt the same. It was always too cold—too quiet. Like grief had already taken up residence there. I remember standing over her, just like this. Watching her chest rise and fall, wondering if she knew I was there. Wondering if she ever would again.

That same familiar dread coils around my throat. My vision blurs, my body remembering before my mind can catch up.

Neither of them deserved this.

Evan wasn't mine, but he was a good person. Gentle in ways I didn't know what to do with. He noticed things. Listened, even when I didn't speak.

Just like her.

They're both broken in ways that can't be seen, but Evan's pain is painted across his flesh.

His head is wrapped tightly in gauze, but his face is visible. Both eyes are painted in a hue of yellowish blue, and his pale skin blends in with the white sheet that's draped over him. There's a mess of wires connecting him to monitors and pumps, and a slow and steady beat is masked by all the shouting happening around me.

"What did they do to you, Evan?" I whisper.

Resting my hand over his, the eerie coolness of his skin sends a shiver through me.

Then...his finger lifts, causing my breath to catch in my throat.

"You guys." My voice cracks before propelling forward. "You guys, he moved!"

And then, he does it again. Only this time, his whole hand lifts, fingers twitching before stretching outward like he's reaching for something—like he's reaching for me.

In an instant, Liam is at Evan's side. I look at him, catching the glimmer of hope in his eyes.

"He moved," I tell him again, my pulse racing. "And right before you came in, he blinked."

Liam nudges me to the side and he takes Evan's hand in his. "Evan," he says softly. "Evan, are you with us? Wake up, bud. It's me. It's Liam."

The worry and love in his tone make my heart ache, knowing the feeling all too well of holding a loved one's hand while wishing you could have them back.

Liam's eyes go wide as if the weight in the room just shifted.

"He squeezed my hand," he whispers, his voice thick with disbelief.

Before I can process what's happening, I'm yanked backward, colliding with Callan's chest. His fingers close tightly around mine, pulling me to the door. "We gotta go," he mutters, his tone low and frantic.

"No!" I shout, shoving him away from me. "I need to be here when he wakes up!"

The shock of my actions is etched into his features, and when he tries to reach for me again, I slap his hand down. "Don't touch me!"

I spin on my heel to go back to Evan, but I slam straight into

Liam's chest. He doesn't push me off, doesn't curse under his breath or shove me away. Instead, he tucks me into his side like his body is my shield.

Glowering at Callan, he jabs a stern finger at the door. "You need to go, right fucking now." Callan moves to close the space between us, but Liam is faster and meets him halfway. "I said fucking go," he shouts.

Callan's nostrils flare, his fists clenched so tightly at his sides that his knuckles turn white. "Not without my girl, asshole!" he grinds out. "Let's go, Avery."

Liam snaps his head around, his quizzical gaze pinned to me. "Avery? As in Evan's ex?"

I don't respond, or even get the chance, before he turns back to Callan. "If you don't get the hell out of this room right now, I'll call the detective on my brother's case and let him remove you."

Knowing this is going to explode if Callan doesn't leave, I begin toward him, ready to diffuse the situation before it gets worse. But I'm stopped by Liam's steady hand on my shoulder. "You don't have to go," he says, his glare still on Callan. *"That fucker needs to go."*

"Give me a minute," I tell Callan, hopeful he'll just go outside and wait for me.

Callan bares his teeth, his eyes locked on to me. His jaw tightens, and his gaze goes darker. It's clear that he's worried if I stay, I might open my mouth and tell Liam something I shouldn't. The best part is, he knows he can't stop me right now.

"I need to get the nurse in here," Liam seethes, his patience hanging on by a thread. "So get your punk ass out of this room right fucking now."

Callan doesn't move at first. But then I see a flicker of uncertainty in his eyes. Liam isn't playing games. And for the first time, I think he's worried he's losing control.

Gritting his teeth, and with a sharp step forward, he bumps his chest against Liam's in a last-ditch show of dominance. "I'll go," he growls. "But this isn't over, asshole." His gaze flicks to mine with a silent warning. "Let's go. Now!"

"I'll meet you in the hall," I say firmly.

With a final glare, Callan spins on his heel and storms out. As soon as the door clicks shut behind him, I feel like I can finally breathe.

Looking over my shoulder, I see Liam standing beside Evan, his fingers wrapped gently around his brother's hand. There's something about the way he holds on to him, like he's afraid to let go, that has me wanting to be here even more. I step closer, joining him.

"I pushed the call button. Someone should be here soon," he murmurs, his voice softer now.

I nod, my chest tight with emotion. "I can't believe he's waking up. I'm just so glad I was here to see it."

Liam lifts his head, his eyes knowing. "Why are you hanging around Callan? You do realize those guys are dangerous, right?"

I let out a slow sigh, the weight of everything pressing down on me. "I'm starting to realize that. It's just...complicated."

His eyes narrow. "Complicated how?"

I have no doubt that if I told Liam the truth, he would do everything he could to protect me and his brother. It makes me feel comfortable, but I also don't want to put him in that position. As much as I want to tell him everything I know, I don't have the full story. *Yet.*

"It's not important," I tell him. It's a lie, but I can't tell this stranger the truth. Not with so much at stake. A heavy moment of silence passes between us before I finally say, "Do you think they did this to him?"

Liam's jaw tightens, his answer immediate. "Oh, I know they did this to him." His voice is laced with certainty. "Now it's just a matter of proving it. That fucking society they run is ironclad. They've got people everywhere, connections in every damn corner. From what I've heard, they get away with everything, even murder."

I don't say anything because I don't want Liam thinking I'm a part of this. Instead, I steal a quick glance at the clock. "I should go before Callan gets too pissed." I take a step back. "I'll be waiting for an update on Evan. I'm sure the news will spread like wildfire."

Liam reaches into his jeans pocket and pulls out his phone. "Let me get your number so I can text you if there's any news."

I hesitate, but there really is no harm in Liam having my number. And I would love to hear if there are any updates on Evan's condition. So I nod. "Sure. That'd be great."

I rattle off the digits, and immediately after, my phone buzzes in my pocket. I glance down at the screen.

Liam: Now you've got me, too ;)

Before I can even register the nerves in my stomach, the door swings open and a nurse steps in. Liam shifts his attention to her, giving her every detail of Evan's movements.

I slip my phone back into my cross-body purse and use the distraction to slip quietly out of the room, before Callan decides to make a scene.

The end is near, but this isn't over yet.

CHAPTER 11

AVERY

THE RIDE back was dead silent.

For the first time ever, I think Callan was at a loss for words. His usually untouchable ego is obviously bruised, and the power he speaks of so often is slipping away from him, little by little. Everything he's built with his newfound family is about to be ripped apart, and he's petrified. As he should be.

When he pulled up to my dorm, he didn't linger. No smug remarks, no grip on my wrist, no cruel words. He just shoved me toward my car with an order to finish the task I've been assigned, *tonight*. Which is complete and utter bullshit.

Evan is waking up. Soon, he'll open his eyes and tell everyone the truth. The truth that Callan and his precious Lords have been so desperate to keep buried. And yet, despite the inevitable fall of his empire, he's still sending me out into the woods to burn evidence. As if the ashes of my music box can silence Evan when he finally speaks.

Now, it's pitch-black out, and I'm expected to drive twenty minutes out to some desolate lot in the woods and destroy what I can only assume is evidence in a serious investigation.

My headlights cut through the thick shadows as I pull up to the clearing. With my engine still running, and my lights still on,

I whip open my door. After slipping on a pair of black leather gloves, I grab the spade Callan threw in my car, my box, and my flashlight from the passenger seat.

I knew the world wasn't sunshine and rainbows, but I never imagined secret societies running around in the dead of night beating people up or killing them.

Welcome to the dark side, Avery. Not only are there no snacks, there are three broody assholes hell-bent on controlling your every move.

With a sigh, I get out of the car, feeling the dried arousal in my underwear with each step. It's about as annoying as the man who put it there.

A shiver runs down my spine when I think about our shameful act. How could I have been so weak?

A sharp gust of wind has the trees bustling, making my nerves feel even more on edge. Crisp leaves rain down, scattering all around me. It's early winter, and thankfully, there hasn't been any accumulating snow, but the crunch beneath my shoes makes me feel exposed. Like someone might hear me. Or worse, like someone might be watching me. I clutch the box tightly, the light of my flashlight bouncing off the trees.

Then, relief washes over me when I see the post with the weathered red ribbon.

Not wasting a single second, I stand to the right of the marker, muttering the instructions under my breath.

"Six steps forward. One…two…three…four…five…"

I see it. My heart jumps into my throat as I crouch down beside the black rock. Reaching into my coat pocket, I pull out the spade. My fingers tighten around the handle as I plunge the blade into the solid ground. It's cold, so I have to really work to even make a dent in it.

My breaths cloud in the night air as I dig, and once I've got a decent-sized hole, I drop the spade to the ground. Reaching for the box, I run my gloved fingers over the delicate details, tracing the design one last time.

A pang tightens in my chest. After tonight, I'll never see it again. Much like everything tied to my mom, it's just another piece of the past that I have to let go of, whether I want to or not.

I can't help but wonder if the picture of my mom and I is still in there. Or, if I'll ever see it again.

The whistle of the branches sends a shiver down my spine, making my nerves pulse with awareness. My head snaps up, scanning the darkness for any sign that I'm not alone.

When I don't see anything unusual, I chalk it up to the wind.

Still, my pulse doesn't settle as I glance back down at the box resting in my lap. Curiosity coils inside me. I've had this box for days, temptation gnawing at me. Now, with only moments left before it's buried forever, this is my last chance to see what's inside. To not only look for my picture, but to also uncover another secret. *Do I dare do that to myself?*

Moments pass before I finally cave, the cool night pressing in on me until I'm almost numb to it.

With a shaky hand, I lift the clasp, drawing in a deep breath before flipping the lid open.

My heart gallops when the ballerina begins twirling to the rhythm of the almost haunting melody. Panic grips me and I slap the box shut. My breaths are uneven as my gaze darts around, scanning the woods to make sure I haven't drawn any unwanted attention.

Still, nothing. But the uneasy feeling lingers as I open the box again.

When it's fully raised, the ballerina twirls again. Lying beneath her is something wrapped in brown butcher paper. But before I inspect it, I close my eyes.

I let the music wash over me, pulling me back to a time when life was simple. It hurts because I can see the moment so clearly.

I'm sitting on the floor of my bedroom, Barbie dolls dancing in my hands. Mom is behind me, gently humming the tune as she braids my hair.

I felt safe. I *was* safe.

Her warm voice and the way she was so gentle with me. The smile on her face and how mine mirrored hers so perfectly. It was almost like we were twins. She never wore a lot of makeup and her hair was always braided. I wanted to be just like her, so I always did the same.

Her soft eyes and perfect smile were all I ever needed to get through a rough day, and it's something I wish I could have back more than anything.

But that was then, and this is now.

I snap out of the memory and open my eyes, face to face with the reality of what's happening.

Reaching down, I pick up the wrapped object inside. It's got weight to it, like a rock, but it isn't hard. Curious, I give it a gentle squeeze. A sickening realization creeps in as my fingers sink into the soft, mushy texture beneath the paper.

I have to know what I'm burying.

With trembling fingers, I slowly peel away the layers of tape, my pulse hammering. The paper crinkles beneath my touch, each movement feeling heavier than the last.

I take a deep breath, then pull it back.

Oh my God.

A strangled gasp rips from my throat as I hurl the object away, my body lurching to the side in shock. I catch myself before collapsing to the ground, only to feel my hands sink into damp, cold moss.

Chest heaving, I lean forward, forcing myself to look at the object now lying on the crumpled paper.

A tongue. Not just any tongue—a *human* tongue. It lies there, raw and pale, streaked with drying blood. The edges are uneven, but the end is clean, like it was cut straight out of someone's mouth.

My stomach twists violently, knots tightening so hard it feels like I might snap in two.

Bile burns as it rises up my throat. Then, I turn to the side and vomit until there's nothing left inside me.

Wiping the back of my arm across my mouth, I force myself to breathe…to think. I need to put these missing pieces together before I completely lose it.

That's not Evan's tongue. At least, I don't think it is.

A person can live without their tongue, sure. But if someone had actually cut his out, rumors would've spread. There's no way this would still be a quiet investigation. Everyone would immediately know someone was responsible.

It belongs to someone else. Which means the Lords didn't just target one person. A cold realization hits me, the fact wrapping around my heart. Callan was right, no one fucks with them and gets away with it. I am holding proof of it. Proof that could bury them even deeper. Proof that could bury me right along with them.

Oh, God. I'm half tempted to dig a bigger hole and just climb in it so they don't have the satisfaction of doing it themselves.

Why the hell would they put me in this position? Leverage? Blackmail? *That has to be it.*

This isn't just about trust anymore. It's about control. They hold the power, and now, I'm locked even tighter in their iron grip. And the worst part is, I have no idea what they'll want from me next.

Forcing down the nausea that threatens to resurface, I brace myself and fold the paper back over the tongue, hiding it, as if that could erase what I just saw.

I stretch both hands out, gathering a bundle of twigs and dried leaves, piling them beside the hole I just dug, the rustling sound unnervingly loud in the silent night.

Reaching into my pocket, my fingers fumble until they close around the box of matches I brought. I slide it open, plucking a single match between my fingers.

With a quick flick, I strike it against the box. A tiny flame dances to life, the scent of sulfur cutting through the cold air. I drop it onto the pile, watching as the kindling catches fire. Leaves curl at the edges, and twigs crackle under the flames.

I strike another match, feeding the small fire to keep it alive. Then, I swallow down the bile rising in my throat and shove the wrapped tongue into the heart of the flame, watching as the evidence of the Lords' heinous act disintegrates. The scent of burnt flesh clings to the air—to my clothes, to me.

Nausea churns in my stomach again, but I shove it down hard, willing myself not to lose the plot, because I'm not finished yet.

There's one thing left to do.

I look down at my music box, feeling a pang in my chest. I can't do it. I can't burn the box. The thought alone feels like I'm setting fire to the last piece I have of her—the old her.

Instead, I break one miniscule rule and I push it into the hole. The sound of it landing sends a chill through me.

I wait, and I watch. Seconds stretch into what feels like hours as the flames consume every last trace of evidence. When I'm certain the contents of the wrapper are nothing but ash, I push myself off the ground and stand.

Lifting my foot, I stomp out the lingering embers, grinding them into the dirt. Then, I pick up the small shovel and scrape the remnants into the hole on top of the box.

Working quickly, I pile the dirt back on with my hands. My entire body is trembling, but I don't stop until every trace of evidence is underground.

Once it's completely covered, I lift my foot and stomp down hard, packing the dirt in place before tossing some brush onto the area so you can't tell something was freshly dug up.

My eyes dart to the rock—the last piece of this twisted task. I grab it, shove it into my pocket, and spin on my heel.

Without looking back, I get the hell out of here.

CHAPTER 12

AVERY

Me: It's done.

I hit send before tapping out another message to Callan.

Me: I'm exhausted. I'll bring you and your miscreant friends the rock tomorrow.

He responds almost instantly.

Callan: Good girl. Now, ice your thighs, Little Devil. You're gonna be aching tomorrow after that finger-fucking.

Heat rises up my neck, settling in my cheeks. He's never going to let me live this down. I knew that the second I let it happen. There was nothing tender or sentimental about what we did in that hospital room. It was raw, depraved, and laced with hate.

It is what it is.

I'm done looking back. Done dragging the past behind me like a corpse I refuse to bury. Callan can taunt me all he wants, but I can throw it back just as hard.

> Me: Fuck off, Callan. My vibrator does a better job than you. The first time…and the last.

With the knees of my leggings caked in dirt and my hair a tangled mess, I trudge toward my dorm room, silently praying Brogan isn't inside. I'm too physically and emotionally drained to even muster the energy to check her location on my phone.

Dragging my feet, I move closer to the door, but just before reaching for the handle, I stop when I realize it's cracked open.

A chill runs down my spine as the low murmur of masculine voices seeps through the gap. I lean in, trying to make out the conversation…

"Do you know when she might be back?" a man's gruff voice cuts through the silence. "It's imperative that we speak with her as soon as possible."

Instinct screams at me to turn around and walk away. Lately, every surprise lurking around the corner has been bad.

But then another thought creeps in. What if it's important? What if it's about my mom? I don't know why my mind jumps to her, but it does.

With my heart racing, I take a breath, push the door open, and step inside.

A man stands in the center of the room, dressed in black slacks and a matching jacket, his posture stiff and professional. He's holding a notepad in one hand and a pen in the other.

My stomach sinks when I see the badge clipped to his belt. *He's a detective.*

This is bad. This is *very* bad. He's likely here about Evan's case. Or worse, the mysterious tongue.

"There she is now," Brogan sings, completely unbothered, as if having a detective in our dorm room is just another Monday night.

But when she catches the flicker of fear in my eyes, her expression drops.

I swallow hard, forcing my shoulders to relax as I pull my

lips into a tight smile. "Hi there," I say smoothly, stepping past him like his presence doesn't send ice-cold panic through my veins. "Were you looking for me?"

My head stays down as I move to my nightstand, pulling the contents of my pockets free. In one handful, I set down my keys, a piece of gum still wrapped, and—*shit*—the rock. It lands with a faint thud against the wood, blending in like it's just another meaningless item.

Keep it together, Avery.

"I was," he responds dryly. "Fortunately, you weren't as hard to track down as some of the others we've needed to speak with." His eyes flick over me in an assessing manner. He clicks his pen again before extending his hand to me.

"Detective Klein," he continues, sliding a hand through the air toward me. "I just have a few questions. Shouldn't take long."

I shake his hand, hopeful he doesn't notice the tremor in mine.

I don't hesitate. "This is about Evan Sanders, isn't it?" No need to beat around the bush. If I dance around the obvious, it'll only make me look guilty. Everyone knows what happened to Evan, so there's no world in which I wouldn't know.

Klein studies me for a beat before nodding. "It is." He tilts his head slightly. "I understand you and Mr. Sanders were close at one point. Would you mind answering a couple questions?"

"Of course. Anything I can do to help, Detective Klein. How is he doing, anyways?" I say, sounding chipper, almost *too* chipper for someone being questioned by a detective.

Dial it down, Avery. Act normal.

"We'll get to that," Klein says casually, like he's already five steps ahead of everyone else. "Would you mind telling me a little about your relationship with him?"

Brogan steps up beside me, her gaze locked on the detective. She leans in, her voice barely above a whisper. "What's this all about, Ave?"

I silence her with a quick step away, putting distance between us as I shift my full attention back to Klein.

"There really isn't much to tell," I say, keeping my tone apathetic. "Evan and I met through mutual friends." I gesture toward Brogan. "My roommate and her boyfriend, who plays on the same hockey team as Evan." I shift my weight, offering a small shrug.

"We hung out for a couple of months, and when we both decided we didn't want more, things ended. No drama, no hard feelings." I meet the detective's gaze evenly. "That's really all there is to it."

Fuck. Did I say too much? It felt like I was rambling on and on and on. Oh, for the love of God, please let this end soon before I faint.

In between scribbling something onto his notepad, his eyes pull up. "And did you two keep in touch after things ended?"

Every time he looks away, relief washes over me. At least then I know he's not analyzing every twitch and every tweak of hesitation.

"Sort of," I say carefully. "I mean, he's good friends with my roommate's boyfriend, and I go to their games. Sometimes I hit the bar with them afterward. So, yeah…we see each other around." I shrug, like it's no big deal.

There it is again—that flash of a glance. My lungs restrict until he finally looks back down.

"And how are those run-ins?" he asks with his pen poised over the notepad. "Would you say they're friendly? Or is there tension when you're in the same room together?"

"Oh no." I chuckle, forcing out a sound that I hope sounds natural. "There's no tension. Evan and I are friends. If you'd call it that."

Detective Klein hums, then his gaze snaps up, this time locking on to mine. "Well, I'd say so," he muses. "I mean, you did go visit him at the hospital today, correct?"

My stomach plummets. I steal a quick glance at Brogan who's

mirroring the same wide-eyed *oh shit* expression that's plastered on my own face.

Fuck. Fuck. Fuck.

"That's right," I manage, swallowing thickly. "I've been meaning to visit since he was brought in last week, but was nervous to see him like that. A friend helped me find the courage today, so we went."

Klein doesn't break eye contact. Instead, he flips a few pages in his notepad, scanning something before raising a brow. "This friend..." he says slowly, his voice measured. "Would that be Callan Cromwell?"

I feel like I'm being played like a damn fiddle right now. This man already has all the answers; he just wants to hear me say them. Worst of all, Brogan is watching it all unfold.

I swallow thickly before saying, "That's right."

"Wait a damn minute," Brogan huffs, suddenly right at my side with a demanding presence. "You went to the hospital with Callan? Why didn't I know about this?"

"It was a last-minute decision," I mutter, trying to steady my voice. "I'll tell you about it later."

"Tell me about this rock?" Klein says, tone stoic as he approaches my nightstand.

My head literally feels like it's spinning from lack of oxygen. "Oh." I laugh. "That little thing. I umm...I found that when I went for a walk this afternoon. Thought it was pretty cool."

Brogan shakes her head but stays silent. She knows the words spilling from my mouth are bullshit. And I know it too, because I can feel my bottom lip trembling through the lies. It's something I'm well aware of ever since Callan pointed it out.

Klein clears his throat, the sound deliberate as he rolls the rock between his fingers. "Was this walk before, or after, you went to visit Evan?"

"Before," I blurt out, the word slipping past my lips before I even have time to think.

Klein nods slowly, like he's filing the answer away. "I see." He holds up the rock between his fingers, turning it slightly as if he's inspecting it under the light. Then, with an unsettling calm voice, he asks, "Mind if I keep it?"

Panic surges through me, twisting my thoughts into a tangled mess. *What the fuck do I say?*

The silence nearly suffocates me before Klein cuts through it. "It's just a measly rock, right? Nothing of sentimental value?" His voice is smooth, but I know better. There's something calculated lurking beneath it.

"That's right," I force out, nodding a little too quickly. "Sure. You can keep it."

"Wonderful." He grins, slipping the rock into his pocket. Then, with a cheerful tone, he adds, "Well, I think that's all the questions I have for now. If you think of anything that might be of relevance, call me." He passes me a business card before turning toward the door, moving at an unhurried pace. "Have a good night, ladies."

The second he's out the door, relief crashes over me, but it's fleeting. Now I have to face Brogan and all her unanswered questions.

I look down at the card, reading his name over and over, desperately grasping for time because I know what's coming.

"What the actual fuck, Avery!?" Her words hit like a slap.

I walk to the door, giving it a firm press to make sure it's closed. Drawing in a slow breath, I steady myself before turning back. "It's not what you think," I say firmly, but my words feel flimsy against her storm-brewing eyes.

She closes the distance between us, ripping the card from my hand and holding it in the air. "Then tell me what it is because from where I stand, it looks pretty damn bad." Her voice drops to a low plea. "Do you know what happened to Evan?"

"No," I spit out, no thought process behind it. "I have no idea what happened to him." It's the truth. I really have no idea who pushed Evan, or why. I know some of the Lords' players had something to do with it, but I don't know to what extent.

"Was it Callan?" Her voice wavers. "Please tell me it wasn't him."

"It wasn't him," I say softly, a knot forming in my stomach.

Callan's hands are far from clean, but for some strange reason, I believe him when he says he didn't push Evan. The problem is, I still don't know where he fits into this twisted puzzle.

Hell, I don't even know where all the pieces are. All I have are jagged edges of half-truths and stolen secrets I wish I never overheard.

If only I could rewind time and go back four days. I'd be a little more patient and just wait outside that locker room until Brogan found me. If I had, none of this would be happening. Now I have to do everything in my power to protect my friend from these dangerous men—one of whom is her own brother.

I have to lie to her so I can keep her safe from them.

"You want the truth?" I ask, raising my brows, feigning something close to sincerity.

"Hell yes, I want the truth!" she fires back.

I nod toward my bed and meet her on the edge of it. We both sit and I press my lips together, my mind racing. I have to choose my words wisely because once the lies start, there's no taking them back.

I take a deep breath and begin. "Callan and a few of his friends from the Lords' team asked me to help them with something for school. Once the other guys left, Callan and I started talking. As you know, we've never really gotten along, but he was actually being nice. Almost human, really."

I force a small laugh, like I'm still in disbelief myself.

"So, I told him how I was feeling about Evan being in the hospital, and in return, he told me about something he learned in rehab—how you have to face what's holding you back in order to move forward. And somehow, he convinced me to go see Evan."

I pause, watching her reaction, making sure she's buying this. When she rolls her hand through the air, I keep going.

"While we were there, Evan started moving. He even reached for me. I don't know if he actually knew it was me, but he reached nonetheless."

I lower my voice as if the next part is an unfortunate sidenote.

"Then his brother, Liam, showed up, and he and Callan got into it. I think Liam tried out for the Lords at one point and didn't make the cut, so he's been butthurt about it ever since. That's honestly it. All I can guess is that Liam told Detective Klein we were there, and the guy just ran with it."

She doesn't look entirely convinced, her brows knitted together as she searches my face for any sign of deceit. "And the rock?" she presses.

"It really is just a stupid rock. I don't even know why he wanted it." I keep my voice casual, as if I'm just as confused as she is. "Maybe he has a kid who collects them."

The seconds stretch as I wait for a response.

"Okay," she quips, shoulders lifting in a quick shrug. "I believe you."

"You do?" The words tumble out too fast and too desperate.

She nods, her expression open and trusting, which feels like a knife straight to the chest. "Of course I do. I mean, you have no reason to lie to me."

My stomach twists into a thousand tiny knots of guilt. I'm the worst. Lying to her, keeping secrets, pretending I have this under control. Everything just keeps stacking up, one deception after another.

"This whole situation is just so fucked up," she continues, twirling the ends of her blonde hair around her finger. "I can't believe anyone would ever want to hurt Evan. Hayes thinks it was his brother, Liam. Apparently, Liam's always been jealous of him."

My eyes widen. *Liam?*

That's impossible. Liam was far too kind and protective.

Besides, I know it was the guys. But it seems I'm the only one who connected the dots. No one else suspects a thing. Just me—alone with a truth I can't share.

CHAPTER 13

CALLAN

"Get her out of your head, man," Aidric scoffs, passing me the puck with a flick of his wrist. "Her living up there isn't doing you any favors."

I growl just before slamming the puck right back at him. It slides across the ice, landing against his stick with practiced ease.

"I'm not thinking about her," I snap.

It's a lie.

The echo of her voice still lingers in my fucking skull. This isn't about feelings, though. It's not about heartbreak or jealousy or any of that emotional bullshit. This is about what she knows, and what she might do with that information.

It's about the risk and exposure.

I worked my ass off to get where I am today, and I'll be damned if I let Avery fucking Castle be the one to take it from me. One wrong move on her part, and everything could come crashing down. Not just for me, but for all of us.

This isn't about today. Hell, it's not even about tomorrow. This is about my future as a member of The Ice Society.

Not just as an Ice Lord playing hockey, but something bigger —something that lasts. For the first time in my life, I've been accepted and given a place to belong. And I don't just want to keep it, I want to expand it. Bring others in. Build something that'll outlive us all. Wrap this legacy around people who were just as lost as I once was. I want to give them something to fight for, like they've given me.

The majority of my teammates don't give a fuck about The Society. It's a temporary shortcut to protection, wins, and solidarity. They'll leave this school, forgo being a permanent member of The Society, and move on with their lives in the NHL. But not me. I'm in it for the long run. I want something bigger than just the ice and the temporary high of power.

And yeah, maybe she's on my mind, too. What we might do to her—what *they* might do to her. Some of our boys aren't all about our secret organization, they just want to play the game, but the ones who are dedicated their soul to it.

I've seen what they're capable of, and she's yet to see the worst of it. Avery has no idea what kind of storm she's dancing with. And if she starts playing nice with Liam Sanders and my boys catch wind of it, she'll be standing dead center in a goddamn hurricane.

I still don't get why she was so chummy with Liam in the first place. She doesn't even know the guy. Just met him at the hospital, yet there she was acting like he was her goddamn savior. Like he was some knight in shining armor, swooping in to shield her from big bad me.

It's laughable. Yet the thought of that asshole putting his dirty hands on her—touching what isn't his—makes my skin burn. The moment he stood in front of her like a shield, something primal rose in my chest and I can't quite swallow it down.

"Cromwell!" Coach's voice booms across the rink. "Get your head out of the fucking clouds and focus!"

I snap out of it, glancing behind me just in time to see the puck slide across the ice, nowhere near where it should've gone.

"Told ya," Aidric laughs, skating up beside me with that shit-eating grin. "You're still fucking thinking about her, aren't you?"

I shake my head hard, trying to clear the fog. He's not wrong, but I still want to make him eat his teeth just for that stupid look on his face.

We pass the puck a few more times and my mind slowly finds that steady focus. The glide of the ice beneath my blades, the way it feels to slap a shot to Aidric knowing he'll circle the goal and bring it right back to me so I can send it into the net.

When the whistle blows, we launch into some rounds of power skating. By the time we're done, my legs are burning, and my lungs are on fire.

After drills, we huddle near center ice, and Coach barks out some plays for the Cloverville game.

"White attacks. Blue blocks. Now move!" The whistle sounds and we fall into our positions.

As soon as the puck drops, it's game on.

I intercept the puck, eyes locked on the defense, and I send it down the ice without hesitation. It's not about trying anymore; it's a reflex that's built into my bones.

We cycle through some power plays, penalty kills, and defensive stacks—all of which are tailored to Cloverville's style.

For a while, I forget everything—even her. *Almost.*

Once the team wraps up, I yank off my helmet, sweat dripping down my neck.

"You killed it, man," Aidric says, giving me a solid pat on the back. "After you finally got that chick outta your brain."

I shake my head, grinning. "You're fucking delusional."

"Just calling it like I see it."

Seb glides up to us with his helmet tucked under his arm, sweat slicking his hair back. I'm glad to see he's not raging right now. At least they're still letting him practice with the suspension hanging over his head. Seb got into some shit with one of the coaches and they really laid it on him hard. He's bouncing back, though.

Near the exit, a couple of the ice girls are lingering. They're all smiles, and their eyes are pinned to me, Sebastian, and Aidric like we're the main attraction.

"Hey, boys," Lani calls out, her voice sweet with a hint of mischief. She twirls a strand of her dark hair around her finger, eyes flicking between us. "You all look hungry. Care to grab a bite?"

Aidric doesn't hesitate to chime in. "Depends on what we're biting." He grabs a firm handful of Jasmine's ass, making her squeal. "If it's this, then count me in."

I, on the other hand, shoot a thumb over my shoulder. "I'm out. Got things to do."

I don't, really. But I'm exhausted and the last thing I feel like doing is entertaining puck bunnies with too much makeup and not enough personality.

"What the fuck, bro?" Aidric huffs, clearly offended. "Since when?" He leans in, dropping his voice to a near whisper.

"Did you *see* that ass?" he says, eyes wide like he's talking about a damn miracle. He reaches out and gives Jasmine another squeeze, making her giggle.

"Come on." He grins. "I'll even let you tap it first."

I just shake my head because no amount of ass grabbing, or tapping, is changing my mind.

Then, Seb casually raises his hand like he's in class and the teacher just asked for volunteers. "I'll ride that train."

Jasmine and Lani smirk as they link their arms around Aidric and Seb's, claiming them for the night.

Lani tosses a glance over her shoulder, a playful pout on her lips. "You sure you don't wanna join us?"

I click my tongue against the roof of my mouth, offering a half smile. "Nah. Maybe next time."

I watch them disappear, laughter and bad decisions trailing behind them.

What the fuck did I just pass up? More importantly, *why* did I just pass it up? This isn't me. I live for tits and ass and girls who serve it up without hesitation. That's my thing.

Something's holding me back, though. Maybe it's…

No. Hell no!

It's not fucking Avery.

Don't even let your mind go there, Callan. Don't be that guy.

Thankfully, I'm yanked out of the spiral when Slade drops onto the bench next to me. I start unlacing my skates, and he does the same, both of us quiet for a moment.

"Can I talk to you for a minute, bud?" Slade asks, his voice low with a tinge of unease.

"Of course," I tell him, setting my skates aside and giving him my full attention. "What's going on?"

His fingers drag through his hair, slicking it back, and he exhales a sharp breath. "I'm struggling...bad," he admits. "I think all this shit is starting to get to me."

I didn't expect that. As council advisor, I've had plenty of these conversations with guys who are cracking under pressure, buckling beneath the weight of our expectations, and all the secretive dark shit we're wrapped up in. I just didn't expect it from Slade. He's always been so resilient and strong.

The sound of the door opening catches my attention, so I lean in. "I know it's a lot," I say quietly. "But I promise you, it's worth it."

Slade doesn't look convinced. His eyes are distant, like he's trying to balance something that won't stop tipping.

"Is it, though?" he murmurs. "I mean...yeah, the team's great. No question about that. But the price tag that comes with all this..." He shakes his head. "It's high, Callan. Really fucking high. Can you honestly say you'd go back on everything you believed in, and everything you were, just for these guys?"

"Yes," I say without question. "I absolutely would."

"Well, I can't." His hands shoot up before slapping down on his thighs. "I took my oath without knowing how bad things could get. I was branded under the belief we were one—unified, in solidarity. But whatever is going on behind closed doors is starting to make its way out of the closet and I'm terrified about what that means for all of us. You, Aidric, and Seb are all keeping shit from the team and we wanna know why."

The team is questioning us? That's not good. If we're going to get through this mess with Evan, we have to stay united. With Klein lurking, we can't afford to slip up. There's no room for mistakes.

"We are trying to protect the team," I say carefully, not wanting to give too much but also knowing he needs something. "We took an oath too, one to guide you. Let us handle it."

"That doesn't make us one, Callan. It makes it *us*...and *you three*."

I get what he's saying. I really do. Normally, things aren't this intense. The lines between our team and The Society are not always so blurred. But lately everything's been chaotic. First, it was Evan's fall, then Avery crashed into our lives like a wrecking ball, tearing through the foundation we've spent years building.

On a typical day, we're just college hockey players playing the game we love while living the dream. This isn't normal for us; it's damage control. And like it or not, it's on me, Aidric, and Seb to keep the storm contained—to make sure no other Society member gets caught in the crossfire. Slade might not see it from the outside, but we're the ones carrying the weight because it's our job to do that.

I keep my tone low and my face unreadable, so I don't come off like I'm judging him. "I get it, man. I've been in your shoes. I've felt that doubt."

I shift slightly on the bench, eyes on him. "This is only my first season as council advisor, but I remember what it was like to watch from the outside and wonder what the hell's really going on. But I can promise you, you don't want to trade places with any of us. The secrets we keep are not about control or exclusion. They're about protection—for all of you. We carry the heavy shit so you don't have to."

His jaw flexes, but I push on.

"Your payday is coming. We're going to bring home the W at nationals, and after that, offers will start coming in. We'll all have deals and contracts coming out of our asses. That's the whole point of all of this, right?"

"But at what expense?" he snaps, suddenly on his feet. "Our lives? Our morals? A friend's life?"

I stand up, placing a hand on his shoulder and pressing him gently back down on the bench.

"Hey." My voice drops to a whisper, eyes scanning the room. "You gotta watch your tone. We're not in The Chamber, and we shouldn't even be talking about this here. But I am because I give a shit about you, Slade."

He drags his hands down his face, frustration bleeding through.

"Look," I say, bluntly. "What happened with Evan was a fuckup. A threat that went too far. It never should've happened." I shake my head slowly. "We're snakes, I'll admit that. But we're not slimy. We're fixing it, quietly and carefully. No one's asking you to do more than what you already signed up for when you became one of us." I add a little enthusiasm to my tone, hoping to take him out of whatever pit he's spiraled into. "So sit back. Reap the benefits. And play some fucking hockey."

"All right," he mutters with a shrug. "I guess it is what it is. I just hope you all know what you're doing because I hear detectives are sniffing around everywhere. I'd hate to see Noah, or any of us, go down because *that* wouldn't be worth it."

I pat his shoulder a couple times. "We'll be fine. Try not to stress yourself out."

He chuckles, a light sparking in his eyes as he looks out over the ice. This is why we do it. The Society might do some fucked up shit, but if it keeps me on the ice, I'll do it with my bare hands. Gladly.

We both stand, and I feel like I actually got through to him. Maybe not completely, but enough to take some weight off his chest.

"Now," I say with a wide grin. "Let's get ready to kick some Cloverville ass so we can celebrate."

"Thanks, Callan." He slaps his hand into mine, and I pull him in for a firm chest bump.

"Anytime. Seriously. And if you wanna talk again, hit me up. Let's just make it somewhere a little more appropriate next time."

He nods, and I notice the tension in his shoulders has already eased.

This role comes with a hell of a lot of baggage, but moments like this make me feel like I made the right decision when I stepped up to council advisor.

CHAPTER 14

CALLAN

After practice, I came home to two half-naked girls draped across the couch like decorations. They tried to get my attention with their arched backs and pouty lips, but I didn't even blink. Just walked past without a word.

They were dressed and out the door within minutes. Guess the party ended the second the attention did.

It wouldn't surprise me one bit if Aidric and Seb kicked them out of bed before the cum even dried between their thighs.

Now, the living room's empty except for the three of us and the energy has shifted dramatically.

Seb and I are doing our best to get Aidric to chill the fuck out, because he's pacing and muttering about how he needs to *take care* of Evan. Which could end really bad for all of us.

"So, he's awake." Seb shrugs as he grabs the barstool beside him. He spins it around before straddling it with his arms draped over the backrest. "Big fucking deal. He's not talking, so we're good."

"No!" Aidric snaps. "We're not fucking good. Just because he isn't talking now, doesn't mean he won't be soon."

Out of all of us, Aidric is the most upset about this. If the Lords get blamed for the mess then he'll be the one taking the heat from The Society. And after what I saw happen to Julian, I have no idea what they would do to him, or even to all of us.

"Wait, wait, wait, guys," Seb says, holding up a hand, his eyes locked on his phone screen. "I just got another update."

Aidric and I turn to him with bated breath—me pacing and him fuming. Each second feels like it's stretching unbearably long as Seb reads over the message. We watch his face for any sign of hope, or maybe the kind of hopelessness that tells us we're screwed.

"Fuck, man," he grumbles, dragging his hand down his face. "I think we just bought ourselves some more time. Turns out, our boy Evan isn't going to be saying anything for the time being."

"Let me see that." I snatch the phone from his hand and scan the message from Olivia, a girl who leeched on to Seb after he fucked her. She's a student at Rosewood U and works at the hospital as a nurse's aide.

> Olivia: I just heard the doctor talking to his family and he told them Evan has what they call trauma-induced paralysis. From my research, that means he's in a state of catatonia. He's awake and his eyes are open, but he's not talking or moving. When I went in, he was just staring at the wall.

A weight settles in my chest. He's awake, but he's lost to the world. Seb is right—this gives us more time.

I scroll up, skimming through the texts to read the previous updates. I have no idea who this chick is or how we are getting these very detailed updates that are one hundred percent a breach of patient privacy.

> Olivia: Vent is out. He's definitely awake.

> Sebastian: All right. Keep me updated.

Another...

> Olivia: He's got visitors. I think it's one of your
> teammates and a girl I've seen around on my
> campus.

Fuck. She saw me and Avery while we were there.

> Sebastian: Keep your eyes on them.

> Olivia: Hard to do when they just pulled the
> curtain on the window shut.

Hell yeah, I did. I pulled that curtain shut and reminded Avery who was in control here. I will never forget the sight of her coming on my fingers like that. The way she tried to hold back, how she bit her lip so hard I thought it might bleed. Then, how her walls gripped my fingers while my other hand silenced her, keeping her cries of pleasure for my ears only.

Yeah, that probably wouldn't have gone well if the curtain wasn't shut.

I keep scrolling…

> Olivia: I've been missing you, baby.

> Olivia: Every time I close my eyes, I swear I can
> still feel you inside me. I don't think I've ever
> wanted someone like this before.

> Olivia: I hope I get to see you again soon. I
> NEED to see you again soon.

> Olivia: You didn't just rock my world that night.
> You WRECKED me. I've never been touched
> like that. My body still remembers you, and I
> already know one night wasn't enough.

> Olivia: You've been on my mind all day. Have
> you been thinking about me, too? Please tell
> me you have.

Jesus, this bitch is obsessed. And the messages just keep going without a single response from Seb. That is, until he needed something from her in return.

"Hey, man," Noah calls out as he steps into the kitchen, oblivious to the storm brewing in the room. "How much booze do you want me to pick up for our guests? And did you have a theme in mind this time?"

I tear my eyes away from the phone, the weight of everything pressing down for a split second before I remember the party I told Avery we were throwing. The one I ordered a few of the guys to throw together and to make sure she shows up.

I level Noah with a look. "Enough for at least a hundred people," I say, barely giving it a thought because my mind is anywhere but on fucking party planning right now. "As for a theme..." I lean back, thinking.

Then, something clicks—something that mirrors the chaos we're currently drowning in. "Let's go with death." I raise my hands, drawing out a scene of mayhem. "Skulls, coffins, tombstones. Black lights and dark corners. Face masks and haunting music. You get the idea, right?"

Noah raises a brow but doesn't question it.

"Can't you see we're in the middle of an important meeting?" Aidric growls, his patience thin. "A meeting that's being held because of *your* fuckup."

Noah's dull expression drops. With his tail tucked firmly between his legs, he turns and leaves the room without another word.

A little harsh for one of our own, but Aidric isn't exactly in the mood for leniency. Not when the pressure of being our leader is demanding he prevents everything from falling apart.

The Ice Lords look to him to hold this shit together. And I can tell the pressure is really getting to him.

Once Noah's out of listening range, I pass Seb his phone back just as my own buzzes in the pocket of my hoodie. I reach in and pull it out. Without hesitation, I swipe open the message from Avery.

Little Devil: I need to talk to you. I'm on my way
over.

My fingers move fast as I type out a quick response.

Me: Bring us our fucking rock!

I stare at the screen for a response. Seconds pass, but still no reply. With a sigh, I shove my phone back into my pocket, rolling my shoulders before looking up.

"Avery's on her way," I tell the guys. "Says she needs to talk."

I glance at Seb, then Aidric, reading their expressions easily. We may not have grown up together, but there is a certain bond that is created when you fight together.

Seb looks amused, eyes glinting with mischief like he's ready to play with our new toy. Like this whole thing with her is just entertainment to him.

"Wonderful," Aidric growls, voice low and venom-laced. "She better be bringing us our fucking rock. At least then, one loose end is tied."

Aidric might say she's a loose end that needs to be tied, but I know better. I see the mischievous glint in his eye and I know the way his fucked-up mind works. I've watched him wrap his hands around girls' throats just to see the fear flicker in their eyes. He doesn't just crave chaos, he orchestrates it. Control isn't a means to an end for him—it's the whole goddamn game.

As long as she exists within reach, he's gonna keep her dangling just close enough to manipulate. The thought stirs something unexpected inside me. It's not quite jealousy. No, it's something worse. Something more depraved.

The idea of him thinking he holds the reins on her makes my blood boil. If anyone is going to keep her within arm's reach, it's gonna be me.

Before I even have time to untangle the twisted thoughts in my head, a knock at the door snaps me back to reality.

That was fast. She must have texted when she was already on her way, which means whatever she needs to talk about is important.

Aidric's eyes stay cold as he leans forward. "Go get her," he hisses, each word laced with ill intent. "Then bring her down to me in The Chamber."

"What the fuck?" Seb snaps, his jaw tight. "She's not a member. She should have never been down there in the first place, and as the Lord speaker, I'm putting my foot down. Rule is members only. She can say whatever the fuck she needs to say in The Vault."

My eyes widen, surprise flickering through my features. "The fuck?"

The Vault is rarely used as it's reserved for only the most serious situations. It's a place for outsiders who know more than they should—a place for snakes and liabilities. Since my initiation, I've only been in that room twice and neither of those times ended well for the person on the other side of that door.

"The Chamber," Aidric barks. "Now!"

Seb shakes his head, frustration rolling off him in waves as he spins around, barely containing his anger.

Not gonna lie, a wave of relief crashes over me. Had Seb pushed harder and she ended up in that black hole of a room, things could have taken a wrong turn.

The kind of fear that room instills doesn't just paralyze, it breaks people and makes them wish for death.

Avery isn't stupid, she's cunning and smart. If we take her in that room and she really does have shit written down about us, we'll be screwed. The thing about controlling people is that they still need to have something to live for to keep them under your thumb. If they have nothing to lose, then there isn't anything to fear. Not even death.

I make my way to the door, my steps slow and deliberate

because truth be told, I'm not exactly eager to hear whatever the hell she has to say. Any news from that girl is bound to be bad news. Unless, of course, she has our rock. But somehow, I doubt that's why she's here.

Avery may be fire, but she's never been one for face-to-face confrontation. If she had the rock, she'd more than likely toss it in the mailbox, shoot us a text, and pray like hell it ended there.

Flipping the lock, I pull the door open and come face to face with our little devil. Her hair is damp and clinging to her face like she jumped out of the shower, threw on some clothes, and drove here without a second thought. She's wearing a pair of gray joggers that hang loosely on her hips and white sneakers. The light pink sweatshirt hangs loosely from her shoulders and has *in my archery era* sketched across the front.

The sight of her *almost* makes me smile. Her face is free of makeup, yet she remains flawless—on the outside, at least. There's something about seeing her without her mask and armor that has my chest stirring. I actually prefer it. She comes off as weak and vulnerable—more destructible.

A slow smirk tugs at my lips as I lean against the doorframe. "Well, well, well," I sing, dragging it out just enough to get under her skin. "To what do we owe the pleasure of your unexpected visit?"

With a scowl carved deep into her face, she shoves past me, brushing against my shoulder like she owns the damn place. "We need to talk."

I arch a brow, turning slowly as I push the door shut behind me. "Better be good news, Avery."

"It's not," she deadpans.

Her words hit like a match to gasoline, and a force of rage heats my skin. More than her words, it's the lack of fear on her face that has my fists curling at my sides. If she has bad news, she needs to feel the weight of it as much as we do.

"What the fuck did you do?" I spit, knowing she had to have

done something that only benefits her. If not, she'd be terrified right now.

"I don't have the rock." She shrugs casually, too casually. "I did have it, but someone took it from me."

Everything inside me begins to erupt at once—hatred, fury, pure fucking evil. Someone took *our* fucking rock?

Without a second thought, I grab her by the back of the neck and pull her toward the door to The Chamber. My footsteps thud against the hardwood, each one sounding like the slow toll of death. Not just for her, but for all of us.

She curses and fights, trying to shake off my hold, but I only dig my fingers in harder, imagining snapping her pretty little neck. The only thing holding me back from that is knowing my boys want a piece of her too. All I see is blinding rage as I practically drag her down the stairs to the dimly lit chamber. She tries to put her hands out to stop us from descending, but I laugh maniacally and push her forward until she's exactly where she needs to be—directly in front of our leader.

CHAPTER 15

AVERY

THIS WAS EXPECTED. I figured Callan would be livid once he found out I lost the rock, or had it taken, rather.

Now, all I can do is brace for the impact because Aidric doesn't look like he's in the mood to offer olive branches. In fact, he looks like he's ready to burn the whole fucking tree down.

"Tell 'em," Callan grumbles in frustration, shoving me forward. "Tell them what you just told me."

There's really no point in dragging this out, so I steel my shoulders as Callan's hand drops from the back of my neck. Lifting my chin, I lay it all out there.

"I had the rock, and now I don't."

The words barely leave my mouth before Aidric is seething right in front of me, our bodies not even an inch apart while his height casts me in his shadow. His chest is taut, shoulders strained, and the veins in his neck are pulsing.

Jesus. These guys are intense.

Sebastian is right there beside him with a firm stance and his jaw locked so tight it looks like it might shatter.

"What the hell do you mean you had it and now you don't?" Sebastian grits out.

"Ugh, exactly what I said." Sarcasm drips from my tone

because if they want to take me down, I sure as hell won't be going quietly.

Aidric sucks in a deep breath, fingers raking through his hair as he paces like he's trying to keep himself from snapping. I can see his hands shaking, rage pouring off him in waves.

Callan just stands there, idly like a little bitch—watching and waiting, but doing nothing useful.

All the while, Sebastian is showing he might actually have some balls, after all. So far, I had him pegged as the quiet one of the group, but apparently Aidric gets that title because he still has yet to say a word.

Great, he's silent and deadly. Perfect combination for a serial killer.

Sebastian levels me with a glare, clearly trying to communicate that my attitude isn't something he wants to deal with at the moment. Well, too fucking bad, because they are the last thing I wanted to deal with, *ever.*

I roll my eyes at him, but before I can cross my arms in front of me in defiance, he grabs my wrist and hauls me into him, his grip punishing before his other hand goes to my hip, fingers grazing just under my sweatshirt. His sinister eyes bore into mine as he leans into my space, his breath hot against my face and jaw clenched so tightly I think I actually hear the grinding of his teeth.

"Where the *fuck* is it?"

With a no-nonsense attitude, I tell them the truth. "The detective on Evan's case took it." I pause, letting the words sink in while I watch the fire in his eyes come to life. "That's right. Detective Klein came to my dorm last night and questioned me. He saw the rock, and he took it."

Worry crosses his features and I can't help my curiosity any longer. I'm already part of this, I might as well know the whole truth at this point. "Care to tell me why he might want it?"

Callan's eyes lock on to mine as he steps up to me, his nostrils flared, but Sebastian puts an arm out, blocking his path.

"You can have her when I'm done with her," Sebastian mutters, eyes never leaving mine.

Sebastian's grip on me tightens, and I know for a fact that my hip will be wearing bruises from his fingers tomorrow. Just when I'm about to cry out in pain, unable to take any more of the pressure, he releases me with a shove, making me stumble as he throws his head back, and roars, "Fuck!"

Aidric has distanced himself from me, as if he's afraid to be too close. He's sitting against the far wall, nearly blending in with the shadows. But I can see him, breaths heavy with fury, and fingers clenched tightly into a fist as if he's restraining himself.

I expect him to march over to me and seethe in my face. But he stays where he is, making the tension in the room feel as if it might boil over. I'm not sure if it's a power move, but both times I've been down here, he's been quiet. I'd call it a coincidence, but something tells me it's not.

I should be afraid of him, of all of them. But that's the thing, I know I have some of the power now. And if their reactions are anything to go by, I'd say they are treading carefully.

"You better be fucking joking, Avery," Callan hisses. "Tell us you're fucking joking."

I tilt my head, a knowing smirk tugging at my lips, all sass and zero fucks given.

"Nope," I quip. "Not joking. Seems you three have a mess on your hands."

Callan jabs a finger into my breastbone, hard and unforgiving. "A mess you're gonna clean up."

"And what exactly do you expect me to do?" I scoff, crossing my arms as I dare them to say it out loud. "Break into the evidence room and *steal* the fucking rock?"

Sebastian doesn't hesitate. Doesn't even blink. "If that's what it takes."

They act like it's my problem to fix. Like they have no issue throwing me headfirst into a suicide mission just to save their asses.

The truth is, I don't think Klein took that rock as evidence in Evan's case. I think he took it because he knows exactly who it belongs to.

Klein isn't just piecing together what happened to Evan—he's building something bigger. Something that I'd bet has everything to do with these guys and this stupid little cult they have going on.

That rock could be a key piece of whatever the hell he's working on. I mean, the number eight carved into it has to mean something. If this is the eighth, then that could mean there were seven before it.

I let the tension sit, allowing them to feel the weight of their own predicament before I tilt my head and smirk.

"Or," I start, voice smooth as I tap a finger on my chin. "I could forgo the risk of prison time for stealing evidence and just tell the detective everything I know."

I watch their reactions, feeding off the shift in energy as I continue. "Sure, I might get slapped with a misdemeanor charge for tampering with evidence. But at least you guys go down way harder than I do. Doesn't that sound like a better deal?"

Before I can take a single breath, Sebastian grabs me by the arm, yanking me forward until my chest collides with his. His cheeks flush a dangerous shade of fire-red, veins straining beneath his skin as his teeth grind. "We could just end it all right here and now."

"Do it." My breath fans against his skin and I grin as I call his bluff. "Kill me. I *dare* you."

Just like that, I'm thrust back and out of his reach. Shaking my head, I exhale a mocking breath before adjusting my stance.

"That's what I thought," I mutter, just loud enough for him to hear.

Sebastian tsks, rolling his shoulders, but his eyes stay glued to me. "Something's up with her," he muses, head tilting slightly. "She's not usually this feisty."

"She is," Callan retorts. "She puts on a good show, pretending to be tough and untouchable, but slowly, the cracks begin to surface just before she breaks completely. And I must admit, she looks so pretty when she's broken."

I scoff, folding my arms while my glare slices straight through him. "You don't even fucking know me."

"I know enough." Callan smirks, leaning in, his breath hot against my ear. His voice drops to a whisper. "Starting with how it feels to be buried deep inside that pussy. Fingers, too."

My stomach turns, a wave of disgust rolling through me. I let out an exasperated breath before howling in laughter, throwing my head back just to make a point. "So we fucked, and I told you to kick rocks," I sneer. "Get over it already."

The guys exchange looks, a flicker of surprise written all over their faces.

"Oh, you guys didn't know?" I flash a wicked grin at Callan. "Your buddy here got a bruised ego after we slept together, so he made it his mission to make me miserable for years. Our rivalry is nothing new."

I watch the weight of my words settle into their thick skulls. They might've believed Callan was just a passenger in their twisted game, but they didn't know he was a front seat rider.

"Bruised ego?" Callan growls. "I'd hardly call it that. I fucked you and that was that. You're the one who showed up where you weren't wanted, and look where it landed you…right back in the palm of my hand so I can toy with you even more."

Callan wraps an arm around my waist before turning me so that I'm facing Sebastian while he whispers in my ear, his hand slowly moving down my stomach. "Did you miss me so much that you had to come back for another round? Tell me, Little Devil, do you like it when I make you squirm?"

His hand moves down farther, just over the hem of my loose joggers. "Just like the way I did in front of your boy Evan while he was comatose. Back then I used my words to bring you to your knees, but in that hospital room, it was my fingers in your pussy that had you begging for mercy."

"Well, well, well," Sebastian drawls, crowding in front of me while Callan's fingers continue their torment of playing with the top of my pants. Refusing to let him get a reaction out of me, I remain perfectly still.

A sinister smirk stretches across Sebastian's face. "I think it's only fair that if you got to fuck her, then we do too."

My blood runs cold. "Over my dead body," I snap, my limbs tensing, ready for a fight. Surprisingly, Callan pulls me more into him, almost protectively. Nothing in me takes comfort in that action, but it does catch me off guard. Then again, he could just be a jealous asshole.

Sebastian doesn't even flinch, his smirk only widens. "That works too," he murmurs. "Less attitude from you that way."

Aidric bites back a laugh, but there's no humor in his expression. If anything, I have a feeling that he's imagining Sebastian fucking my corpse. No doubt that's exactly the kind of depravity his twisted mind would conjure up.

I glare at them, my stomach churning with disgust. "You guys are fucking sick."

"That we are," Sebastian says, his eyes dark with amusement. "Now, unless you want to make that a reality, I suggest you get us our rock, or you bend over and let us take turns with you. Either way, it's your ass on the line."

Nausea coils in my gut, but I push past it and shove out of Callan's hold. I take a step forward, closing the space between us, my jaw clenched. "No, asshole," I snap, eyes locked on his. "It's *our* asses on the line. I've accepted that. And it's time you all accept it too."

"We..." Sebastian waves a hand between the two of us. "Are not a team. We don't work with outsiders; we punish them for sticking their noses where they don't belong."

I shrug, unfazed. "Maybe that's how it was before me. But

I'm here now." I take a step forward, my gaze locked on Sebastian. "And this isn't just about me going down anymore, it's about all of us getting actual fucking jail time with an attempted murder charge hanging over our heads. So I think it's high time we figure this shit out together. If one of us falls, we all fucking fall."

"She's right," Callan cuts in. "As long as she buried that box like she says she did, we have enough leverage to ensure her silence." His gaze flicks between them. "Now, it's time we use her to our advantage."

A slow, dangerous smirk tugs at Sebastian's lips, sending a trickle of fear running down my spine.

I scoff. "Not exactly what I had in mind, Callan."

"Like it or not, that's the way it is." Callan shrugs, his tone casual. So we'll let you go for now." He pauses, eyes locked on to mine. "But you need to find a way to get that rock back."

I cross my arms, tilting my head and silently considering his offer.

"I'll do my best." I let the words hang for a beat before adding, "Under one condition."

Callan's jaw tics, but he doesn't interrupt.

"Tell me why it's so important." I meet his sharp gaze. "I need to know before I can give a damn."

The guys exchange another loaded look, before Callan says, "Let's just say that it will lead that detective straight to the box you burned—straight to you."

My stomach drops. *Shit.* That thought never crossed my mind.

"But how?" I ask, panic creeping in.

Sebastian steps forward, closing the space between us. "Because those instructions I gave you?" He pauses, smirking. "They weren't the only copy. They were a miniscule part of a much bigger—for lack of a better term—treasure map, if you will."

I'm not exactly following, but the way he's explaining this

makes me think I should be scared. Yet, I'm not. I'm just picturing a bunch of hockey players searching for treasure. Though, I don't think that's anywhere close to what he's saying.

"If I had to guess," Sebastian continues, "you said Detective Klein took it, yeah?"

I nod.

"Well, he's been on our tail far longer than he'd ever admit. Go ahead and let him keep the rock. Just know that means he has evidence linking you to a crime."

My throat tightens as the realization settles over me. He's right. I did have the rock and if it somehow leads Klein to the box in the woods, that tongue will be traced back to me. Or rather, the ashes of it could.

But whose tongue is it?

That's a case for another day. Right now, I have to deal with the current situation.

Sebastian's smirk widens, like he's enjoying this far too much. "That number is now ingrained in his memory, right alongside a picture of your face. Doesn't matter if you get it back or not." His eyes glint with darkness. "He knows."

"Then why do *you guys* want it back?" I choke out, my throat tight as the weight of his words are damn near strangling me.

"Because," he drawls, stepping even closer, his breath warm against my skin. "It's not just a rock, Little Devil." His fingers twitch at his sides like he's itching to grab me, to make me understand. "We want it back because it's symbolic of something much bigger than hockey, much bigger than this house, and much bigger than this chamber. It's a marker. A piece of a legacy you don't belong to, but now, thanks to your little mishap, you're tied to it forever.

Chills dance down my spine, and for the first time this evening, I'm scared. Really fucking scared. Not of them, but of the outcome of this entire situation. It's gonna unravel. I have a bad feeling we're all going down.

It's official. I'm theirs now—a peasant to the Lords, their own personal plaything. While I hold a little power here, it isn't much anymore. No matter what, I'm now part of this twisted game.

I shake my head, a bitter laugh escaping me. "You guys did me dirty." My voice is thick as the cracks begin to surface, just like Callan said they would. It's embarrassing how quickly it happened too. "You did me so fucking dirty."

Callan doesn't even flinch. "We did what we had to do," he says, cool and detached, like this was always the inevitable outcome.

My fists clench, nails digging into my palms as my voice drops lower. "And what now?" My gaze flicks between them, my pulse hammering in my ears. "When does it end?"

A long beat of silence stretches between us before Sebastian delivers the final blow. "It doesn't. That's the beauty of what we've built here. It *never* ends."

The words slam into me, stealing the last shred of hope I had left.

Aidric and Sebastian exchange a silent look, and when Aidric gives the slightest tilt of his chin, a fresh wave of chills runs down my spine.

"Cromwell," Sebastian says, his voice shallow, but rough. "Do me a favor and go grab my phone."

Callan scoffs, annoyed. "Where the hell is it? It's normally glued to your fucking hand."

Sebastian shrugs. "Not really sure. But I've got no doubt you'll figure it out."

Callan grits his teeth, muttering something under his breath as he turns and disappears up the stairs. And just like that, I'm alone with the two men even more unhinged than the one who just left.

I swallow hard, my gaze flicking between them as slow-building smirks spread across their faces.

"What?" I mutter, backing a step instinctively. As much as I know I shouldn't show any fear to a predator, the chill in here is starting to bleed into my bones. Something about this room makes them appear even more dangerous than when we are upstairs. Up there, they are just two dudes who play hockey; down here, they are monsters born of nightmares.

"What's with you two?" My voice shakes no matter how hard I try to remain strong. There may be cracks in my armor, but I refuse to shatter.

Aidric jerks his chin toward the far side of the room. Before I can piece together what it means, a hand clamps around my arm and I'm suddenly being dragged in that direction, my heart slamming against my ribs.

"Seriously," I scoff, "enough with the manhandling. It's getting real fucking old."

But my words die in the air because in the next breath, I'm being hauled toward the altar.

Everything inside me locks up, fear coiling tight in my gut the closer I am dragged toward what looks like a torture bench. Callan told them that I was feisty, so I prove it with every ounce of might I possess. I fight, digging the nails of my free hand into Sebastian's wrists in an attempt to break free. A string of curses leaves his lips, but his fingers only tighten around me.

I yank, shove at his shoulders, twist—my body bending in ways I didn't know it could. My foot kicks out, trying to get him in the back of the knee, but he dodges it just in time, a chuckle leaving his lips.

"Fight me all you want. It only makes me hard."

He presses my hand to the top of his jeans and I try to pull away, the bulge clear as I am forced to touch him. My eyes narrow and I flatten my palm, ready to crush his balls, but he must sense my movement coming because he lifts my fingers away while tsking in my face.

"Such a naughty girl. You might need to learn some manners."

"Fuck you," I spit, seething. If I let the anger take over then my fear is shoved to the side. So I give in to it and continue to fight. But it's useless. Aidric moves in to help, and between the two of them, resistance is nothing but wasted energy.

Aidric grips my other wrist and lifts my arm. The clanking of chains fills the room, slicing through the air just before cool metal replaces his even colder touch.

The cuff snaps shut around my wrist with a finality that vibrates through my bones.

"Stop it!" I scream, my voice cracking as it rips from my throat.

Tears sting the corners of my eyes, but I refuse to let them fall. I thrash harder, yanking against the chains, my muscles feeling like they've been set on fire as my hands groan in pain, digging into solid metal.

"The harder you fight, the harder you'll fall," Sebastian says as he repeats the action on my other wrist. The moment his clasp clicks into place, reality slams into me.

I'm chained.

A prisoner to their twisted games in this dark chamber. I might not have a choice here, but I do get to decide whose side I'm on in the end. They want to see me fall at their feet, so I'll fall. But when I get back up, they better be ready to face the fury of a woman scorned, and I think we all know how those stories end.

Suddenly, a podium slams into my chest, knocking the breath from my lungs and sending my thoughts scattering. I'm forced to hang over it, straining against the chains that hold me in place as determination fills me. I'll prove to them that I am not someone to be tested.

Sebastian crouches in front of me, a sinister grin carved deep into his face. His eyes lock on to mine, burning with something so twisted, it steals the breath right from my lungs.

"Well, well, well," he croons, voice dripping with menace. "Looks like Callan's going a little soft. Care to tell me why?"

I don't flinch. I spit, hitting him square in the face. "Fuck you."

He chuckles, low, amused as he drags two fingers down his damp cheek, wiping away the spit. Then, in a slow, deliberate motion, he slips those fingers into his mouth.

My stomach churns, but his grin only grows wider.

"Bad move, Little Lamb."

I scoff, eyes narrowing. "Oh, now it's Little *Lamb*? What happened to Little Devil?"

"Little Lamb feels more fitting, considering you'll be our sacrifice for the next..." He taps the face of his watch. "...ten minutes or so, while your boy tears the place apart looking for my phone."

I don't need to see Aidric to know he's behind me. His presence creeps in like a cold front. Suddenly, rough fingers brush against the waistband of my sweatpants, causing a shiver to run through me.

I kick back, warning him. "Don't fucking touch me!"

Sebastian laughs. "That's not fair. See, we figure if Callan got a piece of you..." He leans in, voice dropping to something more dangerous. "...it's only fair we get one, too. We are brothers who share, after all."

I growl, lips curled in disgust. "You're disgusting. Every last one of you."

Sebastian tilts his head, unfazed. "Disgusting or not, we own you now. Besides, we all know getting dirty just makes it that much better."

He stands slowly, takes a few steps to the left, then returns with something shiny and silver in his hand.

"See this?" he asks, that wicked grin still etched on his face. "This is one of my favorite toys...aside from you."

When he brings it into view, I realize what it is. A wheel of spiked needles that's used for pleasure, pain, or both. I've seen one before, but never in person.

He tsks, slow and mocking. "Scared yet, Little Lamb?"

I lift my chin, defiance burning in my eyes. Pain isn't something that scares me, lack of control is. So if he thinks waving his fancy toy in my face is going to make me cry, he has another think coming.

"Bring it on, asshole," I seethe. My voice holds steady, but hot unrelenting fury boils beneath it. I'm done playing their game. They want to see me break. They want my tears. But I won't give them that satisfaction.

A low rumble vibrates behind me. Then I feel the tug at my waistband as Aidric slowly slides my sweatpants down. His fingers slip beneath the hem of my panties, making my breath hitch as they lift from my skin. Then he lets go, snapping them back into place. I flinch, and before I can stop myself, a muffled sound escapes my lips.

He's chasing a reaction. They both are. And I just gave them exactly what they wanted.

I turn my head slightly to try and steal a glance at Aidric, but Sebastian's hand snaps to my cheek, guiding my gaze back to his.

"Pay him no attention," he croons, voice smooth and unsettling. "You might feel him, but you won't hear him."

"Why?" I gasp, the word slipping out on a breathy tremor.

A devious glint sparks in his eyes as he drags the pinwheel slowly down the curve of my cheek. "Because that," he whispers, "is his power-move down here. He doesn't waste energy on words unless it's necessary. I speak for him. And right now?" He leans in just a little closer. "I think he'd tell you to stop talking."

His fingers clamp around my chin, forcing my head up. His touch is cruelly gentle, like he's savoring the control he has.

I guess the only way they feel powerful is to chain me up. *Fucking pussies.* I dare them to take me on without chains holding me back.

The pinwheel grazes my throat in a slow drag. Each tiny needle whispering across my skin, leaving a trail of goosebumps in its wake. It's strangely thrilling, and likely not the reaction he'd hoped for.

I hold my head high, the scowl on my face never dropping.

They can strip my clothes, but they won't strip me of my defiance.

Aidric's fingers glide slowly between my ass cheeks, and something unexpected stirs inside me—a mix of threat and twisted excitement. I find myself clenching my muscles as they're all zapped to life.

I don't know whether I should fight, scream, or enjoy it. Maybe all three. If I let the pleasure distract me, then they can't use this moment to control or manipulate me—not if I willingly hand it over.

Sebastian hums, still trolling the pinwheel down my body, awakening every nerve like fire licking across my skin. "How about a safe word for this little punishment, Little Lamb?" he murmurs, his voice smooth but wrapped in venom.

I scoff, lifting my head with fire in my eyes. "First of all, I'm a lion, not some weak lamb. Unclasp my arms and I'll rip both of your fucking heads off as proof."

His smirk twitches, but I don't stop. It's clear that he wants to use his words to make me feel small, the same way Aidric's lack of words is an intimidation tactic. I can see right through their bullshit, though, and I think it's starting to really piss them off.

"Second…punishment wrapped in pleasure? That's your idea of control?" I laugh, sharp and bitter. "You clearly don't know me. I don't need a damn safe word." I lean forward, meeting his gaze. "Whatever you two give me, I can take it."

"Well, fuck," Sebastian croons, his grin widening. "Seems we've got ourselves a challenge."

Before I can form a response, a sting between my legs steals my attention. Aidric pushes two fingers inside me without hesitation. There's no gentleness or buildup. Just raw intrusion. I was already wet, though, not ashamed of the fact that pain happens to be one of my biggest turn-ons.

My body jerks forward against the restraints, an airy gasp slipping from my lips before I can stop it. I grit my teeth, furious at myself for making a sound because I know what it does to them.

But there's a twisted and unhinged part of me that wants to see how far they'll take this—how far this will go before someone folds.

And it sure as hell isn't going to be me.

Sebastian presses the pinwheel to my collarbone, dragging it with just enough pressure to send tiny pricks of pain blooming beneath the surface. "Let's see if we can peel those secrets out of you, Little Lamb."

"Give it your best shot," I gasp, as Aidric's fingers work deeper, like he's the one who's about to pull secrets from my body, one knuckle at a time.

I shouldn't like this. Not when it's him making me feel this way. I should be begging him to stop while clawing my way free, but that's what they want. They expect me to cry and beg, to turn into a submissive puddle.

Instead, my back arches, chasing the pleasure even as my mind screams against it. This will not be a game of humiliation— at least, not for me. If they want to offer up orgasms as punishment, I'll ride that line till the end.

Sebastian quirks a brow, something depraved flickering in his eyes like I've just given him permission to have his way with me. In a way, I guess I have. He offered a safe word; I could say no or claim it's too much. But it isn't.

I began studying neuropsychiatry because of my mother, but I have learned a lot about myself and how my brain works in the process. We are as strong as our thoughts tell us we are, so I keep chanting my mantra that I adopted freshman year.

I am in control.

When Sebastian pops the button on his jeans, I'm certain he's about to push for more. The sound of his zipper coming down is drowned out by the erratic cries tearing through my vocal cords as Aidric presses the pad of his thumb to my asshole, his fingers plunging feverishly inside me, curled at just the right angle to hit my G-spot. I've never felt anything like this before.

Oh, God. Right there.

What I crave in the bedroom is not an easy thing to ask for as a college student who's only dated men my age. Most of them can't be trusted to understand the line between masochism and abuse, case in point, these guys.

But for some reason, that doesn't bother me with Aidric and Sebastian.

My skin prickles, every nerve in my body being zapped with pleasure. I've never felt quite so alive, as if every one of my needs were being met at once.

The next thing I know, Sebastian's fingers are gripping my cheeks, possessively guiding my mouth open. The blunt heat of him nudges my lips and I part for him instinctively. This is where I hold the power, bringing him to ruin on my tongue. He knows I could bite off his dick, and I tease him with my teeth while my eyes glance at his face.

Sebastian grits his jaw, understanding flashing in his gaze that this is exactly what I wanted. He thought this little move would put me at his mercy, but it is quite the opposite.

The bitterness of salt hits my tongue, followed by the faint taste of his cologne clinging to his skin. It's both heady and intoxicating.

I seal my lips around him, my tongue tracing along the underside as he pushes deeper. His raw, masculine scent wraps around me, caging me in—holding me hostage.

"That's right, Little Lamb," Sebastian murmurs as his fingers twist into my hair. He's not gentle, but he's not cruel either as he tugs, lifting my head until our eyes lock. The heat in his stare burns into me. My lips are slick, trembling around the weight of him.

"Suck my cock," he says, his voice a low growl. "And tell me I'm your Lord."

His words ignite something inside me, an intoxicating experience I have wanted to chase for so long now at my fingertips. My throat tightens, not from fear, but from the thrill of surrender ripping through me. Because the truth is…I want to do this. I want Sebastian to fall apart on my tongue so hard that he can't shake me from his thoughts. I want him obsessed, chasing this high over and over again until I can turn the tables and make all of them bend to my will.

A hum vibrates in my throat as I take him deeper, my words muffled. "You're my Lord."

His grip tightens in my hair, and a satisfied growl rumbles from his chest. "Damn straight, I am."

My moans wrap around him while his girth stretches my mouth. He is huge, longer and thicker than any guy I have been with before. But I just take that as a challenge, letting him test my gag reflex as he pushes into my throat. My breath hitches, eyes watering—but I don't stop. I want every relentless second of it.

I'm enjoying this more than I have any right to—the thrill of having these men at *my* mercy.

Aidric's fingers are relentless as they ruthlessly drive into me. Each curl sends a spark ricocheting through my spine that resonates down to my fucking toes. The stretch, the pressure, the way he finds that one spot again and again. It's almost too much.

Then there's Sebastian, thick and hot on my tongue, every slow thrust silencing my moans as he claims my mouth. All my senses are on high alert, making me dizzy. And fuck, it feels so good. I'm lost in it. Drowning, and I don't want to come up for air.

"Oh, God," I whimper, without thought.

"Not God," Sebastian growls. "Lord. *Your* Lord."

Before I can even brace for it, my orgasm slams into me. Sounds of pleasure rip out of me, raw and unfiltered as they echo through the room.

Aidric's fingers don't stop, dragging me deeper into the high, while Sebastian grips my hair tighter, fucking my mouth harder —demanding more, taking more.

Then, he pulls out. One strangled breath later, and I feel his hot release painting my skin. My cheek, my tongue, but thankfully it misses my eyes.

My walls clench, pulsing as the last waves of my orgasm shudder through me. My body trembles as I fall breathlessly from the peak of ecstasy.

And still, there's a sick and twisted part of me that craves more.

I'm a mess, shaking, drenched in sweat and everything... *them.*

The sharp thud of footsteps against the concrete has my head jolting up. Callan storms toward us, his jaw clenched and his cheeks blazing red. He's fucking livid.

"What the hell is this?" he roars, his voice cracking like thunder.

Unbothered by his presence, Sebastian calmly tugs up his pants, not sparing Callan a glance. Instead, he slides a hand into his pocket and pulls out a phone.

My stomach knots, a sick twist of realization curling in my gut. *Did Sebastian and Aidric plan this?* While Callan was up there searching everywhere, he had his phone this whole time?

Sebastian's lips curl into a wicked smile as he swipes the screen. Then, he slowly turns the phone to face me.

I freeze, watching as a video plays. Not just any video—it's me tossing the severed tongue onto a heap of sticks. I light the match, setting it on fire before placing the untouched box in the dirt. Every fucking second of it was captured.

By him.

"You were there the entire time?" My voice is a fractured whisper and all of the control I thought I gained turns to ash before my very eyes. My body turns cold, numb even as I try to process this.

"But...why?" I ask, even though I already know the answer.

Blackmail. Leverage. Control.

They never planned to let me go, and I played right into their stupid game.

Sebastian crouches in front of me. "You see, Little Lamb," he tsks softly, dragging a finger up my cheek, wiping away a streak of his release. "We own you. Every twisted little piece." Then, without hesitation, he slips his cum-slick fingers into my mouth. This time, I bite down.

He rips his hand away quicker than Callan could when I did the same thing to him, clearly seeing my monster rise to the surface. A monster Callan has yet to acknowledge.

Suddenly, Callan lunges at Sebastian with enough force to send him crashing off the altar. The sound of his body hitting the floor echoes, but it feels so distant as my ears start to ring. Everything is pressing down on me so heavily, it's like the air itself is trying to drown me.

I swallow as a sense of shock takes over. When I came over here, I thought this would go badly, but I never could have imagined this.

One of my wrists breaks free and I stare at the floor, a noticeable scratch on the concrete from where a secret door must open. My mind becomes so focused on it that everything else fades away. What is behind that door? Could I use it to gain leverage?

I don't even realize Callan is unclasping the cuffs until I feel the cold metal slip away. I don't move—I don't even speak. Part of me wishes he'd just leave me chained here because when I leave this place, I have to face the reality of how everything's changed. I have to face it all—*feel it all.* And right now, that seems impossible.

So for just a minute, I let myself take a breath and adjust to my new reality. I am the Ice Lords' newest accomplice. But the thing they don't tell you about being an accomplice is that they have all of the information they need to burn the entire fucking plan to the ground.

And these men just reminded me that I am not afraid of a little fire.

CHAPTER 16

CALLAN

I can't wrap my head around what I'm seeing. My thoughts are running rampant, my body shaking with rage. Nothing makes sense except the fury boiling in my veins.

What the fuck did they do to her?

Better yet, why is she so calm? Why isn't she screaming or panicking? Her goddamn pants are around her ankles.

All the while, Aidric is grinning from ear to ear as he sucks on his fingers. And Sebastian is pulling his pants up, adjusting his noticeably hard dick.

I'm going to kill him. *I'll kill both of them.*

The second her wrists are free, I yank her sweatpants back up, and pull her into me, wrapping my arms around her as if I can shield her from everything, like I can somehow undo whatever just happened.

I lean down, voice shaking. "What did they do to you?" I whisper harshly. "Tell me they didn't rape you, Avery. Please. I'm begging you. Tell me they didn't."

What the hell is the matter with me?

"I'm fine, Callan," she says calmly—too calmly. But I don't buy it. She's not fine. She's shaking just as badly as I am.

Her pants were fucking down, for crying out loud!

That image is seared into my brain like a brand. I can't stop seeing it. Can't stop wondering what they did. What *he* did.

If Aidric touched her—if he fucked her—while she was chained, while she couldn't even fight back, I swear to God…

I. Will. Fucking. Kill. Him.

I glance over my shoulder, eyes locking on Sebastian. He's back on his feet, teeth grinding, as he shakes his head at me like I'm the one who crossed the line. Like I'm the problem here.

But if Aidric did something and Sebastian just stood there and let it happen, then he's no better.

"I see you've got your fucking phone," I spit at Sebastian. "Real fucking cool, man."

He throws his hands up, smirking like this is all some twisted game he's already won. And that makes me want to knock his teeth in even more. This is a game, sure, but rape is not on the table. Murder? Fine. But rape? Fuck no.

"What can I say?" Sebastian chuckles, low and dry. "She wanted it."

My blood turns to ice. "Wanted what?"

He shrugs, casual as ever. "All of it."

I don't know what the hell that means, and right now, it's probably best I don't.

These are supposed to be my brothers—my family. But I don't play dirty like that. Yeah, Avery's a loose cannon who needs to be silenced.

But not like this.

I know this girl. I've known her for a long time. Long enough to remember the way she smiled before the world hardened her, long enough to still feel the wreckage she left when she shattered my heart. She gave me every reason to want revenge. And yeah, I want that.

But not like this.

These guys don't know a damn thing about her. They see fire they want to snuff out, a wild animal they think they can tame. They don't care if she ends up taking the fall for all of this. They don't care about her. Not like I do...*did*. Not like I did.

Refusing to spare them another second of my time, I wrap an arm around Avery, keeping her close as I guide her toward the stairs, my body still buzzing with rage.

I keep expecting her to burst out in tears, tremble, something. But she remains stone-faced as we climb the stairs one at a time. Like being chained to an altar by two sadistic bastards was nothing more than a slight detour in her day.

She has to be in shock. It's the only explanation for the emptiness in her eyes.

Then suddenly, she shoves me to the side. "Get your hands off me," she hisses.

I stumble back, stunned as I catch myself from falling backward. "Excuse me? I'm helping you."

"Helping me?" She spits out a bitter laugh, turning to me with an accusing glare that is so intense, I almost flinch. "You're not *helping* me, Callan. You're just as bad as those two. Probably worse."

Her words cut deeper than any blade because, once again, I put myself out there for her, and she has the audacity to push me aside like I'm nothing better than the dirt on her shoe.

"You've been playing me this whole time," she grits out. "You pretended this would all blow over, like I wasn't being hunted. And all along, you knew. You fucking knew they had a video of me in the forest."

"Video?" I spit. "What video?" I have no idea what the hell she's talking about, but I get the feeling my boys have been keeping shit from me.

She shakes her head in disbelief. "Don't do that. Don't play dumb with me, Callan. You know exactly what I'm talking about. You guys all fucking played me. But what happened on that altar doesn't even come close to the level of betrayal I feel from you." She jabs a finger hard into my chest before turning and jogging up the stairs.

And just like that, she's gone, while I'm left standing in the wreckage of everything I never meant to break.

As her footsteps pound up the stairs, I turn to face the guys who are lounging like nothing happened, mid-conversation, probably reliving the fun they just had. "What the hell is this video she's talking about?"

They share a look, and their silence is telling. "You guys fucking recorded her burning the box?"

"Had to." Sebastian shrugs. "You might trust her, but we sure as hell don't."

I suck in a deep breath, forcing down the rage threatening to spill over.

Not now. I'll deal with this bullshit later. Right now, I've got more important things to handle.

Taking my time, I trail behind Avery. She needs a few minutes to process what just happened. Hell, I need to process it. I need to figure out what the fuck just happened, and what the hell I'm supposed to do about it.

Once I make it upstairs, I spot a couple of my housemates lounging in the living room, talking shit like nothing's out of the ordinary.

Ignoring them, I make a beeline for the front door.

Then, a voice stops me cold.

"She's not out there," Slade calls out.

My head snaps around. "What?"

"She's upstairs. In your room."

I blink, caught off guard. "Why the hell is she in my room?"

Slade just shrugs, like it's no big deal. "She asked where it was. I pointed her in the right direction. She's fucking hot, man. Go tear that shit up."

I grit my teeth, a low grumble leaving me as I head for the stairs, taking them two at a time.

The last thing I'm thinking about right now is *tearing that shit up*. What I need is answers.

My feet don't stop as I power down the long hallway, passing six bedrooms before finally reaching mine. Without hesitation, I throw open the door.

And there she is.

Standing at my desk like she owns the place, flipping through the pages of *Notes from Underground* like she wasn't just chained to an altar while my two brothers fucked with her.

"Did you read this?" she asks, her voice almost bored. She doesn't even look up, like she knew I was there the second my hand touched the doorknob.

"Twice, actually," I say, leaning into the doorframe, arms crossed, trying to read *her* now.

Avery's eyes flick up before dropping back to the book. "Interesting."

She snaps it shut with a sharp thud, placing it back on the desk before her gaze begins to sweep around my room. Like she's sizing me up through the objects I keep.

I arch a brow. "Why's that interesting?"

She shrugs, not looking at me. "Just didn't peg you as the type to read something from the 1800s. You strike me more as the psychological thriller or gore kind of guy. Actually..." She tsks softly. "...I didn't see you as a reader at all."

I step into the room, closing the door gently behind me. "Like I've said many times before, you don't know me, Avery."

She turns to face me, eyes sharp. "Seems we've got that in common. Because you don't know me, either." Taking a step closer, fire burns behind her calm exterior. "You and your savage little crew think you can break me, like I haven't already been shattered. But here's the thing," she says, pointing to her chest. "It's the broken parts that keep me from giving a damn. You'll soon find out, like your friends just did..." She steps past me, her shoulder brushing mine. "...I'm just as fucked up as all of you."

I don't let her get far. Before she's more than a step past me, my arm shoots out, wrapping around her waist and yanking her back against my chest. She stiffens, but I don't let go.

"What did they do to you?" I grit out, my breath hot against her ear.

She doesn't answer right away, and the silence between us is louder than any scream.

"Nothing I didn't want," she says, tone maddeningly casual, like we're discussing the weather and not the aftermath of something that's tearing me apart inside.

"If anything," she adds. "You should be asking what I did *for* them. Sebastian specifically."

Her words hit like a punch to the gut. "What the hell does that mean?" My voice is broken and raw. "What did you do for Sebastian?"

"I sucked him off," she says flatly. "And he came all over my face."

The room tilts. My blood runs cold, then boils. Every part of me screams.

She said it like it meant nothing. She's not just telling me to tell me. She wants to hurt me—*again*. And damn if it isn't working.

I'm not supposed to care. I swore I was done caring. If anything, I should want my boys to use her—to wreck her body, twist her mind, and leave her hollow and begging. That was the plan. Break her down and make her pay.

But I can't shake it.

These fucking emotions keep clawing their way to the surface, no matter how hard I try to drown them.

No. I won't allow her to sink her hooks into me again. *I can't.*

Reaching out, I wrap a lax hand around her throat, not squeezing—just controlling. Tilting her chin up, I bring those sharp honey eyes to mine. "Did you like it?" I ask, cutting straight to the point.

My gaze drops to her lips. The ones that were just wrapped around my best friend's cock. "Did you like him fucking your mouth?"

I relish the way she swallows against my palm, like she's

caught in the crossfire between fear and pride. Terrified to admit she liked it, but just twisted enough to want to brag about how much she did.

Because I know she did.

Avery won't say it out loud—at least, not yet—but she's got a freaky side to her. She's a wicked little thing who thrives under attention, especially when it's on her body. She radiates confidence—wears it like armor. She knows exactly what she's working with, and she's never been afraid to flaunt it.

I figured that out the night we had sex.

"Go ahead, Callan. Touch me," Avery rasps, her sultry voice igniting something primal in my chest.

This is the shit I've fantasized about since the first time I saw her strut down the hall at Rosewood High like she already owned the place. She wasn't just confident—she commanded attention, and she got mine, instantly.

Then Brogan brought her home and introduced her as her new best friend.

Her. The girl of my dreams.

Man, I fell harder than I could have ever fucking imagined.

Our flirty hallway glances turned into something that took root and started growing, fast and wild. I know she felt it, too.

The way her fingers are trailing down my abs like she's memorizing me with her touch is proof that she wants me as much as I want her.

But this isn't about just one night. Not with the way my name rolls off her tongue like a promise. This is about the long run. At least, it is for me.

She bites the corner of her lip, sending heat straight to my core. "Fuck, Avery," I groan. "What the hell are you doing to me?"

But I already know what she's doing. She's unraveling me piece by piece, and I'm letting her.

She smirks, all confidence and sass. "Whatever I wanna do to you, Callan. I just want...you," she says breathlessly between open-mouthed kisses on my neck.

Everything about that night was magical. It was like time had bent just for us.

Until it didn't.

When we finished, Avery jumped out of my bed and snatched her phone off the floor like it was burning a hole in the carpet. One glance at the screen, and everything changed.

She didn't even have the nerve to look at me. She just said what we did was a mistake and it could never happen again.

For weeks, I tortured myself, overthinking every look, every word, every touch—replaying all of it on a loop in my head.

But fuck no. I didn't do a damn thing wrong.

I treated her like a fucking queen and she still walked away like none of it mattered.

When that realization hit, I snapped.

I fucking broke because of her, and I haven't been the same since.

Just thinking about it all pulls me back into that headspace I swore I'd never return to. After her, I made myself a promise to never let anyone hurt me like that again. To never let someone twist me up so bad I didn't recognize myself.

And I'll be damned if I let the same girl do it twice.

I'm not even sure why I repeat the question she still hasn't answered.

"So," I ask again, "did you like what my boys did to you on that altar?"

She meets my stare, a wicked smirk tugging at her lips. "I didn't like it," she says, each word slowly. "I fucking loved it."

Something snaps inside me. I shove her back instinctively, disgust rising in my throat. I can't even look at her. That grin—so twisted and so proud—makes me fucking sick.

I hope to God she's just saying this to get under my skin, because if she's not…if she really enjoyed whatever twisted shit Seb and Aidric did to her, then we've got a bigger problem on our hands than we thought.

Avery isn't just some reckless girl with hardcore shooting

skills. She's unpredictable and uncontainable. And right now it looks like she's prepared to burn our whole fucking world to the ground with a smile on her pretty little face.

I could tell her Seb and Aidric have been conspiring behind my back. That I was no part of what they did today, or the video, or much of anything they've been up to. But she's made up her mind. She can go ahead and glorify what they did to her like they're fucking saints.

Fuck them, and fuck her.

"Get the hell outta my room," I growl, my finger jabbing toward the door. "In fact, get the hell outta my house. I can't stand to look at you a second longer."

"Aww," she mocks, as her hand runs down my arm. "Is someone jealous?"

I slap her hand away, fury flashing through me. "Not a chance in hell. I just don't want to watch my boys fall for a vixen who's gonna break their hearts the same way you did mine."

Her smirk drops, and for a split second, something real flickers in her eyes. "I broke your heart?"

"What?" I snap, the word shooting out like a reflex. "No. Fuck no!"

I grab her arm, jaw clenched so tight it hurts. Then I drag her toward the door. "Just fucking *go*."

I shove her out and slam the door behind her. The second it latches, my back hits the wall as I breathe through the silence.

No, Avery. You didn't break my heart.

You ripped it out of my fucking chest barehanded.

CHAPTER 17

AVERY

It's BEEN two days since I've heard from any of the guys. No unexpected visits, no stolen things, no threats scribbled across my mirror in red.

My life has been eerily quiet.

And yet, even in the silence, they haunt every corner of my mind. I keep replaying what happened on that altar. I've been cycling between disgust and a sick sense of intrigue. I should be ashamed of what we did. Yet, I've masturbated to the memory of it...*twice*.

Is something wrong with me? Am I so broken on the inside that the thing I needed to truly wake me up from the mundane life I forced myself into was *that*?

What's worse is that even more than the phantom feel of Aidric's fingers, or Sebastian's cock in my mouth, it's Callan I can't stop thinking about.

That look in his eyes. Those words. It's all lodged in my chest.

"I just don't want to watch my boys fall for a vixen who's gonna break their hearts the same way you did mine."

He's never said anything like that before. Never hinted that I hurt him. And now I can't stop wondering how I possibly could have.

Is that why he's always been so cold? So cruel? Did I break his heart and never even realize it?

"Good afternoon, sweetie," Winnie says softly, snapping me out of my thoughts.

I blink, refocusing. "Hi. How is she today?" I ask my mom's nurse at Juniper Heart, the psychiatric facility where she stays.

Stays. That's the word I cling to. It's less final than "lives" here. This place isn't her home. It's a detour until she's well. At least, that's what I tell myself. Yet, with each visit, it feels a little more permanent.

Winnie offers a gentle smile. "Today's been a good day," she says. "This morning was a little rough, but after her meds, she settled. She's actually outside right now…with a visitor."

I blink. "A visitor?"

That doesn't make sense. My dad and I are the only ones who come to see her. And he hasn't been here in over a year.

My chest tightens, hope pressing against my ribs as I punch my name into the digital keypad. I murmur a quick thanks to Winnie before making my way toward the garden doors, my steps picking up speed.

I can't believe he came.

As soon as I step outside, my eyes search for her—*for him.* A gentle breeze wraps the scent of lavender around me, and I take in the calming landscape.

In the heart of the garden is a circular seating area with a fireplace in the center. On the outskirts are beautiful shrubs with flat tops. Littered throughout the garden, hostas mingle with a colorful array of flowers. There are tulips, daisies, zinnias, and some others I don't know the name of.

On the far right, there's a large, three-tiered stone water fountain. Its weathered look only adds to the charm. I wonder how many wishes were made in that fountain. I'd toss endless pennies into it if I knew my one wish would come true.

Then I see her.

Seated in a wheelchair, on the side of the fountain, my mom has her hands raised in the air. Her fingers move around like a conductor orchestrating an invisible symphony. All to the sound of the trickling water as she's lost in a melody only she can hear.

Her short, thin brown hair is pulled back into a ponytail, revealing the smile on her face. She's wearing her favorite color—a lemon-yellow sweater adorned with white knitted sunshines scattered all over it.

I scan the area around her, searching for my dad. Then as I start toward her, a figure steps out from beside the fountain. But it's not my dad.

It's Sebastian.

My heart plummets, crashing into the pit of my stomach. The sight of him gripping the handles of her wheelchair sends a sharp jolt through me. My breaths turn heavy, each one fueling the fire rising in my chest. With every step I take, the space between us shrinks, and so does my restraint.

"Get away from her!" I shout, my voice cutting through the hum of the fountain. He's wearing a navy suit jacket with a white collared shirt, looking as composed as ever even with all of his tattoos. He's a wolf in sheep's clothing if I ever saw one.

Just as Sebastian begins to turn his head, I catch him off guard, and without hesitation, I shove him hard against his side. He stumbles back a few steps, but his grip on my mom's wheelchair remains firm.

If it weren't for a dozen people surrounding us with their loved ones, I'd punch this fucker square in the face.

"What the hell are you doing?" I grit out.

Sebastian's smirk doesn't falter. If anything, it deepens, like he's enjoying every second of this.

I can't believe there was even a sliver of a second when I actually considered trying to befriend this piece of shit. I don't even know how he knows...

Callan. That asshole.

I shouldn't be surprised, but I am. I never fully trusted Callan to keep my secret, or at least one of them, but I didn't expect him to spill it to Sebastian. And if Sebastian knows, then Aidric probably does, too.

Betrayal settles in, pressing against the anger already burning inside me.

"Hello.there, Avery." He smirks. "Glad you could join us."

I ignore him, my focus locked on my mom as I round the wheelchair and crouch in front of her.

"Hey, Mom," I say, my voice gentle, despite the storm fuming inside me.

She doesn't react, her gaze fixed on the fountain, looking straight through me while she's lost in a world of her own. Her hands keep moving in the air, a small smile lifting the corners of her lips. She seems to be okay. For now.

I rise to my feet, every muscle in my body wound tight and ready to spring. But I hold my ground because my mom is my priority.

Sebastian's grin stretches wider. "Just came to check on your mom. Make sure she's doing all right. Seems to be great." His eyebrows lift. "In fact, just before you got here, she was telling me a story about you. And let me tell you, it was quite an interesting tale."

My cheeks burn with indignation, my pulse hammering in my ears, but I refuse to let it show. I keep my expression unreadable, locking eyes with him as I dare him to push further.

If this is a game, then fine. I'll play. But he's gonna regret ever dealing me in.

"What do you want?" I growl.

His fingers ghost my cheek. "Just checking in. How's the jaw? Is it sore from being stretched so wide?"

I slap his hand away, rage flashing hot beneath my skin. "Fuck you."

"Avery Castle," he croons. "That's no way to speak in front of your mother."

"Cut the bullshit, Sebastian. Why the hell are you here? Aren't you supposed to be with your team in Cloverville?"

"Nah." He waves his hand lazily through the air. "They had to go on without me. Couldn't leave our girl unsupervised. Besides, I've been suspended for two games. Turns out, telling your coach to suck your dick isn't great for team morale." He reaches for me again, fingers grazing the air between us, but I step back. "But you like it. Don't you, Little Lamb?"

"You need to leave," I grit out, jaw clenched so tight I'm surprised I haven't cracked a tooth. "Right now, Sebastian."

I grab his arm, trying to drag him away, but he doesn't budge. My chest tightens, hot tears threatening to fall because he now knows something very few people know—not even my best friend.

And I don't know if it's shame, or embarrassment, or just pure, blinding panic, but whatever it is, he can't be here. Not in this place. Not anywhere near my mom, or this version of me.

In one smooth motion, Sebastian rips his arm from my grip. "Come on, Avery," he says, mockingly soft. "I just wanted a little glimpse into your personal life. You keep everything so bottled up. What's the problem here?"

"The problem?" I snap, voice rising. "The problem is I can't fucking stand you, Sebastian. You're the last person I want near my family, especially my mom."

My throat tightens, and I force the words out past the lump forming there. "You can't hurt her the way you're trying to hurt me. Please."

He tilts his head, confusion flickering across his face like he genuinely doesn't get it. "What do you think I am, Avery? Some kind of monster?"

"Yes!" I shout. "That's exactly what you are."

A sinister smile curls on his lips just before he laughs menacingly. "You're right," he says. "I am."

I shake my head, completely mind-blown by the fact that any

human can be so damn cold. And to think I gave this asshole an orgasm.

"Fine," I say firmly, arms crossed over my chest. "What do you want from me, Sebastian?"

He taps a finger against his chin, pretending to think, dragging it out like he's enjoying every second of watching me squirm.

While he's wasting my time, I use the moment to steal a glance at my mom. The sight of her tugs at my heartstrings. She's so beautiful. Even now, like this. She might appear lost, but she's at peace in her own mind. At least, she is today.

Then, I'm torn away from the moment by the gruff sound of Sebastian's voice.

"I've made up my mind," he says, all too casually, like he's about to ask me to fetch the morning paper for him instead of detonating a bomb. "I want...*you*."

I gulp. "Excuse me?"

"That's right." He steps closer, and closer, until his shoulders brush mine. "I want you, Little Lamb. And you might not know this about me, but I always get what I want."

And here, all this time, I thought Aidric was the more debauched of the three. Hell, they're all a coldhearted fucking mess.

"Well," I say, steeling my voice as I press a finger to his chest and shove him back a step, "I'm not up for grabs. So you'll have to try again."

Sebastian throws an arm around my neck, pulling me in close like we're old friends. My skin crawls, and the minute I try to pull away, he tightens his grip. "Take a walk with me, Little Lamb."

Knowing better than to make a scene here, I force my feet to move, matching his steps until we're tucked within a row of tall trees. I push myself up on my tiptoes, making sure I have a clear view of my mom, and when I see her, my nerves settle a tad.

Sebastian leans in, his breath a whisper in my ear. "When I

say I want you," he murmurs, "I mean I'm *going* to have you. And if you fight me...well, I might just have to do exactly what you begged me not to do."

My heart splinters. *My mom.*

"Don't you dare touch her."

His nose scrunches up before he crowds me. "I would never physically hurt your mom, Avery. Despite what you may think of me, I have *some* morals."

I scoff. "So what are you threatening here, exactly?

"You see," he continues, casually brushing something off his sleeve, "the connections we've formed in our society run far and wide. We're handed opportunities most billionaires can't buy."

He smirks, eyes glinting. "One phone call to the administrator, and your mom's gone. Moved out of this cozy little facility in a matter of minutes."

"You wouldn't," I say breathlessly as my mind scrambles to put together a coherent thought.

Who has that much power? Who *needs* that much power?

"I would." He tilts his head. "Is that what you want, Avery? Your sweet, helpless mom displaced just because her daughter doesn't know how to play nice?"

Every damn time I think I'm two steps ahead of these assholes, they remind me they're the ones pulling the strings. I've never been a quitter, but I'm so damn close to just throwing in the towel.

Not yet, though.

Reaching up, I dig my fingers into the skin of his forearm, and peel him off me with every ounce of strength I have left. My body snaps back as I shove myself free.

"What the hell do you want me for?" I growl.

"Many things, actually," he says smoothly. "Your talents on the archery field could prove useful." His eyes drop to my lips. "And that mouth of yours." He groans. "That mouth works wonders."

"You're such a fucking pig."

"And you're my little lamb," he purrs, smug and disgusting.

I plant my hands on my hips, tapping the toe of my shoe against the dirt, and fake an exaggerated yawn. He knows he's getting to me, and when it comes to Sebastian, indifference is the game I need to play. Aidric is easy; I can talk him to death. And Callan, all he wants is to make me miserable.

"In all seriousness," he says, tone shifting. "This isn't just about sex, or even your body. As much as I do enjoy that part. It's about compliance. You learning how to stop being so fucking defiant all the time. Play your part, and who knows, you might actually find that you enjoy our company."

"The hell I will."

He smirks. "You'd be surprised."

Taking a deep breath, I throw my hands up in mock surrender, hiding the fire still burning inside me. If *playing my part* gets him out of here, I'll fake it till I make it.

"Fine," I say, forcing the words out. "I'm yours. You win. Can you go now?"

"Not so fast," Sebastian says, his arrogant expression pinned in place. "First of all, I don't believe a single word slipping through those pretty lips of yours."

He steps closer, voice dropping. "Second of all, to kick-start this little deal of ours, I need you at our house tomorrow at eight o'clock, *sharp.*"

I arch a brow, but he keeps going.

"You see, my boy Callan is pretty fucking pissed at me right now. So to make it up to him, I'm giving him what he wants… and that would be you."

"Oh." I laugh, dry and sharp. "So now I'm Callan's, too?"

He nods, so certain of himself. "You belong to all ranking members of our society—me, Callan, and Aidric."

Society. Every time I hear that word my pulse spikes. I still don't know what it means, or what they do, but I know it's dangerous. And now I know that these guys are all ranking members.

Interesting.

Maybe going to this party is exactly what I need to do so I can dig into this society they keep talking about. I may not be able to bring them down without torching myself, and now possibly my family, but at least I'll know what I'm now part of now.

"Okay," I say, the word laced with fire. "I'll be there."

"I know you will." His arm hooks around me again, leading me back in the direction we came. "Walk me out, Little Lamb."

I practically choke on the bile rising in my throat before swallowing down the burn.

The second he walks through the doors, disappearing from the garden, I unravel.

My face falls into my hands and I stifle a scream. I've never handled a lack of control well. Something I learned the hard way when my mother fell ill. The chaos of that time left me grasping for anything steady. My therapist encouraged me to empower myself through activities where I held the reins—hence, archery.

Turns out, when I clung to something like a lifeline, I could be pretty damn good at it. Too good, maybe. Because now, all that control I worked so hard to build has come back around and bitten me in the ass.

After a few deep breaths, I wipe my face and collect myself. Then, I put on another one of the masks I wear so well and go back to my mom, because I really need her right now. She might not be able to hear me or even speak at the moment, but sometimes, just being close to her is all I need to soothe the ache in my heart.

CHAPTER 18

CALLAN

Scratch that. Now, we're down by two.

Borgman, Cloverville's center, is on fucking fire. But not for long.

His ass is mine.

I skate back onto the ice, eyes zeroed in on my target. Borgman's been taking cheap shots during the entire game, and I think it's time to put an end to that.

With my stick in hand, I glide straight toward him, and when the gap between us is closed, I don't hesitate. My shoulder slams into his chest, driving him right into the glass with a satisfying crack.

Then, just like I knew he would, he erupts.

"What the fuck?" he howls, shoving his gloves into my chest.

I slide back a few steps, then eat the space right back up.

Fuming, we go helmet to helmet, breath to breath.

"Bring it on, pussy," I growl, letting the name sting. Fitting, since he plays for the Cloverville Cats.

The next thing I know, he's ripping my helmet off my head. It hits the ice with a hollow clatter.

That's step one.

All I need is for him to throw the first punch.

I smirk and tap my cheek. "Go ahead, pussy. Gimme me your personal best."

I watch as his fist flies through the air, but I don't even attempt to block it. He lands a hard shot right to my jaw. Knuckles meet bone, and pain radiates. But that's the only one he's getting.

I flex my jaw, working out the ache just before lunging at him and taking him down onto the ice.

I strip his helmet off before whaling on him. Punch after punch, no hesitation, no mercy. The crowd blurs and the noise fades until it's just my fists and his blood.

Without my permission, the memory of Avery chained to the altar glazes over my vision and I'm lost to the rest of the world around me. All I know is anger.

Her body trembling. Sebastian in front of her with his signature post-orgasm smirk. Her mouth wrapped around his dick.

I see Aidric behind her, his filthy hands gripping her ass like he owns it while his fingers move in and out of her.

Something inside me snaps. Suddenly, this isn't just a fight, it's a fucking *purge.*

My knuckles crash into his face again and again, rage spilling out. I'm not even aiming anymore, I'm just releasing.

Then, I'm yanked off by an on-ice official, reality returning in pieces. My heart is fucking pounding. Adrenaline courses through me.

I know I went too far. But fuck it, I don't care. Borgman will reap the consequences and I'll just get a slap on the wrist. One of the many perks of being an Ice Lord.

"Off the ice!" the ref shouts. "Now!" He hauls me away from the bloody mess of a man, and all I can do is smile at my work of art spilling onto the ice.

I scoop up my helmet and gloves and skate out of the rink without argument, hurling my gloves into the penalty box before

I even reach it. Blood drips from my fingers and all the players are called off the ice for cleanup.

I catch the official holding up five fingers out of the corner of my eye, and a slow smile tugs at my lips. Normally what I did would have me sent out of the fucking building. But this ref is in the Ice Lords' pocket, and he knows better than to take one of the top players out of the game for too long.

"Five minutes," Coach roars from behind the bench. "And don't pull that shit again or you're done for the day!" I can see his pride for what I just did, though. If Avery thinks I'm twisted, she should meet our coach. His senior year as an Ice Lord is written about in our society's journal, and you don't get to be a legacy in there for the small things.

I don't sweat it. Five minutes is nothing. Especially if Borgman is out for the rest of the game. That's the kind of trade I'll take every damn time.

Unfortunately, the first minute is too quiet. Sixty fucking seconds trapped in my own head. As the adrenaline fades, the thoughts of her creep in again.

Where is she? What's she doing? Who is she with?

The questions gnaw at me, and no matter how hard I try to shake them, they sink in deeper, like she's pulsing underneath my skin.

I warned Seb to stay the hell away from her while we were gone. Even begged him to come with us while reminding him that suspension or not, he's still part of this team.

He insisted on staying back, though. Said he needed to catch up on schoolwork, but I call bullshit. We both know the real reason was her.

Fortunately, before my mind spirals too far down the dark hole, the athletic trainer steps in for a quick assessment. I'm handed an ice pack and a rag to wipe the blood from my hand since I can't start a new play while actively bleeding.

As I swipe over the marks on my knuckles, I take a few deep breaths and try to regain my focus.

We have to win this fucking game.

A few minutes later, my penalty's up and I'm back in the game. My head is clearer. My focus is locked. And it's time to finish what I started.

With Borgman out, there's not a chance in hell we're losing this.

The second the puck hits my stick, I'm cutting down the ice. I see the opening, clear as day, a shot I can't miss. I swing my stick back, but...

I hear her.

Her voice. My name rolling off her tongue. She's here.

My head snaps toward the crowd, eyes searching, like they know exactly where to look.

The next thing I know, the puck is stolen right out from under me.

I blink hard, trying to refocus my attention.

It wasn't her. Just some random girl in the crowd cheering me on.

Avery's not here. Of course she's not. She's probably at campus or out at Faraway Archery Range. She's anywhere but here.

What the fuck is wrong with me?

Coach calls me off the ice, waving Slade in to replace me. I hit the bench hard, jaw clenched as Coach tears into me—as he should.

The trainers mention that I was hit in the head during the fight and could have concussion daze, but Coach stares at me too hard. He doesn't believe it. I wish I could. I wish this had nothing to do with Avery. She isn't even here and she's still ruining my life.

I don't say a word. Nothing will suffice for my fuckup. Luckily, Coach doesn't go too hard on me. Or maybe he did. I wouldn't know because I barely heard anything he said before he waved me back in. I was somewhere else. Stuck in my own head, where the real punishment was taking place.

Shoving all thoughts of Avery, Seb, and everything else into the back of my mind, I pour my heart and soul into the final period.

Aidric and I both score, bringing it to a tie.

Then the buzzer sounds and we're in overtime.

Make it or fucking break it.

The crowd is on high alert. Chants roar through the arena, but when the puck drops, it falls dead silent. It's like the world is holding its breath, and it feels like all eyes are locked on me.

I live for this shit. Pressure isn't my enemy; it's my fuel. If I fail here, I'm not worthy of wearing this jersey on my back. So I give it all I've got.

Blades scrape across the ice, sticks clashing together. I react instantly, the puck snapping against my stick like it belongs there.

I cut through their defense like they're simply standing still. Bodies close in, but I don't feel them. Crossing the blue line, I wind back and send the puck slicing through the air, past the goalie's glove, and straight into the net.

Goal.

The arena detonates, red lights flashing, horns screaming, and helmets flying. My team swarms the center ice to celebrate our sweet victory.

We fucking did it. Just like I knew we would.

There was one minor hiccup. Avery seems to be stuck in my head like a bad habit I can't quit. But even she won't throw me off this high.

Not tonight, anyways.

CHAPTER 19

AVERY

AFTER GRABBING some food between classes, my dad calls and I figure since it's been two weeks, I should probably answer so he knows I'm still alive.

I know I've been tough on him, but it's hard not to be. Even though he left my mom like she was too much to carry, he tries with me. And he's still my dad. So yeah, I love him and every now and then I pick up his calls. But that doesn't mean I let my animosity go unnoticed.

"Yeah, Dad," I sigh, weaving through the sidewalk crowd, earbuds pressed tightly in my ears. "I told you I'll try to make it home soon for dinner."

The thought of another meal with just the two of us, hunched over our phones, not once making eye contact, makes my stomach sink. Occasionally he'll toss out a random question such as, *Thinking about changing your major yet? Still shooting that bow around?* It's like he's fishing for something, but he doesn't really care what bites. No matter how I answer, he always ends the conversation there.

It's painfully awkward. But I go because he's alone and I'm all he's got.

"Wonderful," he says, flat and direct. "There's someone I'd like you to meet."

My stomach drops. My feet freeze mid-step.

"Who?" I blurt, my voice choking on the word.

I yank out an earbud and dig my phone from my jacket, killing the Bluetooth. Whatever this is, I need to hear it without a filter.

"Her name is Dina," he says smoothly, a sudden shift in his tone like he's been rehearsing this. "She's a lovely lady, Avery. I think you'll like her a lot."

"Doubtful," I mumble.

"What was that?"

"Nothing. Someone just bumped into me," I lie quickly.

Dina. What kind of name is that, anyway? Sounds like a stripper. Wouldn't shock me if that's where he met her. I can see him in some velvet-lined club, dressed in a three-piece suit, swirling bourbon while women dance in circles like he's the king of sad, lonely men. He probably played the part well.

"Move," some girl hisses as her shoulder clips mine.

I barely register her glare as she passes because I'm too busy spiraling.

Stepping out of the foot traffic, I let the crowd pass while my thoughts try to catch up. "You're…seeing someone?"

A pang hits my chest, sharp and unexpected. My thoughts snap to Mom. My poor, beautiful mom. How could he do this when her heart still beats for him? Maybe it's not the same rhythm it once was, but it still does. I've seen it. Sometimes when I visit, I watch her eyes wander, searching for him as she calls out his name.

I love my dad. I really do. But lately, it feels like every day I hate him a little more.

"I am," he admits. "It's fairly new, but we have a really nice time together. She has a daughter, too. She's eleven. Name's Grace."

Fuck my life.

"Eleven?" I spit. "How old is this Diana lady, anyway?" I ask, deliberately getting her name wrong, just to make it clear I don't give a single damn about her.

"It's Dina. And she's thirty-one—"

"Thirty-one?" I cut in, a dry laugh slipping out. "Dad, you're almost sixty!"

Unbelievable. Either my dad's bagged himself a gold digger, or she's got a pussy carved from solid gold.

Whatever. I can't deal with this shit right now.

"I gotta go, Dad. I'll talk to you later."

I hang up, head shaking in disbelief. I don't care what he does, or who he dates, but if my mom gets better—*when* she gets better—she's going to be devastated.

Forced to push away the emotional wreckage laying heavy on my heart, I stroll up to the Ruth Hill Health building for my human genetics class.

As I make my way toward the doors, the sound of whispers and laughter wrap around me.

I catch a few students pointing across the street. Curious, I follow their gaze and see what it is they're all staring at.

Someone's standing there, still as a statue, wearing a black cloak with their face hidden behind a white hockey mask. The kind you see in the *Halloween* movies. It's cheap plastic, but it looks like there's a smear of fake blood under the left eye, and it makes my skin crawl.

The mask doesn't move, but I swear it feels like their eyes are locked on me through the dark holes.

"What the fuck?" a guy murmurs nearby.

"Should we chase him out of here? Beat his ass?" His friend laughs, acting tough.

I don't say anything. I just stare a second longer because it's too creepy not to.

If I don't get into class right now, I'll be late. So I shake it off, chalking it up to a late Halloween prank. Probably some punk-ass loser with too much time on his hands.

A drawn-out yawn escapes me, forcing me to put a hand over my mouth. I return to taking notes, listening to Professor Reynolds speak on mutations and DNA.

Without my permission, and for no reason I can fathom, my mind drifts to fucking Sebastian, of all people. The prick's got this talent for showing up uninvited, whether it's in person or clawing his way into my head.

I still can't believe he showed up at my mom's facility. Who the hell does that?

A psychopath, that's who.

A shiver runs down my spine when I think about what he and Aidric did to me. Sometimes, I swear I can still feel Aidric's hands, and taste Sebastian on my tongue. The ghost of their touch haunts my skin like a secret I'll never say out loud.

It's fucked up. I know it is. What's even worse is that I want it to happen again.

Sure, Callan has talented fingers, but Aidric and Sebastian zapped electricity into me. Man, I couldn't even begin to imagine what the three of them could do to me at the same time. I'm forced to clench my thighs just thinking about it.

It's not even about them as people because they're the absolute worst. It's about the way they made me feel. It's the darkness in them, and not the kind that hurts, but the kind that seduces. The kind that whispers promises you know you shouldn't want but do anyway.

I'm not ashamed of what I did because it was just a sexual act, and it doesn't matter that I can't stand either of them.

The buzz of my phone snaps me out of my thoughts. My hand jerks across the page, sending a straight line right through my notes. I sigh, reaching into my pocket to pull my phone halfway out.

Llam: Hey. You busy?

I shove it back in without replying.

Dragging the eraser on my pencil over the page, I attempt to erase the line without smudging my notes.

Then, just as I get back into the lecture, my phone buzzes again.

I glance down, *again*.

> Liam: Just wanted to check in and see how you're doing.

Unless it's about Evan, it can wait. We've got a huge exam coming up, and I already feel behind.

"For the love of God," I mutter under my breath when my phone buzzes, yet again.

> Liam: If my brother were awake, I'd ask him if it always takes you this long to respond.

That's an odd thing to say. Maybe he's trying to be funny, but it lands wrong. It's only been two minutes since the first message.

Before I can stuff the phone back in my pocket, another text comes through.

> Liam: I was wondering if you wanted to grab dinner later? I've been at the hospital all day and haven't eaten. What do you say? Hungry?

His persistence is almost sweet, but these texts came out of left field. I don't know anything about this guy. I remember Brogan telling me about the rumor going around—how some people think Liam pushed Evan out of jealousy. It sounded ridiculous at the time, and it still does. But I can't help wondering what made people think that in the first place. He seems decent enough.

I type out a quick response to keep him from blowing up my

phone any longer. Maybe I'll reach out again later, but I prefer to keep the conversation strictly on Evan. I don't have the energy to let anyone new into my messy life right now.

> Me: In class. Talk later.

Before I can even swipe out of our messages, another one pops up

> Liam: My bad. Didn't mean to interrupt. Let's talk after?

I pause, waiting to see if this is the end, and when I'm convinced it's safe, I put my phone back in my pocket.

With a heavy sigh, I force my attention on the lecture, but my mind is miles away.

For a while, I was desperate for Evan to wake up. I needed to know what happened to him. I wanted justice.

Now, he's starting to come back and instead of relief, I'm teetering. Part of me wants him to tell everyone the truth and bring those guys down. But there's another part, a selfish part, that wants him to stay silent and keep their secret buried forever.

If Callan, Sebastian, and Aidric go down, there's no doubt in my mind they'll burn everything on their way out. Including me, my mom, and anyone else they can grip tight enough to drag down with them. That's the kind of people they are.

Class wraps up, and while I managed to take some good notes at the start, I failed miserably at the end.

As I step out into the hallway, I pull out my phone to see if Liam sent any more texts. But a message lights up the screen from someone else.

> Benson: What time should I pick you up tonight?

I type out a quick response...

Me: See you at 8 o'clock. Sharp.

A wicked smile spreads across my face when I think about how this is all going to play out. What I'm doing might be a little evil, but when you're playing with Satan's children, sometimes you have to get your hands dirty. Because in their world, kindness is weakness—and I don't plan on bleeding for any of them.

CHAPTER 20

CALLAN

Music pounds through the speakers, bass shaking the floor, and everything is just the way I pictured it. Noah and the boys really outdid themselves. It looks like gothic Halloween exploded in our house, even though Halloween was three weeks ago.

Black lights beam down, casting everything in a violet glow. Skeletons hang from the ceiling. Bleeding hearts are squished into glass jars. Tombstones line the walls.

The cherry on top is the full-sized coffin. It's even got a fake corpse inside that looks pretty damn real. At least, I think it's fake. The whole scene is twisted and depraved, just like I asked for.

I linger near the door, bottle of water in hand, nerves buzzing as I wait for our VIP guest to arrive. I'm half expecting her to bring Brogan because it's hard to imagine her showing up here alone. Then again, she might not want anyone to know she's showing up here at all.

"You sure she's coming?" I ask Seb, who's already halfway through a six-pack.

"For sure," he says, lifting the bottle in the air. "Not that I gave her much of a choice."

I should probably be pissed, but I'm not. I didn't even ask him what he said to her to get her here. Truth is, I'm just glad she's coming.

When I first planned this party, it was meant to be a scare tactic—a way to show her how our fucked-up minds work. But at this point Avery's seen enough to know better than to turn on us. She's not fucking stupid. I'm actually learning she's pretty damn smart.

Now, this party has become something else. An invitation into our world of drinking, puck bunnies, and pure fucking chaos. The kind you never want to leave, and rarely come back from.

"Remember what I said earlier," I tell Seb. "No more fucking secrets."

"I gotchu." He raises the bottle to his lips and takes a swig, his trademark smirk tugging at the corner of his mouth.

That look says everything.

I've always trusted Seb and Aidric. They're my brothers, on and off the ice. But when it comes to Avery, I feel like I don't even recognize them. I still haven't figured out if their motives are for us as a whole, or for themselves individually.

They said the video was for leverage, and the altar scene wasn't planned. That it just happened when the opportunity struck. According to them, she didn't just allow it, she wanted it. She backed that part up too, and that shit still blows my fucking mind.

I stopped them before they got into the details because I definitely didn't want the visuals burned into my head. Had I been included and got to experience it for myself, I might be singing a different tune, though.

Fuck it. What's done is done, but I'm keeping a close eye on both of them. And next time one of them crosses the line, I won't be so forgiving.

The fact that Seb is standing here beside me, waiting for her to arrive, speaks volumes. Normally, he'd be upstairs in what we call *The Lords' Lair.*

It's a massive room, strictly reserved for more private festivities. The kind that involves bodies, liquor, and absolutely no rules. Some stick to the walls and watch. Others fuck, drink, and indulge in whatever sordid game is on the table that night.

The door opens, and a few more people pile in, none of which are Avery. Just as it's about to close, it pops back open, and there she is.

I'm not sure what the hell is going on in my chest, but I chalk it up to excitement that she actually followed the rules, and not because I'm genuinely happy to see her. She's holding a six-pack of some fruity bottled shit, her hips already swaying to the music. It seems she came for a good time.

I start toward her, but everything inside me comes to a dead stop when I see she's not alone.

"Whoa, whoa, whoa," I growl, indignation ripping through me like wildfire. "What the fuck is he doing here?" I raise a hand, pressing it firmly to Benson's chest to stop him from coming in any farther. "You weren't invited."

Avery's brows knit together, but the grin tugging at her lips tells me she's anything but confused. "Is there a problem with me bringing a friend?"

Benson stands tall like he's not the least bit intimidated, which only pisses me off more. I dealt with this prick once before and he gave me shit. Over my dead fucking body will he do it again. Let alone in my own damn house.

"Yeah," I spit, eyes locked on Benson. "Big problem. No unwanted guests."

Seb doesn't wait for a response. He steps in, grabs a fistful of Benson's collar, and drags him toward the door without breaking a sweat. Seb's got at least six inches on him, and twice the muscle, so Benson would be a fool to put up a fight.

"Pretty sure my boy said you weren't invited," Seb says, calm and collected, before shoving him out the door.

"What the hell?" Avery snaps. "He was invited by me!"

She storms after Benson, brushing off his shoulder like he's some fragile treasure we just chucked out with no care.

Her blazing eyes lock on me. "If he goes, I go."

I could stand my ground, prove we don't back down from anyone, and remind them exactly who the fuck we are. Let everyone think we're a bunch of assholes—which is accurate.

Except, I know that means I'd have to deal with Avery's whiny ass and I really didn't have that on my agenda for the night.

So instead, I let it go.

"Fine," I quip. "He can stay."

Now, he can watch Avery melt under my thumb all night while wishing he'd never come with her in the first place.

Avery flashes a side smile, pleased with herself, like she just won this round.

Seb steps aside, motioning for them both to come back in. And when they do, I'm at Avery's side instantly.

"What the hell is this shit?" I scoff, grabbing the six-pack from her hand. I lift it up, pretending to inspect it, but really, I'm guiding her deeper into the house and away from Benson.

"My drinks." She reaches for it, but I hold it back. "Do you really think I'm stupid enough to drink whatever poisoned beverages you psychos have on the menu for the night?"

"You think we spiked the booze?" I laugh.

She shrugs, cool and unapologetic. "Wouldn't put it past you." The grin on her face says she's half kidding. But the look in her eyes says she's not.

I pluck one bottle from the cardboard ring and hand it to her, fingers brushing hers just long enough to make sure she knows it's intentional.

"Whatever keeps you satisfied," I murmur, watching her closely.

Before handing it over, I hook my thumb under the cap and pop it off with a flick. The scent snakes up my nose and settles in my chest, burning like a memory. I inhale once, temptation gnawing. The craving is still there. But I know better. I'll never go down that path again.

Seems Seb's got Benson handled since neither of them are in sight. Probably his way of having my back after the shit he and Aidric pulled. He'll spend some time making it up to me, and eventually, I'll forgive the fucker. Because that's what we do. We screw up. We clean it up. And we move the hell on.

I walk Avery farther away and into the kitchen, stopping in front of the fridge. I drop her now five-pack inside and snatch up another bottle of water because I'm not sure where the hell my other one went. Since I don't drink anymore, it helps keep temptation at bay when I have something to hold in my hands at all times during parties like this.

After the fridge door shuts, I press my back against it while Avery stands in front of me. She's close, almost too close, but still not close enough.

I watch as she lifts the bottle to her mouth. Her top lip dips inward, bottom one resting on the rim. She tips it back slightly, letting a shot's worth slide past her tongue.

I lick my own lips, jaw tight. I'm not sure if it's the booze I'm thirsty for, or her mouth. Probably both. And right now, I'm not sure which one would ruin me faster.

"So," I say smoothly. "What'd Seb do to convince you to come?"

"Oh, you know," she begins casually. "Threatened my life, my mother's life, and basically told me he'd burn the world to the ground if I didn't come." A glint of a smile plays on her lips. "I figured any party with those stakes had to be worth showing up for."

Her mother's life? That's odd. Seb doesn't know anything about Avery's family, and definitely not about her mom.

Unless...

That rat fucking bastard went digging. My jaw tightens. *Of course he did.*

At least Avery's not pointing the finger at me this time. I shove the thought aside, refusing to let this ruin the night.

I force a laugh, waving my hands out like I'm presenting a masterpiece. "Well, now that you're here, what do you think?"

Her eyes sweep the kitchen, taking in the bodies that are packed in under the same black lights in the entryway and living room. She smirks. "I could've done better."

Savage. But somehow, it makes me smile wider. Of course she couldn't just admit it's impressive. That'd be too easy. But, honestly, I wouldn't want her any other way.

"Hey," she says, voice low, pointing her bottle at me like it's loaded. "I don't know if it's the booze or the vibe in here, but I, umm…wanted to say thank you." She pauses, then smirks. "And just so we're clear, this is probably the only time you'll ever hear me say that."

I lift my brows, hands to my chest. "Thank me? For what?"

"The other day, in The Chamber," she says, eyes glancing away for just a second. "I know you had no idea what you were walking in on. And I swear, I really was fine." She lets out a breath, half a laugh, half something heavier. "Well, as fine as someone can be after being shown a video that could destroy their entire life. But I was fine. You didn't know that, though. And you…" She shrugs, her voice dipping softer. "…rescued me. I guess."

My shoulders tense. I'm not used to this non-feisty, almost vulnerable version of Avery. And, honestly, I have no idea how to respond. We don't thank each other. We don't apologize. Hell, we barely hold conversations without a verbal knife in one hand.

So instead of overthinking it, I just mutter, "Don't sweat it."

Because more than anything, I want to forget that whole thing ever happened. Every time it's brought up, it drags something I don't want to admit to the surface. That maybe I do carry some residual feelings for this girl. And that maybe, *just maybe*, I don't really hate her at all.

"I should go find Benson," she says, already turning away.

Before I can stop myself, my arm is shooting out in front of her. "Wait," I blurt, sharper than I intended. "Why'd you bring him here, anyway?" She pauses, but doesn't look me in the eye. "Come on now, Avery. You had to know it wouldn't go smoothly."

Her walking into my house with him lit something up in me I didn't expect, and I need to know if she did it to hurt me, or to piss me off.

"I don't know what you're talking about." She shrugs, cool as ever. But I know. I see the smirk playing on her lips.

"Benson's a good friend," she adds. "We have fun together. Does that bother you?"

Ah. There it is. She's flipping it. Turning the spotlight on me now. Maybe that's why she brought him. Just to see if I'd be jealous.

"Not at all," I lie. "Don't really care much for outsiders, but the more the merrier."

"Bullshit," she scoffs.

I shrug, playing it off. But she's not letting it go.

"I'm an outsider, Callan. Yet, I was forced to come. And you can drop 'the more the merrier' crap. I know better than that."

"You're not an outsider," I say, plain and simple. "Not anymore."

Her head pulls back, brows knitting. "Then what am I?"

"I don't know," I answer honestly. "But whether we like it or not, you're a hell of a lot closer to us than anyone else in this house." I hold her gaze. "And that makes you anything but an outsider."

"Hmm." She tilts her head, thoughtful. "Guess I didn't see that coming."

I nod. "Yeah. I didn't either."

A beat passes.

"But here we are. No road map in hand."

Her expression shifts in an instant, brow furrowed. "Hey.

Why'd you tell Sebastian about—" she begins, but before she can finish, Aidric steps in between us, cutting her off.

"Slade's looking for you," he says, eyes locked on mine.

Fuck. Slade must be spiraling again. I should probably check on him and make sure he's not toeing the edge of self-destruction like last time.

"All right," I sigh, dragging a hand through my hair.

"Don't worry," Aidric adds, taking Avery's empty bottle and handing it to a random passerby. "I'll take care of our girl."

Wasting no time, he slides his hand around her waist, his expression smug like he's daring me to react.

And just like that, we're back to reality. Back to the game.

CHAPTER 21

AVERY

"I'LL BE RIGHT BACK," Callan says, as if he could offer me any real protection against Aidric.

He said 'our girl' and that makes my hackles rise. I might have made a stupid deal with Sebastian, but I'm not really theirs. I guess Aidric just hasn't realized that. But he will soon.

I really wanted to ask Callan why he shared my secret with the guys. The way they know things they shouldn't has really been eating at me. But of course, I was rudely interrupted by none other than the head dick Lord himself.

I glance down, scoffing at Aidric's fingers pinching my waist. It's not rough, but it's not gentle either. It walks that line of too casual to call out and too deliberate to ignore.

Regardless of what it is, his hand shouldn't be there. And it sure as hell shouldn't drag my mind back to the way those same fingers made me come. But it does, and I fucking hate that my body remembers what my mind is trying so hard to forget.

I look up and fall right into his deep, sea blue eyes. For a second, I forget to breathe. Aidric might have the personality of a brick wall, but even I can't deny he's gorgeous. He's really got that brooding, mysterious thing down pat. Girls probably die for those eyes and that mess of dark, disheveled hair. And don't even get me started on his body. But once you get to know him, you realize he's nothing more than a pretty face with a hollow center.

Aidric reaches behind me, opens the fridge, and grabs another one of my drinks like he knew exactly where they were. Like he's had his eyes on Callan and me the entire time.

He flips the bottle impressively, then catches it with a smirk before handing it to me. "Ready for some fun, Little Devil?" he hums against my neck, his arm already snaking back around my waist, pulling me flush against him.

I growl under my breath, but it's too quiet to matter.

Satisfied with my lack of response, he guides me out of the kitchen, through the haze of the living room, past the entryway, and up the staircase, which is crowded with bodies moving in every direction.

I scan the faces, but aside from Aidric, Callan, and Sebastian, they're all strangers.

Shit. Benson. I completely forgot about him.

The day Sebastian ambushed me while I was visiting my mom, I called Benson. I didn't have much to say, but I needed to talk to someone on the outside to keep me grounded.

I told him I owed the hockey guys a few favors, played it down by saying they were letting me use their archery field, which he got insanely jealous over.

When I mentioned the party, he offered to come with me and be my backup. I warned him the guys wouldn't like that, but he wasn't fazed in the least. But now I've gone and left him alone.

The second we reach the top of the stairs, I stop short, placing a hand on Aidric's chest.

"I need to find my friend I came with," I say, hoping he'll let me go.

Aidric smirks, head tilted slightly while his bright eyes drink up my soul. "No worries, Little Devil," he purrs. "I know exactly where he is."

I swallow hard, hesitating, but my feet move anyway. One drink in and my dumb ass is already being more trusting than I should be.

The dim, never-ending hallway stretches ahead, pulsing with the bass from downstairs. Aidric leads us forward without looking back, and I follow because I'm a glutton for punishment.

We pass Callan's room and I notice the door is cracked slightly, and the light is off. The scent of him wafts out and without meaning to, I breathe in deeper.

God, I hate that I know him by smell alone.

After what feels like a quarter-mile trek, we reach the end of the hall, and Aidric pushes open a door that reveals another staircase leading up to another level.

This house is fucking ginormous. Like, secret passages and body hiding space ginormous.

Aidric doesn't say a word. He just starts climbing the steps, guiding me at his side. Like an idiot, I follow. Hell, if curiosity doesn't kill me, Aidric will still get his shot.

The closer we get to the top, the thicker the air gets, and the unmistakable scent of booze and sex floods my senses. A trifecta of poor decisions and morning regrets.

My pulse kicks up, and I'm not sure if it's because I'm excited or terrified for what's to come. Maybe a little of both. It's clear this isn't like that dungeon of a room in the basement.

As soon as the door at the top opens, someone barrels through, heading down the stairs and bumping hard into my side.

Aidric grabs me in an instant, placing me behind him as he lunges for the person who almost sent me flying.

Seething, he fists the guy's shirt in one hand. "Watch where you're fucking going, or I'll throw your ass down these damn steps. Got it?"

I freeze, eyes wide. My breath catches somewhere between my chest and my throat. I knew Aidric was dangerous, but right now I can feel his dark side practically bleeding into the air.

The guy nods quickly, turning sideways to squeeze past us without another word. The second he's clear, he bolts down the stairs.

I scoff. "Little over the top, don't ya think?"

He may be terrifying, but I apparently have no idea when to keep my mouth shut.

Aidric pauses at the top step, while I stand just one below him. "He almost knocked you down twenty-three stairs, Avery," he deadpans. "I think a thank-you for saving your life is in order."

"Oh," I snap back. "My bad. I didn't realize that little outburst was on my behalf."

I do find it odd that he reacted that harshly for me, but part of me wonders if the only reason he stopped me from eating shit down those stairs is because he'd rather it be his hands that take my life.

Without another word, Aidric snares my wrist and yanks me up the last step, his controlling presence back in full swing.

My jaw nearly hits the floor the second I step inside.

The walls are all glossy black, the floors matching them like polished obsidian. A huge glass chandelier hangs in the center, the lights bleeding from it casting a purple haze.

Against the back wall is a huge, fuzzy black couch that looks more like a throne than furniture. To the left, a bar glows under dim backlights, each stool occupied.

At least two dozen people are up here, each moving to their own rhythm. Some are dancing, some chatting, and some just watching.

In the far corner is a butt-ass naked girl. Her body is moving to the hum of the sensual instrumental music coming from the speakers on the walls. Her eyes are closed, one hand holding a glass filled with nothing but melting ice.

What the…

Is that a guy fucking a girl against the wall?

For a second, I think my eyes are playing tricks on me. But there they are. Her legs are wrapped around his waist, his hands gripping her thighs.

Jesus. My sheltered eyes have never seen anything like this. This isn't just any party. In fact, it's something else entirely.

Aidric comes up behind me and I flinch when his hand ghosts my side. He's barely touching me, but it's enough to send a shiver slipping up and down my spine. "Welcome to The Lords' Lair, Little Devil," he murmurs.

I'm in awe. A little out of place, but undeniably intrigued. My eyes dance around the room, drinking in every detail. It's dark, decadent, and completely unhinged. Yet, something about it pulls me in.

Aidric's other hand grips my chin, tilting my face to the right. "You see that?" he hums. "Told you I knew where your friend was."

My gaze shifts, landing on Benson.

He's sitting on the long black couch, his posture tense like he doesn't know how he got here. In front of him, a girl in nothing but a baby pink bra and matching thong moves to the music.

"How does that make you feel, Little Devil?" Aidric growls low in my ear, his breath hot against my skin. "Seeing the guy you brought here, over there, letting a half-naked girl grind on him like you never existed?" His grip tightens ever so slightly. "Is that really the kind of guy you want to waste your time on?"

I spot Sebastian standing still in the middle of the room, surrounded by girls dancing around him like he's some untouchable god in their orbit. But he pays them no attention.

He's holding a glass of clear liquid, fingers curled around it like he doesn't even realize it's there. He's just standing tall, watching me like he's waiting for an explosion. Like he planned this because he knew I was coming up here.

I glance back at Benson and notice a smile threatening to break free, and when his eyes find mine, it does.

He raises his beer in a lazy toast, shrugs like this is all just a joke, and glances between me and the girl now grabbing his hand and planting it firmly on her ass.

I can't hold it in any longer, I burst out laughing.

Aidric steps around to face me, hand still clamped on my waist, his eyes flicking to Seb, then back to me. "What's so damn funny?"

I snort, nearly doubling over. "You guys have no fucking idea, do you?"

For the first time ever, Aidric actually looks confused. Eyebrows drawn, head tilting slightly. "No idea about what?"

I shake my head, laughter still spilling from my lips. "If you dumbasses seriously thought this whole setup was going to hurt me or piss me off, you're dead wrong."

I slap a hand over my mouth, trying to stifle my giggles.

Aidric's brow furrows deeper. "Jesus Christ, Avery. Just spit it out."

My hand drops from my mouth, but the grin stays firmly in place. "You wanted me to freak out over Benson letting some chick grind on him. And I get it, really good strategy." I nod toward the couch. "But I'm not fazed in the least, and neither is he."

Aidric scoffs. "The hell he's not. Look at him with his hands all over her."

"I see it." I laugh again. "Everyone sees it. But hate to break it to you, Aidric…" I lean in just enough to watch his expression fall. "Benson's gay."

His shoulders drop, right along with his jaw. "Seriously?" He throws a look at Sebastian, then slowly shakes his head.

I pat him on the back firmly. "Nice try, asshole."

Then I turn and saunter over to Benson, drop down beside him on the couch, and enjoy the show like the queen I am in this ridiculous little kingdom of theirs.

He tosses an arm over my shoulders just as a man approaches in a G-string that hardly covers anything, and I instantly lose all of my friend's attention.

But that's okay because my eyes find Aidric and Sebastian across the room, looking pissed off as ever.

Avery Castle, one. Hockey assholes, zero.

CHAPTER 22

AVERY

I HAVE no idea what Benny Boy put in that drink, but whatever it was, paired with the other…oh, three or four I've had, has me feeling really damn good. Warm, weightless, and maybe a little dangerous.

My body sways beside Benson, moving to the beat like it's my own private rhythm. I don't give a damn who's watching. Except, I do, because *they* are.

Aidric, Sebastian, and Callan.

Their eyes follow my every move like they own me. And maybe for tonight, I'll let them think they do.

I wonder what they're talking about, or plotting, rather.

It's hard not to notice that something's been off with Callan lately. That moment in the kitchen when I first got here was almost normal. It felt like I was talking to the old Callan. The one I knew before we had sex. Before everything got twisted and cold.

For a split second, it felt like the old feelings I buried years ago were starting to resurface. The ones I had before he started treating me like I was nothing.

I still can't forget what he said about me breaking his heart. It still haunts me and at the same time, it doesn't make sense. He's the one who turned on me. Maybe one day I'll have the courage to ask him what he meant. But not tonight. Not when his eyes are on me like I never hurt him at all.

I'm starting to realize this is my life now. At least for a while.

To protect myself, and my mom, I'm keeping my mouth shut. I won't tell anyone about the twisted, messed-up shit they've done.

The truth is, I don't even know the full extent of it. I don't know what they've done that I haven't uncovered yet. There are secrets buried in this house, ones my curiosity is dying to unearth.

I watch them just as closely as they watch me. I'm not sure why. Maybe I'm waiting for an opening, a moment to slip past their gazes and dig deeper into whatever shadows they've hidden.

Callan twists the cap off a bottle of water, cool, calm, and collected, smiling at something Sebastian just said. And God, it's a beautiful fucking smile.

Sebastian flicks a glance in my direction, but when he catches me watching, his eyes lock on mine and fire rips through my veins.

He nudges Aidric, who shifts his focus to me. Under the backlights, Aidric's eyes practically glow.

He swirls the glass in his hand, the ice clinking softly in the caramel-colored liquid. Then he lifts it to his mouth, lips curling behind the rim in a knowing grin.

All three of them have their hooks in me, but I've got my claws in them, too. And I'm starting to think they don't just keep me close to protect their secrets. They like the thrill of the chase. The push and pull, not knowing what I'll do next.

Well, if it's a chase they want, it's a chase they'll get. This cat likes to test her nine lives.

I push myself onto my tiptoes, lips brushing close to Benson's ear. "Be right back," I whisper.

I slip into the crowd, heart pounding and a smile on my lips because now, it's my move.

Without looking back, I don't stop until I'm at the bottom of the staircase. I don't know if they're following, but I keep moving like they are.

As I close the door behind me, I stumble a little, catching myself against the wall. A giggle escapes me. Those drinks definitely aren't doing me any favors, but maybe a little recklessness is exactly what I need.

I scan the room, eyes darting past all the unfamiliar faces, "Alone in a Room" by Asking Alexandria vibrating in my chest. The air tastes like cheap vodka, reminding me that I need another drink.

I shoulder my way through the crowd, brushing past bodies, ignoring the conversations and sidelong glances. When I reach the kitchen, I head straight for the refrigerator where my alcohol is.

A pale girl with inky black hair and eyeliner smeared like war paint around her eyes stands in front of it, an angry scowl on her face as she watches a couple flirting directly in front of her. From where I'm standing, it's not hard to piece it together. She's into him, and the girl batting her lashes is probably her best friend. *Ouch.*

"S'cuse me," I murmur, reaching past her, fingers brushing the side of her black trench coat as her glare stays locked on what's happening in front of her.

"Oh sure," she groans, stepping aside. "Go right ahead. Everyone just takes what they want anyways. Take, take, take."

I blink, caught off guard, then roll my eyes and offer a strained smile. "Bad day?" I ask, though I'm not sure why I bother.

She gestures at the scene unfolding in front of her. "Do you see this shit?" Her voice shakes with rage. "My best fucking friend is flirting with my brother—my *twin* brother, for God's sake. Bet they're already screwing behind my back."

I steal a quick glance at them before pulling the refrigerator open and retrieving my drink. The door clicks shut on its own, and before I've even stepped back, Emo Chick slides right back in front of it, reclaiming her spot.

She shakes her head slowly, arms folded over her chest. "How could she do this to me?"

I twist the cap off my drink, take a sip, then glance back at her brother and best friend.

Reality sinks in that this could have been Brogan watching Callan and me years ago, before everything went downhill.

I turn to her again, voice quieter now. "Is it really such a bad thing?" I ask. "I mean, if you love them both, what's the harm in them liking each other?"

Her brows pinch together, but it's the shift in her eyes that gives her away. She's angry, but even more so, she's hurt.

"There wouldn't be any harm if they'd just come to me," she says. "But to go behind my back. It fucking sucks."

"I get it," I start, but the moment I catch the basement door creaking open, my words vanish in midair.

My gaze snaps to the hallway where I see Aidric stepping out. I was sure he was still upstairs. Guess they followed me down, after all. But if he's here, where the hell are Sebastian and Callan?

Doesn't matter.

This is my chance.

Before I can think twice, I'm already moving. Aidric strolls away, thumb pressing the button on the remote in his hand. I see the door start to seal, but I'm faster. I shoot my hand through the narrowing gap, drawing attention to myself, but I don't care.

I rip the door open and slip inside. Instincts kick in and I instantly slam it shut.

I'm immediately engulfed in the warm glow of the lit sconces lining the staircase. My pulse kicks up, and each step down feels more and more like I'm walking into a trap I set for myself. I've always been a nosy person, but this is bold even for me.

When I reach the bottom, I take a second to scour the area, making sure I'm alone. Once I'm certain I am, I let myself breathe. My fingers trail along the rough brick walls as I move, grazing the surface, tracing the details I've seen before but never truly noticed until now.

Symbols and chaotic words are hand-painted on the brick in various colors. It makes no sense to me, but I'm sure it means a great deal to them.

I reach the door Callan once disappeared behind, the memory of him retrieving a skeleton key from somewhere near the altar fresh in my mind. I was curious then, watching from a distance, but now I'm desperate.

This might be my only chance to find out what's hidden in there, so I have to try.

Moving quickly, I go to the altar, taking the two steps to rise on top of it. Leaning over the podium, I look on the backside of the small shelf but all I see is a strange metal rod resting on a silver stand.

I pick it up, noticing a plate at the base and a small on-off switch. I flick it and it instantly begins to warm in my grip. Curious, I turn it over and freeze when I realize it's a branding iron.

There's a shield at the center, surrounded by two crossed hockey sticks, and a hockey mask with vented holes pressed into the middle. Along the top, engraved in bold letters, is *Ice Lords*.

I swear I've heard that name tossed around a few times. I always figured it was because their team is the Lords, but this feels like something else entirely. I'm starting to think the Ice Lords aren't just a simple college sports team, but rather part of whatever secret society this is.

First mystery cracked. Sort of. I need to find that damn key.

After putting the branding iron back, I look around on the altar, noticing the cuffs hanging from the ceiling. I don't have to wonder what they're for because I already know. I remember the bite of the metal, the way it burned into my wrists. I remember it all too well. I wonder how many people hung from there, not to feel pleasure, but pain.

I turn around and notice something I didn't see before. Against the shadows behind the altar is a nearly invisible, black curtain. It blends so seamlessly into the darkness, I almost miss it.

Moving to the end, I pull it open and when I see what's back there, it feels like the air has been sucked from my lungs.

Three metal tables line the space like something ripped straight out of an operating room. Only, I don't think these are meant for saving lives. Each tray holds various tools and weapons used to torture someone.

My stomach curls, heart pounding against my ribs like it's trying to escape before I can.

This is so much worse than I expected. It's not just disturbing; it's downright sickening. Yet, I don't run. I don't even back away. Instead, I enter the room and go over to the items along each table. My fingers hover curiously before picking up a spiked baton. It's cold and heavy, the jagged edges sharp like tiny knives.

Just as I'm about to set it down, I catch something out of the corner of my eye. Beneath one of the sconces, right where the curtain's edge falls, a long, rusted nail sticks out from a brick. And hanging from it, like it's been waiting for me all along, is the key.

I toss the baton onto the tray and it hits with a heavy clank that echoes through The Chamber. Six long strides lead me to the key and I snatch it without hesitation, fingers curling tightly around the cool metal.

A wicked smile curls at the corners of my mouth as I push past the curtain, heading straight for the door at the back of the room.

When I reach it, I slide the key into the lock, noticing the slight tremble in my hands. I can't tell if it's nerves or adrenaline, but at this point, not much should shock me.

Once it's unlocked, I slowly push it open, the sound of creaking dragging through the silence. The only light is a faint glow deep in the room. I can't even make out what surrounds it, but curiosity gets the best of me.

How many lives do I even have left at this point?

Shadows dance across the brick walls like they're inviting me in. And, of course, my dumb ass follows them.

Leaving the door open, I let the little light from the sconces enter. With small, cautious steps, I move toward the light, and the closer I get, the clearer it becomes.

A glass display, the kind you would use for a prized trophy, holds a book on a three-point stand. It doesn't look like any book I've seen before. Its cover appears ancient, almost like a spellbook, though I know better. This isn't a book that grants power, but I have no doubt it's one that hides secrets.

Before I even reach it fully, I notice the gold key slot and disappointment curls in my gut.

Of course it's fucking locked.

My first instinct is to start searching for another key, but I don't have time for that. I'm actually shocked no one's found me down here yet.

So, I do what I have to do. I spin on my heel and make a mad dash behind the curtain. Grabbing a hammer I saw lying on one of the trays, I return to the display. My heart is racing, but the decision has been made. No backing down now.

I swing the tool in one sharp motion, shattering the top of the display while leaving the bottom part with the light intact. Glass goes flying, scattering around on the concrete floor.

Carefully stepping over the broken shards, I stretch my hand out and grab the book.

I find a clear spot near the light, drop the hammer, and sit down. My back presses against the cold brick wall while my fingers graze over the silver embossing of the typography that reads: Where there is a Lord, there is power.

Fitting for these debauched men.

I open the cover and immediately begin flipping through the pages.

Thirty seconds in, and my jaw is already on the floor.

There's a short and dry foreword about the Ice Lords being established in the early 1940s by a man named Edison Einhorn. It mentions that the Ice Lords exist under some paradox of The Ice Society. Whatever that means.

But then it gets interesting.

There's a picture, or maybe it's a sketch, of a black cloak, and above it is a solid white hockey mask, expressionless and cold. It looks exactly like the one I saw someone wearing earlier today. Coincidence? Maybe. But something in my gut says it's not.

Apparently this is what they wear during ceremonies.

This is some seriously messed-up shit. But I keep going, reading more.

There are pages filled with strategies, power plays, dominance tactics, strength-building routines, bonding methods that go way beyond the usual team-building fluff.

A fold-out hierarchy map catches my eye. At the top are three titles: leader, Lord speaker, and council advisor. I don't need names to know those are Callan, Aidric, and Sebastian; it fits considering they've always been the ones pulling strings. Beneath them sit the other members, known as barons.

I flip a few more pages, skimming through the paragraphs about rules and requirements. One detail jumps out: every player on the Lords' hockey team must be a member of The Ice Society. There are no exceptions, and damn...the selection process is brutally ritualistic.

This isn't just a hockey team; it's a brotherhood rooted in blood.

As I thumb through a few more pages, a corner lifts. I pause, turning back, only to realize it's not a page at all. It's a separate sheet, tucked between chapters.

I unfold it carefully, eyes narrowing, then widening when I realize it's a map.

Lines crisscross, but there is no title at the top to tell me where this is. My fingers tremble as I trace a few of the streets and some of the picture begins to come together.

When I look closer, I see why. *It's here.* The same location, and the same marking from the map Sebastian gave me to burn and bury the box.

But this map doesn't stop with the number one, or start at eight, rather. There are multiple locations spanning around the two neighboring campuses, and all are numbered. My mind races when I see the total number is thirty-six.

Holy fucking Batman.

This thing could be the key to everything. Each spot could be tied to a crime the Ice Lords committed. Not just one, but many.

I could quite literally destroy these guys. I mean, I could've before, but now I really can.

I may never know what happened to Evan, but I might be able to figure out just what is happening here and prevent anyone else from getting hurt like that.

Folding the map back up until it's small enough to hide in my cross-body purse, I stick it inside. I didn't uncover any hidden bodies or chained-up chicks who have been kidnapped and held against their will, but I did find this map, and even got a little insight into what their twisted society is. I'd call that a win. And as I've always been told, it's best to quit while you're ahead.

Pushing myself off the floor, I brush off my hands and start toward the exit.

Suddenly, the door slams closed with a heavy thud.

It feels like the room has swallowed me whole and there is no escape. The light behind me is suddenly dim and useless. Panic rises in my chest as I sprint toward the door, my heeled boots clapping against the concrete, heart racing.

"Let me out!" I scream, voice cracking as I slam my fists against the thick wood. My whole body trembles, limbs shaking so violently I can barely stand. This isn't just any door, and this isn't just any room. I know that no one can hear me down here, but I try anyway.

All self-preservation goes out the window as I try to think of a plan. "Please!" I shout even louder. "Just let me out of here!"

There's a long stretch of silence, aside from my labored breathing. I begin to picture things in my head I don't want to think about. Me tied to a torture table, the weapons used on my skin. I'm a tough girl, but no one ever taught me how to hold up under torture.

Tears spring to my eyes as I start to realize this could be the end for me. The buzz I had from the alcohol is already making me feel weak, and now I just want to pass out and try to forget. Forget my life and everything I thought I knew or had planned for myself.

"How's it feel to be in hell, Little Devil?" The voice startles me and I nearly jump out of my boots.

Aidric.

I suck in a shaky breath, forcing down the lump rising in my throat. Using the door to steady myself, I press my palms against it. "Aidric, please just let me out," I ask again, this time softer, kinder.

"Confess your sins," he taunts. "And maybe I'll consider it." His voice is muffled coming from the other side of this door, but I can hear him clearly enough.

Heat rises in my chest. "For the love of God," I mutter before raising my voice. "Just open the fucking door!"

I swing my foot out and slam the toe of my boot into the wood with a loud thud, the impact jolting up my leg. The sound echoes, but the door doesn't budge. And neither does he.

I know this isn't the time to try and be a badass, but it's damn near impossible not show these guys I can hold my own. The moment they see that I might be caving is when they'll go for blood.

Then I hear the soft click of the key turning, and the sound reverberates straight through me.

My head snaps up, shoulders square, and I brace myself for a battle.

When the door opens, I step forward, ball my fists, and shove them hard into Aidric's chest. "You asshole."

I don't wait for a reaction. I push past him quickly because I know these guys love to grab, hold, and torment. And just as I hit the first step, I'm proven right.

Aidric's arm wraps around my waist and he pulls me back, lifting me off the ground. Before I can even twist away, he's already carrying me straight back into The Chamber.

He hauls me to the first row of chairs, and I kick my legs out, knocking a couple over on purpose. Not because I think it'll help, but because I know it'll piss him off.

He drops me down in one of the chairs like I'm a sack of potatoes. "Stay!" he snaps, stern and commanding.

"Oh, now you're gonna talk down here," I scoff. "That's new."

"I talk when I want to," he growls. "My position comes with benefits you'd sell your pussy for, Little Devil. Others speak for me, so I don't have to waste my breath on nosey little bitches."

"So now I'm a bitch?"

I should be offended, but I'm not. Not much this asshole says surprises me anymore.

"You tell me," he says, voice sharp, as he heads to the front of the room.

I roll my eyes and cross my arms, settling in with all the fake composure I can muster. I know better than to run. I already spotted the remote sticking out of his pocket and I have no doubt he's two steps ahead of me, as usual. The door to the upstairs is definitely locked.

My only other option would be to run into the dark room I was just in, but I'm sure as hell not doing that. Although, there very well could be another exit or entry point in there. I didn't really have the chance, or the courage, to look deeper.

Aidric steps onto the altar, and I watch him closely, heart

hammering as he reaches behind the podium. But I was just back there and the only thing on that shelf…

I lose my train of thought when he comes forward holding the branding iron. I notice the switch pushed up and I can see that it's heating fast.

My stomach knots. "What are you doing with that?" I ask, scooting back in my chair as he comes toward me.

His eyes lock on to mine, cold and unreadable. "What did you read in that book?"

I shrug, eyebrows caved in confusion. "What book?"

"Don't play dumb with me, Avery!" he snaps, the name slicing through the air like a whip.

I jolt. He hardly ever calls me Avery, and just hearing it sends a chill down my spine.

"I saw the broken glass and the book on the ground," he continues, seething. "You fucked up, Little Devil. You *really* fucked up."

I swallow hard, panic rising fast. "Okay," I blurt. "I flipped through the book, but I didn't really read anything incriminating. Just society stuff like traditions, ranks, and rules. I swear, it was all just bullshit. I didn't see anything worth hiding."

Aidric tsks, slow and deliberate. "You shouldn't have done that," he says, tone laced with intent. "Because now, I have to do this."

Before I can react, he yanks me to my feet, causing my breath to catch in my throat. In the next instant, he lifts my shirt, and suddenly there's a searing pain.

The iron presses into my side, and a scream rips from my throat as the heat tears through skin. I claw at his arm, at anything, but it's already done.

My knees nearly give out, tears streaming down my face, and I hate myself for letting them break free.

"You want to be someone important, Little Devil? Well, now you are. We're your Lords, and now you're our queen. Stuck with us forever." He pauses for a beat. "Unless, of course, we decide to kill you."

As fast as he pressed the iron to my skin, Aidric pulls it away, but the unforgiving burn still lingers.

"Get your ass back upstairs," he snaps. "And don't let me catch you down here again without our permission." He leans in slightly. "And I don't think it needs to be said, but keep your goddamn mouth shut and your nose where it belongs."

While I can, I run like fucking hell.

Aidric is the worst. He just marked me for life, something I know I will never be able to get rid of. He called me a queen, but I know better. I'm not royalty like them. I'm a simple pawn in their fucked-up game and I just made myself the center of attention for them all.

My boots pound against the stairs, breath burning in my lungs, and then, as soon as I push the door open, I collide with someone at the top.

I crash into him hard, falling right into Callan's arms.

"What the fuck," he mutters, catching me, arms wrapping almost instinctively around my back. "Where the hell have you been?"

CHAPTER 23

CALLAN

I PULL AVERY INTO ME, holding her tight against my chest. My hand finds the back of her head, stroking gently, trying to calm the tremble in her body. She's crying, and not the kind of tears that come from mental pain. I know her, and no words would make her react like this.

"What happened?" I ask, bracing myself for the worst as I stare into her eyes.

She's obviously distressed, shaking uncontrollably and barely holding it together. It's not often I see Avery cry. And I sure as hell don't like that it was at the hands of someone else.

Fuck. Truth is, I don't like it at all.

Not the tears, not the vulnerability, and certainly not the way it makes something twist deep in my chest. No matter how many games we play, how much shit we've thrown at each other, seeing her like this gets to me.

The only sounds that escape her are stuttered breaths as she clings to me.

I shift, sliding an arm around her waist and moving to her side. "Come with me," I whisper as I lead her to the staircase. We move slowly, weaving through the crowd as people pass by, laughing, drinking, completely unaware of the storm curled against my hip.

A minute later, we're at my door. It's already cracked open so I give it a gentle kick and guide her inside, straight to my bed.

She sits on the edge, silently shaking. I pull the string on my bedside lamp and sit beside her.

Her head hangs low, eyes fixed on her lap as she fumbles with her fingers. She's fragile in a way I've never seen and I fucking hate it.

"Hey," I say softly, tipping her chin up with my thumb so I can see her face. "Was it Sebastian?"

She shakes her head.

"Aidric?"

A small, reluctant nod.

Just like that, something manic twists in my gut. I clench my jaw, grinding my teeth to keep the rage from spilling out. My hand fists the sheet beside me, gripping it tightly.

Hold it together, Callan. It might not be as bad as you think.

But that small voice of reason is drowning in a sea of crimson because no matter what happened, Aidric did something to hurt her.

Avery makes a move and I pull back, watching every motion as she grasps the side of her shirt. Her fingers curl around the hem, and she lifts it slowly, pain etched on her face.

That's when I see it.

"Jesus Christ," I growl, forcing myself to stay and not bolt out of this room to hunt Aidric down.

Right below her breastbone, etched into the soft skin of her side, is a stamp. *Our* stamp.

He didn't just hurt her, he branded her. No! He fucking binded her—*to us.*

Rage surges through me, washing out every rational thought. I had a feeling this might happen if she kept stirring the damn pot, but I don't tell her that. The less Avery knows, the better. She's already in too deep. And whether she realizes it or not,

Aidric just sealed her fate. Because once you wear our mark, there's no escape.

"What does this mean?" she asks, voice cracking as she looks down at the burn. It's red and welting a bit around the edges. He clearly pressed too fucking hard and she no doubt fought him every step of the way.

"I'm not entirely sure," I tell her truthfully because I really don't know the details.

What I do know is, The Society's rules have never specified gender, only that the branded shall be one of us.

However this plays out will be a surprise for all of us. I don't think Aidric even realizes the extent of what he just did.

"I'll find out," I say softly. "You'll be fine. I'm not gonna let anything happen to you."

Something's shifted in me over the last couple days. I don't know exactly when it happened, or why. Maybe it was seeing her bound on that altar, stripped of her fire. Whatever it was, something cracked open.

It was subtle at first, but now it's impossible to ignore. I've gone from loving this girl, to hating her, to…whatever the hell this is. I don't even have a name for it. All I know is, I don't like it.

This would be so much easier if I could be like Aidric. If I could just revel in the chaos, break her down piece by piece, and walk away with no guilt.

But I can't do it anymore because somewhere along the way, I stopped wanting to hurt her and began wanting to protect her. Even if that does make me the biggest threat of all.

She doesn't say another word, just lies back, curled into a ball like she's gone numb.

I watch her for a moment, then reach out and gently stroke her hair until her eyes begin to close.

And when they do, I ease my arms beneath her, cradling her against my chest. I lift her carefully to the top of the bed, settling her down like she's something breakable. Because right now, she is.

Moving slowly and quietly, I go to my bathroom and grab a jar of salve. When I return to her, I scoop out a fingertip's worth and set the jar down beside my bed.

Lifting her shirt slowly, I rub the salve on her burn. She winces, but doesn't wake. Once I'm done, I lower her shirt, pull the blanket over her, and lie down beside her.

Close, but not close enough. And that's probably for the best because if I let myself get any closer, I might not be able to pull away.

"Where's Benson?"

I shoot up, panic blooming in my chest. "What?" I gasp, blinking over at Avery, who's now sitting upright beside me.

"Benson," she says again, her voice sharp and urgent. "Where the hell is he?"

I sigh, dropping my head back onto the pillow. "He left after the lap dance with a group of guys he knows."

I watch as the tension in her shoulders drops, but she doesn't lie back down.

"How'd you sleep?" I ask.

She shakes her head. "Slept fine. But please tell me last night was just some twisted nightmare."

"Afraid not," I mutter, rolling onto my side to face her. I tuck my hands under the pillow, keeping my mouth low so she doesn't get a whiff of my heinous morning breath.

She didn't ask, but I slept like the dead. First full night's sleep I've had in a while. No tossing, no nightmares clawing at the edge of my mind. Seems like sleeping next to her was the antidote.

"This is fucked up, Callan," she snaps. "I've got a third-degree burn on my side, which is going to scar in the shape of your satanic cult's branding."

There's the feisty Avery I've grown to like.

I don't respond because she's right, this is fucked up. But I've got nothing to say until I talk to Aidric and Seb and figure out what the hell any of this actually means. Until then, there's no point in diving into a conversation I'm unprepared for.

So instead, I lighten the mood. "Want breakfast?" I ask, like everything's normal.

"No, I don't want breakfast," she huffs, clearly annoyed. "I want answers, but even more than that…" she begins as she peels the blanket off her and stands. "I wanna go home."

She stumbles, grabbing the sides of her head. "Ugh," she groans. "I don't feel so hot." Then, in the blink of an eye, she's hauling ass into the open bathroom. The door doesn't even shut behind her before I hear the sounds of her throwing up.

I swing my legs over the side of the bed and stand, adjusting my morning wood with a sigh. "You okay?" I call out as I head toward her.

She's curled over the toilet, hair draped in front of her face like a curtain. I move beside her, gathering the tangled mess into my hands, holding it back as another wave hits.

I'm forced to look away because suddenly, my own stomach's not feeling so hot either. Funny how blood, bruises, and broken bones don't faze me in the slightest, but the smell of alcohol-soaked vomit curls my stomach like nothing else.

Once she's done, her head lifts and I let go of her hair, watching as it falls into place, framing her face.

She groans, mutters something under her breath, and reaches for the hand towel lying on the floor beside her.

Shit.

I immediately remember using that towel to clean up after I jerked off yesterday morning. I open my mouth to say something, but before anything comes out, she's already wiping her mouth with it.

Fuck it. Not like she won't be tasting my jizz at one point or another anyways. We'll just call this a little preview.

Dropping the towel back down and after flushing the toilet, she murmurs, "I think I'm better." She shifts, pushing herself up, and I slip my hand under her arm, helping her to her feet. Her weight leans into me for a beat longer than she needs to, and I don't move.

"There's some toothbrushes in the top drawer," I say, keeping my tone even. "Clean towels in the cupboard, if you wanna freshen up."

What I don't say is how much I want to pull her into the shower, scrub the night off her skin with my hands, and feel her back pressed against my chest. But knowing her, she'd knee me in the balls, curse me out, then throw up on my feet. So yeah. Maybe not today.

Avery nods and drifts toward the sink. I follow, grabbing my toothbrush and dragging a smear of toothpaste across it.

I catch her side snarl in the mirror, watching me like I'm some stray dog in her territory.

Smirking, I stick the toothbrush in my mouth and start brushing, feeling the coolness of mint against my tongue. For a second, I'm tempted to reach out and poke her side, something stupid to make her laugh like she used to. Back when things were easy. Back when we didn't have to tiptoe around each other like strangers with too much history.

But my hand stays still because that was then and this is now. We're not those kids anymore.

Once we finish in the bathroom, Avery follows me into my room and out to the hallway. There's a guy passed out on the floor three doors down with a beach towel tossed over him. I don't even blink because it's just another morning at this house.

We head down the stairs, but I pause halfway, catching the full extent of the wreckage from last night. There are cups and trash littered everywhere, glitter glistening on the couch. There's a sticky liquid splattered across the hardwood, and someone's shoes are stuffed into the cupholders on one of the recliners.

It looks like a war zone, but the cleanup crew is already on it. By the time I get back from dropping Avery off, I bet it'll look like a party never happened here.

Stopping in the kitchen, I snag a couple bottled waters from the fridge and hand one to her.

"Thanks," she whispers, so soft I almost miss it.

We slip through the side door into the garage, the scent of motor oil thick in the air. With a click of the remote, I watch as one of the sleek black SUVs lights up, and we waste no time hopping in.

As I back out of the garage, one hand grips the wheel while the other slides behind Avery, resting on the headrest. Yeah, I've got a backup cam, but I'm old-school in that way.

Out of the corner of my eye, I catch her unzipping her purse. She pulls out her phone, except something else slips out with it.

My gaze lands on the numbers, the lines. *What the hell?* Before she can shove it back, I reach over and snatch it right out from under her fingers.

"Where'd you get this?" I hold the map up between us, my voice sharp.

Her throat bobs, lips parted slightly. "I found it last night."

My eyebrows shoot up. "You found it?"

She nods.

"Avery, you didn't just *find* this. You went looking. You sought it out, didn't you?"

My foot slams the brake pedal as I throw the SUV into park, only halfway out of the garage.

My head drops back, eyes closed for a second too long. "This is why he marked you, isn't it?" I turn to her again. "Aidric caught you down there. Didn't he?"

She nods again.

Fuck.

I flip the visor down and slide the map into the crease, then snap it shut. She watches me, eyes narrowed like she's already planning how to get it back.

I catch her gaze and level her with a look of warning. "Don't even think about it," I stammer. "Haven't you already gotten yourself into enough trouble?"

I shift into drive and ease us out of the garage, jaw tight. With any luck, the surprises will stop long enough for me to make it down the fucking driveway.

"When the hell will you learn to leave well enough alone?" I ask, tone flat.

"It's hard, Callan," she says, and for once, there's no fire in it —just sheer exhaustion. "I just want to know everything. I need to know what I'm up against."

I let out a dry, bitter scoff. "Up against, huh? So that's still the plan? You still think you're gonna take us down?"

"No," she snaps, fast and hard. "Not really. I mean, I'm not dumb enough to go blabbing about what I know. But I'm also not naive enough to think we're all playing on the same damn field."

"We are now," I mutter under my breath.

She doesn't catch it, or maybe she does and just chooses not to respond.

I don't think she fully realizes it yet. Hell, I'm not sure I do.

This isn't just about the Ice Lords. This is about something older and more powerful. Something even I'm impervious to.

"Look," she says point-blankly as she turns in her seat, one leg tucked under the other. "I'm not angry with you about this part, Callan." She lifts her shirt, a fresh reminder of what she's done. Of what *he's* done.

"I know Aidric and Sebastian pull reckless, split-second shit that's downright deplorable. I don't blame you for that," she says, voice steady but threaded with hurt. "But why the hell do you let them get away with it?"

One hand stays firm on the wheel as my eyes flick between her and the road. "It's not about letting them get away with anything. It's about loyalty, Avery. We've been over this. I have to protect this fucking society at all costs!"

"This isn't you." She shakes her head. "No. This cold, hard exterior you walk around in is just armor, it's not the truth. You think I haven't seen through it?" She leans in. "And don't you dare tell me I don't know you. Because I do."

Her voice cracks slightly. "You might pretend you've turned into this hollowed-out version of yourself. But I've seen it, Callan. I've seen the real you pushing through the cracks again and again. No matter how hard you try to bury him."

Her words hit somewhere deep, a place inside me I don't let people near. Hell, I don't even let myself look there too often.

The worst part is, she's not wrong about me, or the cracks.

They've been showing more lately, no matter how hard I try to patch them over. And now she's sitting there staring right into them like she's not afraid of what she'll find.

Her eyes search mine. "Why do you allow them to hurt me like this when it clearly hurts you too?"

Her words squeeze at my chest. "Have you considered the fact that everything I've done is to try and keep you from getting hurt?"

"No." She chuckles dryly. "Because you've hurt me too, Callan. So if you really believe you're protecting me, well... you're not."

I open my mouth to speak, but she barrels on.

"I just don't get it," she presses. "Why? Why rip into me, push me away, tear me down? Is it revenge because you think I hurt you?"

"You did hurt me." The words slip out before I can stop them, and just like that, I can't even look at her.

She shifts in her seat, straighter and sharper. "How, Callan?" she demands. "How did I hurt you?"

I can't take it.

I swerve the car to the shoulder, tires kicking up gravel as I bring it to a screeching stop. "You fucking walked away from me, Avery!" My raw voice rips out like it's been trapped for years.

"I was crazy about you, didn't you see it? Fuck!" I shout, raking my hands through my hair, heart hammering. "I thought I was falling in love with you," I say, the words landing heavier than I expected. "And then it happened. First time ever for me, I might add."

Her head jerks slightly, eyes widening just enough to tell me she had no idea. Not that I was falling for her, and definitely not that she was my first.

"I had no idea," she says softly, confirming what I already knew.

And maybe that's what guts me the most. Because she didn't mean to wreck me...she just did.

"Anyways," I continue. "I finally had what I'd been craving, and in the next breath, you looked me in the eye, called it a mistake, and ran."

I turn toward the windshield, jaw clenched. "You didn't just leave the room that night. You left me."

There's a long beat of silence that feels like it's wrapped around my throat, cutting off my air supply.

Then, she breaks it.

"You were falling in love with me?" Her voice is soft and emotion-laced.

I take a deep, audible breath, head shaking in small, defeated movements. "Maybe," I say quietly. "Fuck. I don't even know what it feels like to be in love." I glance at her for a second. "But if I had to guess, then yeah, that was probably it."

She reaches toward me, fingers trembling slightly. But when my gaze snaps instinctively to her hand, she pulls back fast, like she thinks I might bite her.

Her hand drops to her lap, and we sit in heavy silence.

Should've just kept my damn mouth shut. My heart's pounding like it's trying to punch its way out of my chest, and my palms are slick, sliding against the wheel. I hate this. Hate the way I'm cracked wide open in front of her, exposed in a way I swore I'd never be again. I just gave her the power to break me for a second time, and I'm not sure I can survive that shit twice.

"Why didn't you just tell me all this?" she asks, finally breaking the silence.

I let out a bitter laugh under my breath, eyes fixed on the road ahead. "You never gave me the chance. And because of that, I was too busy hating you. I guess somewhere along the way, I convinced myself that it was easier than just telling you the truth."

My grip tightens on the wheel, knuckles white as I wait for her response.

It doesn't come fast enough, though.

Say something. Anything, dammit.

"I was supposed to visit my mom that day," she says quietly.

My eyes shift to her, drawn in by the way her fingers wrap around the strap of her purse like it's the only thing keeping her grounded.

"Brogan asked me to stay, so I figured missing one visit wouldn't hurt. Besides…" She lifts a shoulder in a small shrug. "…I was excited to see you. Always was, back then."

I swallow hard, trying to keep it together like I have for so long.

Avery looks at me, eyes red and rimmed with tears. For the first time in a long time, I see her. Not the girl I built walls against, but *her.*

"I didn't see it until after I got out of your bed," she says, her voice cracking. "The text. It was about my mom. She'd gotten into a fight with another resident at the facility. Scratched the woman up pretty badly and took a few hits to the face herself." Her hands tremble in her lap. "They admitted her to the hospital for observation, and all I could think was, if I'd just gone to see her that day, maybe her mood would've been different."

Her tears break free, sliding down her cheeks. Before I can

stop myself, I reach across the center console, my fingers closing gently around hers.

"It's not your fault," I say softly, meaning every word. "There's nothing you could've done. I know this," I continue, voice low, "because I beat myself up the same way, over and over after my mom died."

Her eyes flick to mine.

"I wasn't there," I admit, my throat tightening. "Everyone else was, but not me. I was at a friend's house down the street, playing fucking Fortnite." I laugh, but there's no humor in it. Just self-loathing. "When I came home, she was gone."

"I'm so sorry, Callan." She sniffles, shaking her head like she's trying to undo the weight of everything. "I didn't mean to—"

"No," I cut her off, my thumb brushing over her knuckles. "Don't be sorry. You didn't do anything. Not then, and not now. Back then we were just kids trying to make sense of too much shit too fast."

She nods, and for the first time in a long time, I feel the past loosening its grip on us. It's not gone, but it's not choking us either.

Silence hangs between us. I sit in my thoughts, and she sits in hers. But it's not heavy anymore. It's just…still.

Slowly, I reach across and shift us back into drive, never letting go of her hand.

The car eases forward and I pull out onto the road, driving at a leisurely pace. There's no rush, no pressure.

Maybe this won't last. And I know things will never be what they were. But maybe they can be better.

I pull up in front of her dorm and put the car back in park.

Avery turns to me, her face no longer streaked with tears. "What now?" she asks, a small shrug lifting her shoulder.

I bite the corner of my lip, one hand draped lazily over the wheel.

"I've got a game on Saturday," I say, watching her carefully. "Wanna come watch me?"

She lets out a soft chuckle, eyes dropping to her lap. "Haven't I told you before, I'm not a hockey fan, Callan."

I grin, tilting my head. "Any chance we can change that?"

She lifts a shoulder again, but this time there's a hint of a smirk tugging at her lips. "We'll see."

With that, she pushes open the door and slips out. I wait, eyes following her every step as she crosses to the dorm entrance.

Just before she disappears inside, she tosses a quick glance over her shoulder, and it's impossible to miss the smile on her face.

We dragged a lot of shit into the light today. I don't know what comes next, but whatever it is, it has to be better than what's come before. Even with the unknown still hanging over Avery. Whatever fate's got lined up for her, I'll make damn sure it's better. I'll take care of her.

I flash her a wink then I throw the car into gear to head home. Because as soon as I walk through that door, I'm tearing Aidric's ass apart.

CHAPTER 24

AVERY

"WELL, HELLO, STRANGER," Brogan says with a teasing smile as I slip into the seat across from her outside of Clara's Cafe.

The warm sun hits my cheek and it feels nice after the gloomy couple days we've had. Maybe it's a sign that things are finally looking up.

I smile, flinging my purse off my shoulder and draping it over the back of the chair. "Sorry I'm late. After you left this morning, I crashed again. Lately, I just feel like I could sleep for days."

Brogan chuckles, stirring the iced latte in front of her. "You have been busy." She raises an eyebrow. "Though I'm not exactly sure why. Care to fill me in on what's going on in Avery's world?"

Tapping my straw against the edge of the table, I slide it through the wrapper and pop it into the lid of the sweet tea Brogan ordered for me. I take a small sip, the cool sweetness calming the tight knot in my chest.

"Mmm. Thanks for this," I say, lifting it slightly in her direction.

She narrows her eyes playfully. "Oh no, you don't. I notice that little deflection."

I laugh under my breath, already caught.

"Come on now," she says, a little more serious this time. "My question isn't going to just slip away. What's been going on with you?"

I clear my throat and square my shoulders, trying to summon the kind of gravity this moment deserves. My palms are sweating and my heart is tripping in my chest, because this isn't just a casual catch-up with Brogan. This is *the* conversation. The one I've been rehearsing in my head for two days straight.

Ever since that girl at the party two nights ago—the one in the kitchen who looked like she was one wrong word away from going full *Carrie* on everyone—said, *"If my best friend and brother had just been honest with me, none of this would've happened,"* it's been echoing in my head like a curse.

I took it as a sign and I asked her here to finally tell the truth about me and Callan. So, here I am, a jittery mess of nerves and caffeine, ready to come clean. And it's not just the guilt, which feels like a cinder block sitting on my chest. But it's also the reality that, like it or not, I'm tethered to these guys now. We're bound by secrets we're all desperate to keep buried.

So sharing a half version of the truth with my best friend feels necessary.

"Earth to Avery." Brogan snaps her fingers in front of my face. "On with it, babe."

"Right." I take a deep breath, then begin, "I've been spending a lot of time with Callan and a couple other guys on the Lords' hockey team."

I don't even know why I mentioned the other guys. Maybe I just thought it would soften the blow, like if it wasn't just Callan I was hanging out with, it wouldn't be so wrong.

Not that Callan and I hang out. Well, maybe we do.

Jesus. I'm a mess.

She lifts a brow, not missing a beat. "I know."

That catches me off guard. "You do?"

She nods, still swirling her straw casually, like I'm not about to drop a bomb in her lap. "You said you were helping them study. I found out that was bullshit. Then I found out you and Callan went to see Evan. And I thought that was odd. So yeah, I know."

My throat dries. "But I don't think you fully understand why."

Curious eyes look up at mine. "Then spit it out, silly. Just tell me."

I suck in a breath like I'm diving underwater. Then in one breathless blur, I let it all out.

"Junior year, Callan and I slept together. Once. I told him it was a mistake and ran out of the room. He hated me for it, like, really hated me. He made my last year of high school a nightmare. Then we came here and started clashing again. He recently told me he was in love with me back in high school and I think that maybe…" I let my words trail off. "I might sort of, possibly…like him a little bit too."

It's not really a lie. All of those things did happen. And as for me liking Callan, that's not a lie either. Lately, it feels like pieces of the old him keep surfacing and every time they do, my own feelings for him are brought to light.

The truth is, I did like Callan. Probably more than I ever admitted, even to myself. And if he'd just been honest back then, instead of trying to break me down, I think we could have had something special—something worth fighting for.

Brogan is far too quiet. I watch her closely, anticipating a response. My mouth twists into a grimace and I'm so close to gnawing off every last one of my fake nails like a feral gremlin. Anxiety has my heart doing all sorts of shit and all I can think is, why the hell did I open my mouth?

Brogan blinks, her spine straight against the chair. "Whoa." Her voice is barely above a whisper. "I did *not* see that coming."

"I know," I quip, my eyebrows practically hanging out on my forehead while I wait for her to say something more.

"So…you two are, like…a thing now?"

"No!" The word bursts out of me in a half laugh, half sputter. "God, no. I mean…no. Definitely not." I pause, biting the inside of my cheek. "We've just reconnected. Sort of. And we might hang out again. Maybe. Sometimes. You know, if that's okay with you."

Why do I feel more nervous right now than I did when that detective was grilling me in my own room? I guess it's because Brogan matters more. This isn't about hiding secrets from some stranger with a badge; it's about my best friend. And deep down, I know how much this could sting. How it might feel like a betrayal, not just by me, but by Callan too.

She lifts a brow. "Are you seriously asking me for permission to fuck my brother?"

My whole body stiffens, eyes wide. "No! God, no. Not at all. I swear, we only…there was just that one time. That's it."

She snorts, completely unbothered. "Chill, Ave," she says, breaking into a laugh. "I'm just messing with you."

My shoulders instantly drop, the tension bleeding out all at once. "Jesus Christ, Brogan. Don't do that to me."

Her straw lingers between her lips as she speaks around it. "I don't care if you and Callan…do whatever it is you and Callan want to do." She waves a hand in the air, brushing it off like it's no big deal. "I just don't want the details, like ever."

I chuckle. "Deal."

Then I finally breathe. The air feels a little lighter, but I'm not done yet. There's still more to say.

Only, this next part isn't laced with anxiety, it's soaked in emotion. And I worry it might be a little harder.

There's a heavy beat of silence before I finally say, "There's more."

Her eyes snap up. "Don't you dare tell me you're pregnant."

I laugh, a short, breathy sound that cuts through the tension. "No. Not pregnant."

She tilts her head, studying me. "Then what is it?"

I inhale, bracing myself. "It's…about my mom. Something

I've never told you. Or anyone, actually." I meet her gaze, steady this time. "And since I'm apparently in a full-blown confession arc, I figure, maybe it's time I get this out, too."

I can see the flicker of pity in her eyes. She knows whatever I'm about to say is going to hurt. Not her, but me.

Without a word, she pushes herself up. The screech of metal legs against the concrete cuts through the air. Brogan drags her chair until it's right beside mine, close enough that our shoulders nearly touch. She doesn't say anything as she turns toward me, ready to listen.

So, I tell her.

"My mom doesn't live in the house with my dad. She hasn't for a while."

Brogan's hand flies to her cheek. "Oh no. Are they getting a divorce?"

I shake my head, lips pressed tight for a second. "They're already divorced. But it wasn't your typical *we fell out of love* kind of thing. It was a no-fault divorce."

I pause, letting the words settle, watching her face shift as she tries to process.

"I don't know what that means," she says softly. "But I'm so sorry, Ave."

"It means," I say, swallowing hard, "that my mom is mentally incapacitated. And my dad gave up on her. He didn't want to be married to someone who wasn't really there anymore." My voice cracks slightly. "My mom's not well, Brogan. She hasn't been for a very long time."

"Oh, honey," she murmurs, wrapping her arms around me like this is fresh news—like I haven't been carrying it for years, quietly suffering on the inside. "She'll be okay, right?"

I shrug against her chest, the weight of uncertainty pressing into my ribs. "I hope so. But I don't really know." I pause, voice softening. "She lives in a facility that takes really good care of her, and lately, she's actually been thriving there. It's the best she's been in a long time."

Brogan pulls back just enough to look at me, her eyes full of something warm and aching. "Why didn't you ever tell me this before?"

I swallow hard, blinking through the blur. "I guess I've always been scared people would think I'm going to end up like her." I pause, breath catching. "Or maybe it's me who's scared I will."

"No," she says firmly, shaking her head. "Your mom's fate is not yours, Ave. Don't think like that. Not for a second." She cradles my head again, pulling me close. "I hate that you've been carrying this by yourself, but I'm glad you told me so I can be here for you."

Something in me loosens at that. Just enough to let the words start to flow.

So I tell her everything.

How we moved to Willow Creek the summer before eighth grade, not for the fresh start I always said, but because my mom became convinced our old neighbor had summoned the devil. She swore he'd been pulled straight from hell and possessed the woman next door.

Then one night, she broke into the neighbor's house with a kitchen knife and attacked her.

That was the beginning, but it wasn't the end. Not yet, anyways.

I tell her how every time I said my mom was away on business, it was a cover for the truth I wasn't ready to say out loud.

Brogan doesn't say anything right away. She just holds me tighter, like she's trying to make up for all the years I carried this weight alone.

And I let her. I let myself be held until the tears stop falling, and until my breath doesn't hitch every few seconds.

And by the time it's all out, we're both a blubbering mess. Smeared mascara, red noses, the whole dramatic package.

Yet, for the first time in a long time, I don't feel alone in it.

The conversation shifts naturally, like the emotional storm has passed.

"So," Brogan says, dabbing under her eyes with a napkin, "Hayes has been a total basket case all week over this game. He says if they don't win, they're out of the playoffs."

That jogs my memory. "Speaking of the game tonight, would you mind if I skipped it?"

She groans immediately. "Seriously? Why?"

"Callan kind of asked me to go watch his game. It's home, too. I could catch the first half of the Devils with you, then head over to their arena after?"

In all reality, I could skip it. I mean, there were no demands that I go. And I actually think we're passed that point. But for some reason, I *want* to go.

She narrows her eyes, tone dripping sarcasm. "And just like that, he's already stealing you from me."

I giggle, reaching over to pat her leg. "Never."

She sighs dramatically. "I guess. Just go watch all of his. But don't you dare bail on me. Legends after the game, or die."

"Deal," I say, sticking out my pinkie.

She links hers with mine, sealing it with a squeeze.

We finish our drinks in comfortable silence, the kind that only comes after everything's been said and nothing's been broken.

"I should get to cheer practice," Brogan mutters, like it's the last place she wants to be. She slides her chair back, and I stand with her.

"See you tonight, babe." She wraps her arms around me, and our hug lingers just a second longer than usual.

"You sure will," I say.

I watch her walk away, feeling like the weight of the world has finally eased off my shoulders. Well, some of it, anyway.

CHAPTER 25

AVERY

"Thanks for coming with me," I say to Benson, glancing over as he crams a fistful of popcorn into his mouth.

He nods, speaking as he chews. "No problem. There's actually someone playing tonight I wanted to see."

My brows arch, a slow smirk tugging at my lips. "Oh yeah? And who might that be?"

He swallows and wipes his hand on his jeans. "A man never kisses and tells."

"Oooh, so now there's kissing involved?"

His mouth twists into a tight-lipped smile, but his flushed cheeks give him away. He shrugs, eyes glancing toward the ice, then back to me. "Maybe."

I nudge him with my knee. "Give me the details, dammit."

He shakes his head slowly, and with a pop of his lips, he says, "Nope."

The Lords' team comes skating onto the ice, but my eyes stay fixed to one player. The one who glides out there like this arena was built just for him.

Callan.

Then Aidric comes into view, and my eyes stay on him far longer than they should. I tell myself it's just familiarity. I've spent more time around Callan, Aidric, and Sebastian than I ever wanted to. Enough to notice things I never intended to.

Sebastian isn't playing, but he's here. *I see him.* He's standing off the ice wearing his jersey, cheering on his team like his heart is out there skating with them.

"Hmm," Benson hums. "Seems I'm not the only one keeping secrets."

I look at him, then down in my lap, only now realizing that I was practically levitating off my seat with my palms pressed to the armrests and a stupidly wide grin on my face.

I settle, then scoff. "No idea what you're talking about."

"Just be careful," he says, voice dipping low. "I've heard some not-so-great things about those guys."

"You're telling me," I mutter.

A beat of silence stretches between us as we watch the players skate into formation. The puck drops, and right when the game has my attention, Benson cuts through it.

"So," he says casually, "which one do you have your eyes on?"

I could tell him it's Callan that's been making my heart forget its rhythm for the last forty-eight hours. I could admit I've been watching Aidric and Sebastian just as closely, though for different reasons. Instead, I take the safe route.

"All of them."

It's better than the other lie, which would have been none of them. At least this one gives him room to tease and keep the mood light.

"Well, damn," he croons. "Save some for me."

I laugh.

The conversation shifts to archery and the upcoming competition in three weeks. I admit I haven't been practicing as much as I should, then toss in a casual lie about school being the reason. He buys it, or at least, he doesn't press.

The game resumes, and a strange sense of déjà vu washes over me. Callan barrels into an opposing player, slamming him hard against the glass right in front of us. The crowd erupts, but all I can hear is the thud in my chest.

Callan looks up, and his eyes find mine like he knew exactly where to look.

For a split second, I'm back at the game at our arena when the Lords played the Devils. I remember the way Callan's stare sliced clean through me, cold and cutting. It felt like a warning. Like he somehow knew I was going to walk into that locker room afterward and my world would flip upside down.

But this time, there's no ice in his gaze. This time, it's something else entirely. Lust, maybe. Or a genuine happiness that I'm here. I can't quite put my finger on it, but whatever it is, I prefer this look over every other one he's given me before.

He skates away, slipping back into the game, but my eyes follow him. I can't help but wonder if I'm in his head the same way he's in mine.

I don't know what's happening to me.

All I know is, I haven't felt these strange flutters in my stomach in a very long time, and I'm not sure if that excites me or terrifies me.

Before long, the red light flashes and the final buzzer sounds, announcing the Lords' 4–1 win. Not that I ever doubted it because the game wasn't even close.

The thought of sticking around to congratulate the guys crosses my mind, but we're not there yet. We don't use manners or trade pleasantries, and we sure as hell don't offer congratulations. Callan, yeah…maybe. But the other two, hell no.

Once we're outside, Benson offers to drop me off at Legends but says he won't be sticking around because apparently he has plans. He doesn't share the details, and I don't bother asking. I've learned that Benson prefers to lead a quiet life, which I can respect.

On the drive over, I pull out my phone to text Brogan a quick heads-up that I'm on my way, but a message from Liam catches my eye.

Liam: Haven't talked in a while. Hope all is well. Just wanted to let you know Evan was moved to a long-term rehabilitation center couple days ago. Still no change.

I know I should go visit Evan, show that I care. Truth is, I don't. I don't want to see him like that. I might not want him to ever speak again, but that doesn't mean my heart isn't heavy for him and his family.

I send a quick text back with a simple thank you for the update and a smile emoji, then shift to Brogan.

Me: Be there soon.

She responds.

Brogan: We got tables in the back corner. Hurry up.

Benson pulls up right in front of Legends. There's a crowd gathered outside, probably waiting for tables or just trying to get in. I'm not surprised. The place is always packed after a Devils' home game.

I step out of the car, and the cool night air slides up my jean skirt, making me shiver. My white sneakers hit the pavement with a soft thud as I close the door behind me.

I pull my oversized black-and-white checkered flannel tight across my chest, fingers bunching the fabric over my white crop top. It smells faintly like popcorn and that pine-scented Christmas tree air freshener hanging from Benson's rearview mirror.

A quick wave and a *thanks* later, I'm weaving around bodies out front, slipping through a cloud of smoke as I push through the doors of Legends. The minute I step inside, I'm thrust into pulsing music, pressed bodies, and the scent of alcohol and worn leather. It's overwhelming, but familiar and alive.

I spot Brogan standing tall near the back, one hand raised in the air and a wide smile etched across her face. Her mouth moves, saying something, but I'm too far away to hear over the noise and I've never been good at lip reading.

It takes a minute to get to her as I dodge elbows and sidestep around people, but eventually, I make it there.

Without missing a beat, she pulls out the chair beside her, saved just for me.

"You made it!" she gushes, clapping her hands together in front of her like she's been holding in the excitement. "And I got you this."

She slides a blackberry mojito in front of me, condensation clinging to the glass. It's the same drink she's holding—the same one we get every time we come here.

"Thanks, babe," I quip, wrapping my lips around the straw and taking a sip. It's delicious, one of my absolute favorites. I lower the drink and glance at her. "So, how was the game?"

I already know they lost, but it's an easy lead-in for her to ask how Callan's game went, and I can't wait to tell her the Lords won. Not to boast over the Devils' loss because that really sucks, but to celebrate her brother's win.

Never in a million years did I think I'd be giddy over Callan's team winning a game. Nonetheless, here I am, buzzing like it's my own victory.

"Not great," she says, a frown tugging at her lips. "But I heard the Lords won, that's awesome. Did you get a chance to talk to Callan?"

"Nah," I drawl, leaning back a little. "It was packed, he was busy, and I was just too damn excited to get here to you." My shoulders do a little happy dance as I take another sip.

Brogan throws her arms around me, pulling me into a tight hug. "I've missed you, Ave."

"I've missed you too," I say honestly.

For the longest time, Brogan and I were inseparable. Then we came here, and even though we room together, life got busy. She joined the cheer squad and started dating Hayes. I buried myself in schoolwork and archery. And now, I've been thrust into a life of debauchery with three misfits in a secret society.

Crazy how fast things change.

Brogan drops her arms, eyes snapping toward the entrance. "Oh shit," she murmurs.

I follow her gaze and immediately see why her expression's gone pale.

Moving through the crowd like a storm rolling in, is Callan. He's standing tall, shoulders squared, and jaw tight.

"I can only assume he's here for you," Brogan says, eyes locked on him.

This is bad, and we both know it.

The Lords and the Devils don't play nice. Callan showing up here, of all places, is more than just bold; it's a slap in the face.

I'm the first to push my chair back, Brogan a step behind. But before we can reach him, he's spotted.

"Man, shut the fuck up," Callan grumbles, brushing past Finch, one of Hayes's closest friends.

You'd think Hayes would step in and call off his guys, given that he's dating Brogan, but that's not how it works with them.

Despite Brogan and Hayes's relationship, Callan can't stand Hayes. And even if it's never been said aloud, I'm pretty sure the feeling is mutual.

They don't fight, but they don't defend each other either.

When I see two more guys step up to Callan, looking like they're ready to throw down, I move faster.

Callan might have a build that makes people think twice, and sure, he's strong-willed and relentless. But tonight, he's alone with no backup and one man, even him, doesn't stand a chance against a couple dozen looking for a fight.

I'm being tossed in every direction as bodies press. But I

shove, curse, and refuse to stop until I'm standing right in front of Callan.

He's mid-verbal takedown, ripping into one of the Devils' players, spitting words you don't come back from.

I reach up and grab his face, forcing him to look at me. "Callan! Callan, just shut the fuck up!" I say sternly when his mouth just keeps running.

"Put your money where your mouth is, fucker," he spits over my shoulder, venom aimed at one of the Devils. "You talk a big game, but where's the fucking proof? Sure as hell isn't on the ice because your team lost. Again."

Damn. He's ruthless.

If he keeps going like this, he's going to get his ass handed to him. And, honestly, I wouldn't blame these guys one bit.

Suddenly, I'm yanked back by the arm and shoved hard to the side. My balance slips, heels scraping against the floor as I stumble. When I look up, I see a guy with a twisted expression wearing a Devils jersey.

"This doesn't concern you," he snarls. "Get the hell outta the fucking way."

Before I can react, or even steady myself, a fist comes out of nowhere, cutting through the air and landing square against the guy's nose.

His head snaps back, blood already framing his nostrils.

Callan's arm snakes around my waist, pulling me behind him in one swift motion. "You okay?" he asks, breathless.

I nod quickly, the words *you need to leave* already forming on my tongue. But he turns before I can speak, eyes snapping back to the guy he just knocked out.

He draws his foot back and slams it forward, straight into the guy's ribs.

My head spins. Fists start flying, bodies crashing into each other.

But all I can focus on is getting Callan the hell out of here before this turns into something we can't undo.

I grab him by the waist with both hands and pull hard, panic rising in my throat.

He's fucked if he doesn't run right now.

"Please, Callan," I beg, voice cracking through the noise. "Just leave. I'll go with you."

That does it. Something inside him shifts abruptly, and in one fluid motion, he spins around, grabs my hand, and yanks me toward the door.

Without a shred of hesitation in our steps, we get out as fast as we can.

Still gripping my hand tightly, Callan uses his other one to shove one of the doors open.

The night air hits me like a slap in the face, but it feels so good against my hot skin.

I keep moving, eager to put as much distance between us and those doors as possible before the manhunt comes out behind us. But Callan pulls me back.

Suddenly, he's in front of me, scanning me head to toe like he's expecting to find blood or bruises. He brushes my hair aside, eyes darting over my face, then down my arms. "Are you sure you're okay?" he asks, voice urgent, almost desperate.

"I'm fine," I say on a sharp exhale. "But we need to go, Callan. You can inspect me later."

"I'm holding you to that," he quips.

Leave it to him to crack a joke while we're practically running for our lives.

I tug on his arm, and this time he follows, tangling our fingers together. We make it to the end of the sidewalk before I realize I have no idea where we're going, where he parked, or even if he drove at all. So I let him take the lead.

"This way," he says, pulling me left as he digs into his jeans pocket for his keys. "I'm in the mini-mart lot."

Makes sense. The parking lot at Legends is always a nightmare, and the mini-mart is closed for the night.

The lights on his SUV flash, and we pick up the pace. Callan rounds the car, still holding my hand, and pulls the passenger door open for me.

Once I slide inside, he closes it without a word.

Seconds later, he's in the driver's seat bringing the engine to life.

I shoot a quick text to Brogan, letting her know Callan and I are all right. She responds immediately.

> Brogan: Thank goodness! I was worried sick. Don't worry. Everyone's getting shit-faced and forgot Callan ever came here. And the guy he knocked out started running his mouth and got his ass kicked by someone else right after you guys left. He deserved it, though. Text me later to tell me your plans. I'm likely staying with Hayes tonight.

I send her back a response, letting her know I'll likely just go home, and to be safe. Then, I turn my attention to Callan.

"Why did you go to Legends?" I ask, cutting straight to the only question that matters.

"To find you," he spits out like it's the most natural thing in the world to show up where I am. Like walking into enemy territory for me is just what he does.

"You went to a bar crawling with your rivals...just to find *me*?" I shake my head, disbelief tightening in my chest. "Why, Callan?"

"It's a bar, Avery. Everyone is welcome. The Devils don't own that place."

"Come on," I grumble, turning toward him. "You know damn well that was a ballsy move. You knew it before you walked through those doors."

I pause, giving him a look. "What would you do if one of the Devils showed up at The Effin Bar?"

The Effin Bar is home turf for the Lords after home games. Everyone knows that and it's an unspoken rule not to cross enemy lines.

"I'd fuck 'em up," he says without missing a beat.

"*See*," I drawl, lifting a brow. "And what makes you think the Devils would feel any differently?"

He flashes me a look, all teeth and trouble. "Do I look fucked up?"

I let out an audible sigh, slumping slightly in the seat. There's just no getting through to him. "Forget it."

"All right, all right," he concedes. "It was a bad move."

He glances over at me, something softer slipping into his tone.

"But you came to my game and left without saying hi, or goodbye. So yeah, I figured I'd come check on you. Make sure you hadn't been kidnapped by some Devil scumbag." He scoffs. "Still don't get why you and my sister hang out with those douchebags anyway."

I nod slowly, just long enough to be smug about it. "Interesting."

His brow lifts. "Why's that?"

"Ohhhh…just because you were jealous." I tilt my head. "Or maybe possessive is the word I'm looking for. No," I say, a small grin tugging at my lips. "Jealous works."

"The fuck I am," he grumbles, that playful glint in his eye. "Not so sure about you, though. Shall we pretend you *weren't* watching me the whole damn game?"

He's not wrong, I was watching him. The way his body moved with precision. How he glided across the ice so effortlessly. And don't get me started on how well he handled that puck. Seems he has a knack for controlling things.

"I was watching two teams compete," I say, point-blank. "Same as everyone else."

He smirks, tossing me a quick glance. "Is that so?"

"Yep," I quip, casual as ever.

We pull up to my dorm, and I'm surprised by the tiny flicker of disappointment rising in my chest. I was actually looking forward to cutting loose tonight, spending time with Brogan, letting myself breathe for once.

"Plans for the rest of the night?" he asks, voice low and lazy. But there's something behind it, like he's wondering if I'll ask him to come up.

And maybe I'm getting ahead of myself, but I think he'd say yes.

"Seems my plans took a sudden turn, thanks to you," I say, lifting a brow, a smirk curling my lips.

"For what it's worth," he says, shoulders rising in a shrug before relaxing again, "I really did go there to see you. And… maybe I knew my presence would turn some heads."

"You went there for trouble," I deadpan.

"If you're trouble," he says with a grin, "then yeah…I guess I did."

"Wow," I laugh. "Real fuckin' smooth, Callan."

I shake my head, slow and deliberate. "Shut the car off. You're coming up to my room with me."

His eyebrows shoot up. "I am?"

"You are," I say flatly. "Since you ruined my night, you're now officially my company. I'm not about to spend my Saturday alone in a dorm room."

"Someone's bossy," he teases, but doesn't question it further. He cuts the engine, grabs his phone, wallet, and keys, and climbs out.

CHAPTER 26

AVERY

As soon as we reach my door, something shifts. A strange feeling coils in my chest causing me to look around. My heart is thumping, a sense of doom crowding in that I can't quite place.

"Do you hear that?" I ask, pressing my ear to the door. I know for a fact that Brogan isn't in there, but it sounds like someone is.

Callan stands beside me, hands in his pockets. "I don't hear anything."

He doesn't seem concerned, and maybe I'm just overthinking because I'm the one who brought him up here. We called a truce, and things feel better now, but part of me still wonders if this is all just another move in his game. Is he doing this just to break my heart the way I broke his?

I listen again, one hand digging into my purse for my keys, but the sound doesn't come back.

I could've sworn I heard faint music coming from inside my room.

Weird.

I go to slide my key into the lock, but the door opens before I can even turn the key.

"What the hell," I breathe, panic rising. "We never leave this door unlocked."

Callan shrugs beside me. "My sister can be forgetful sometimes."

My head shakes no because I don't think that's it. My gut tells me it's not that simple. Callan only thinks that way because he's a guy. They don't have to worry about someone coming in while they're sleeping, stealing their things, or taking advantage of them.

Brogan would never forget to lock the door. Besides, I was the last one to leave for the game.

I step into the room, cautious and on high alert, like I'm expecting someone to jump out and grab me. But then I feel Callan by my side, and my nerves settle slightly.

Then I hear it again. And this time, there's no way Callan doesn't hear it too.

His wide eyes scan the room. But the moment I recognize the melody, my world shifts on its axis.

Music. Not just any music, and not just any sound. It's soft, haunting, and all too familiar.

Without hesitation, I flip the light on and the sight that greets me has me wanting to vomit and cry in equal parts.

There, sitting in the center of my bed, muddy and worn, is my music box.

The lid is flipped open and the tiny ballerina twirls slowly to the mechanical tune. It's covered in ash and there's already dirt flaking off of it onto my comforter.

My breath catches and my limbs go stiff. I try to move and reach for it, to slap it shut, but it's like I'm locked in place by something I can't see.

Callan takes two long strides and in a swift motion, he slams it shut, snapping me out of my panic-induced state.

"Who..." I choke on the word, pointing at the box on my bed like it might spring to life and attack me. "Who put that there?"

Callan stares at it for a beat, his fingers dragging through his hair like he's trying to piece something together.

But is he?

"Did you do this?" I snap, the question bursting out of me, rage and panic clawing their way up my throat. "Was this you?"

"No!" he barks, eyes flaring. "Why the hell would I have that box? I thought you burned and buried it." His gaze whips back to me. "You *did* burn the box, right?"

"Does it look like I fucking burned it?" I shout, motioning wildly to the very real, very not destroyed music box on my bed.

"You knew I didn't burn it," I breathe, the words cracking. "The video…the one Sebastian recorded. You saw it. You knew."

Callan presses a hand on my shoulder, sincerity in his gaze. "I never watched the video."

He backs away from me, going to my bed and looking over the box without touching it. "I didn't even know the video existed until you told me down in The Chamber. And I never asked the guys for it because they never gave me a reason to think you didn't follow through with your fucking assignment."

"I did follow through with it," I snap, my voice shaking with force.

"Obviously not!" he shouts back, hand slicing through the air as he gestures to the music box like it's exhibit A in a case against me. "It's right there, Avery!"

"I did what I was supposed to," I say. "I followed the map. I found the post with the ribbon. I dug a hole, and I burned…" My words trail off, because this right here is where I incriminate myself.

"Burned what, dammit?" Callan demands, his posture rigid.

"I burned what was in the box." I swallow hard. "I burned the dismembered tongue."

Just saying it makes my stomach twist. Even worse, that box that was holding it is here, sitting on the bed where I sleep.

"I couldn't do it," I admit, and the words rip through me. My knees hit the floor as I crumble under the weight of them. Being forced to burn that flesh, the scent of it, the tune in the box out there with me on that cold and dark forest floor. I try to take a breath, but my lungs refuse to let it all in.

"I couldn't bring myself to burn something that meant so much to me. Even if now it's just a casket for cut-off body parts."

I glance at the bed, but I can't truly look at it. My vision blurs, tears burning my eyes. I'll never look at that music box the same again. That memory with my mother is tainted.

Callan steps closer, crouching beside me. His hand rests gently on my back as I fight to breathe through the tightness in my chest.

"I buried it," I whisper, my voice barely there. "I buried it. So I have no idea how or why it's here now."

"We need to think this through, Avery. You've got to pull yourself together." He holds the back of my neck but I squeeze my eyes shut tight, letting the tears flow.

"I can't," I choke out.

"You can. And you will," he says, his voice sharp and commanding.

He controls my head and when my eyes flutter open, his face is inches from mine.

"Stand the fuck up," he growls. "And face this shit head-on. Don't let it break you down because that's exactly what whoever did this wants."

I flinch at his tone. We were just starting to make up and now he's angry with me. "Why are you being so mean?"

"I'm not being mean," he snaps. His grip on the back of my neck loosens a little and I feel slightly more centered with him forcing my attention onto him. "I'm being realistic."

His voice rises, harsh and unrelenting, but his grip stays soft, like it's an anchor, keeping me here and forcing me to listen to him. "Do you think sitting on your knees crying is going to fix this? No! You're letting your emotions take over, and in this world, that's weakness."

"I'm only human, Callan," I fire back, looking up at him through blurry eyes. *"You're* only human. We cry. We hurt. We bleed."

It's like he's been trained not to react. Not to feel. Or maybe he's been taught to twist fear into fuel, to use it as a weapon.

"I never said you couldn't cry, Avery. Bleed all you need to, but stand the fuck up and let's get this figured out. We can still problem-solve while you process this fucked-up shit. But you can't give in to it. You can't let it be the thing that breaks you."

I feel my shoulders relax as I finally take in a full breath. He may be an asshole sometimes, but maybe this isn't the worst idea he's ever had. Whatever it is, it's working. Because I'm suddenly on my feet, swiping the tears from my cheeks like they have no business being there.

"You swear on everything it wasn't you?" I ask, eyes narrowing as I study his face.

He nods, firm. "It wasn't me."

"And the guys?"

He shrugs. "Doubtful. But I can't be sure."

That's enough for now. While it's clear they don't communicate the best, it wouldn't make sense for them to do this. Sebastian already has the video and this would only make it easier for the detective to get more evidence. I don't think either of them are that dumb.

I march over to my nightstand, yank open the top drawer, and grab a notepad and pen. Without hesitation, I slam them against his chest.

"Put them on the list."

His brow furrows. "What list?"

"The list we're making." My voice is steady now, a plan forming in my head as I take back control here. Someone wants to play, but they forget my major is in studying the brain and human behaviors. If they want to test me, I'll show them who the smarter one is.

"We're figuring this out, Callan."

I cross the room to the bed, bile threatening to rise again as I stare down at the music box. Swallowing hard, I grab it with both hands, keeping my arms locked straight because even the smell makes me nauseous.

"First," I mutter. "I'm getting rid of this damn thing."

"How?" Callan asks from somewhere behind me.

I didn't think that far ahead. So I do the only thing that comes to mind. I go to the window and shove the sill up with one hand. Cold air rushes in immediately, whipping my hair across my face. But before I can even push it away, I launch the box out the window with zero hesitation.

It disappears into the darkness below and I listen, waiting for the crash. Once I hear it, I slam the window shut and brush off my hands like I've just taken out the trash.

I shrug. "I think that takes care of the first problem."

Callan quirks a brow. "We could've dusted that for prints, ran them through a database, collected samples…"

I spin to face him. "What? Are you serious?"

He laughs, waving a hand through the air. "Nah. I'm just fucking with you."

I exhale a sharp breath and shake my head at him.

Callan drops down, back against the wall, and opens the notebook in his lap. He presses the pen to the paper without looking up.

Meanwhile, I start stripping my bed. The sight of that box on my comforter is going to stay in the back of my mind for a while. Luckily, I've got another sheet set in the closet so washing this one can wait until morning.

"Thanks," I say softly as I peel off a pillowcase.

His eyes lift. "For what?"

"For talking me down…again." I pause, offering the smallest smile. "Your method might be intense, but somehow, it works."

He moves the pen steadily across the notepad, focused on something, though I have no idea what he's writing.

"It's a trick I learned in rehab," he says after a beat. "I was a goddamn mess when I got there. Panic attacks all day, every day. Couldn't breathe, couldn't think."

He pauses, eyes still on the page.

"My roommate used to pull me out of them with the harsh truth. He'd stand over me and shout, practically scaring the panic out of my chest. At first, I just thought he was a mean motherfucker." A slight smile tugs at his lips. "But when it worked, I started to get it."

"That's good to know." I chuckle. "Because I was starting to think you were just a mean motherfucker, too."

He smirks. "And now?"

"Now…" I pause, letting the word hang between us. "I'm not so sure."

His brows lift, but he doesn't look at me. He just smiles and turns his attention back to the paper in front of him.

Callan Cromwell is sitting cross-legged on the floor of my dorm room with no shoes, scribbling in my rainbow-swirled notebook like it's the most natural thing in the world.

He seems comfortable, present, and happy.

And my God, he's fucking gorgeous.

I've always known it. But for a while, it was buried by his bitterness and ugly personality. Now, with those walls slowly coming down, I see it clearer than ever.

It's scary how easy it is to want him like I did back then.

"All right," he says, blowing out a breath as he holds the notebook toward me. "I think this is a good start."

I close the space between us and take the notebook from his hand.

Our fingers brush, and for a second, neither of us moves.

Then I sit down beside him and look at his list.

1. Benson
2. Liam
3. Hayes

I look up from the notebook, scowling. "Hayes?"

He just shrugs, rolling his shoulders with that infuriatingly casual grin. "Hey, you never know."

I smirk, clicking the pen dramatically before crossing his name off the list.

1. Benson
2. Liam
3. ~~Hayes~~

"Well, I can tell you right now, it's definitely not Benson," I say, tapping the pen against the page. "He doesn't have a hateful bone in his body." I glance up. "Except toward you."

"I do inspire strong feelings." He nods like that is just a normal thing for him and I guess as a brutal hockey player, it probably is.

I chuckle as I cross Benson's name off. Then a thought occurs to me and I add a name that shocks Callan.

1. ~~Benson~~
2. Liam
3. ~~Hayes~~
4. Detective Klein

"Think about it," I say. "You said he's been after you guys for a while, and he just so happened to show up right after I came back from burying that box with the rock in my hand. What if he's getting desperate and starting to play dirty?"

Callan looks angry, a red tint rising in his cheeks. "He won't get away with this shit if it is him."

"How would we even prove it?" I wonder out loud.

"If it is him, we have contacts who'll take care of it. But I don't think it was. Klein knows this goes deeper than whatever he was sniffing for with the rock."

"And what's that?"

Callan bites his lip. "Another time. But for now, let's just assume it's not him." He crosses his name off, but I'm not ruling him out.

"That leaves us with just Liam," I murmur. "But...I don't think so. Liam might be a little pushy, but he's harmless."

Callan leans back, arms folding behind his head, that knowing smirk tugging at his lips. "We all have secrets. Maybe he's pissed at you and thinks you had something to do with it. Secrets are what make people dangerous."

"Oh yeah?" I challenge, arching a brow. "Tell me one of your secrets."

He goes quiet for a beat, his expression unreadable. Then, without a word, he reaches for the notebook and pen.

I watch as he scribbles something down, then flips the notebook around and presses it to his chest.

"Can I trust you?" he asks, eyes locked on mine. "Like, really trust you?"

"Probably not," I say with a smirk, though my pulse is picking up.

His tongue clicks against the roof of his mouth. "I think I can. You've proven yourself." His tone shifts, low and serious. "But this stays between us. Aidric and Seb can't know."

Something about the weight behind his words twists my chest. He's about to give me a piece of himself, and I don't know what to do with that.

Callan finally passes me the notebook.

1. ~~Benson~~
2. Liam
3. ~~Hayes~~
4. ~~Detective Klein~~
5. Julian

My eyes lift. "Who's Julian?"

Callan leans back like we're just chatting about the weather.

"The owner of that tongue you burned and buried," he says, so casually it makes my stomach flip.

"What?" I gasp, the notebook nearly slipping from my hands. "You're telling me the guy who's missing a tongue is still alive?"

Callan doesn't even blink. "Very much so," he says, calm as ever. "Though I doubt he's giving any speeches anytime soon."

I smack the notebook against his chest, trying to hold back a laugh because this isn't funny. Not even a little.

But judging by the way Callan's laughing his ass off, he clearly disagrees.

"God, you're such a psychopath," I grumble, but the corners of my mouth betray me.

Before I can blink, he's grabbing me, pulling me into him until I'm practically in his lap. His arms wrap around me, fingers digging into my sides with relentless tickles.

I squirm, fighting him off through a mess of giggles. "Stop!" I shriek, laughter breaking free despite my efforts.

It's ridiculously wild that we're laughing over a guy out there with no tongue who may, or may not, have walked out of the shadows, dug up a box, and broke into my room.

Yet, this is the freest I've felt in a long, long time.

CHAPTER 27

CALLAN

SHE FITS in my lap like my body was meant to hold hers. Her skin is warm against mine, in a way that shouldn't feel this natural. The way she laughs lights me up from the inside out, sparking something in my chest that's been dead for a long time.

Suddenly, my hands stop moving teasingly around her body, and we both go still. Her head lifts, her inviting honey brown eyes burning into mine.

It's all fun and games until shit gets serious. I half expect her to crawl off my lap, to make a break for it and avoid letting things get too real. When she asked me to come up here, I wasn't expecting anything. I just knew I needed to see her.

Playing hockey is an adrenaline rush like no other, and after our win, the only person I wanted to share that feeling with was her. It used to be the boys, but they've slipped to the back of my mind. I don't wanna kick it with people I'm not sure I can trust anymore.

The way she's looking at me now, hungry and drenched in need, shifts something inside me. My heart thuds unevenly, and my body trembles from the sheer intensity of her.

Her hand rises to my cheek, fingertips dragging a slow line

that sparks beneath my skin. Temptation gnaws, and when I can't resist any longer, I crush my mouth against hers.

Her lips mold to mine perfectly, and when she parts them, I slip my tongue inside, tasting her. Our tongues dance, tangling with something that feels like more than memory—something new, something better.

One hand finds her throat, gentle but possessive, my thumb grazing the flutter of her pulse. The other moves up her side, catching the peak of her nipple beneath the thin fabric of her shirt.

She arches, barely, but it's enough for me to know she wants this. Then her arms wrap around my neck and I'm all fucking in with this girl.

I slide my hand down lower, tracing the curve of her waist and her hip before sliding up her jean skirt. Her thighs part, skin hot under my touch.

My fingers hesitate just at the edge of her panties, grazing but not yet touching. When I feel the dampness of her want for me and her slight shift forward, I accept the invitation. This isn't like before in the hospital room. I don't want to make her bend to my will right now. I just want *her*.

Pushing her panties aside, my fingers glide between her folds with ease, finding the slick heat of her. I test the waters, curious to see if she'll chase the pleasure I can give her as I trace slow, deliberate circles over her clit.

"Callan." She breathes my name like it's a secret, and I swallow it down. The hand around her throat pulls her closer, letting me deepen the kiss so all she feels is me.

I've kissed Avery before, but it was nothing compared to this. The fire, the intensity, the urge. It's almost too much.

I have to have her.

Her hand grips my shoulder, fingers digging in as she leans closer. I grind against her, my cock pressing hard against my jeans, aching for friction.

My head is dizzy with want and desire. Avery is like a drug, more potent than anything I have ever had before, and I'm already addicted.

Slipping two fingers inside her, she shudders against my skin. Her head drops to my shoulder, body curling into me as I drive deeper, fingers curling to just the right angle. I know my girl and I know exactly what she needs.

Her breath is hot against my throat, soft moans slipping from her as I slide my hand from her neck and pinch her nipple beneath her shirt. When she gasps, it sends goosebumps down my spine, and I can't help the smirk that spreads across my face.

Her hips tilt just right, granting me more space, and I take it, pushing deeper until she clenches around me.

She's so fucking tight and warm, and the thought of being inside her makes my cock twitch painfully.

She moves with me, riding the rhythm, rising and falling with every stroke. My hand returns to her neck, controlling her movements lightly.

Avery leans back and our eyes connect. I feel her pulse around my fingers as she tightens then relaxes like her body's speaking to me.

I glance down and notice her mouth slightly open, breathy moans slipping free like she can't hold them in.

Her lashes flutter and I can feel her unraveling beneath my hands.

"Oh God," she whimpers, and fuck, there's nothing more beautiful.

The sound fuels my need to see her unravel, for me to know I'm the one giving her what she craves and not anyone else. I thrust faster and harder, chasing the tremble in her voice, desperate to pull her over the edge just to watch her fall apart around my fingers...*again.*

Last time, she fought the pleasure, refusing to come undone. She pretended she didn't love it, but I knew better. I felt it.

Now, she's putty in my hands.

Her walls clamp around my fingers, and I curl them again, pressing into that spot I know drives her wild.

"That's right, Little Devil," I hum. "Come for me, baby."

She exhales a heady breath, fingers fisting my t-shirt like it's the only thing holding her together.

She falls forward again, burying her face in the crease of my neck. Her voice cracks against my shoulder with muffled sounds of pleasure. Her orgasm hits hard and I feel every wave of it ripple through her. Shaking against me, her breath stutters, her moans raw and wrecked.

When she finally relaxes against me, I guide her down, lowering her to the floor. My mouth connects with hers and I inhale every breath that comes out of her.

She parts her legs and I slide between, the ache for her twisting tighter as I grind into her.

Avery's scent wraps around me, her fingers dragging down my back before she grips the hem of my shirt. We break apart just long enough for her to pull it over my head. When our eyes lock again, something primal snaps.

We tear into each other like wild animals. It's unlike anything I've ever felt, the burning need between us erupting like a volcano. I devour her mouth, urgency pulsing through every inch of me.

Every emotion I've buried over the last four years crashes to the surface—love, lust, hate, anger, pain. It all hits me at once, and I pour every drop of it into this kiss. Like she's the only one who's ever accepted me for who I truly am, bitterness and all.

My lips move down to her neck, then over the slope of her chest, before stripping her out of her shirt and bra. Her skin is flushed, goosebumps breaking out where my mouth has been.

I keep going, moving to her breasts that fit so perfectly in my hands.

She gasps as I suck on the bud of her nipple, all teeth and tongue. Her back arches, pleasure radiating from her in waves. When I pull away, a devilish smirk curls her lips.

Avery moves her hands between us, lust-filled eyes locked on mine. She unbuttons my pants, and I sit back to kick them and my underwear off completely. When I'm done, I watch as she tosses her shirt across the room.

With almost nothing left between us, I press myself against her, the heat of her bare skin meeting mine. I cradle her face, fingers gently wrapped around her jaw, and kiss her hard before easing her back down, her hair fanning out around her like a halo of chaos.

My gaze drags over her as I slide her jean skirt down her hips, slow so I can savor her reaction.

We may call her Little Devil, but right now, she looks like a saint sent to save me.

Her chest rises, lips parted.

My fingers skim the hem of her soaked panties teasingly before I rip them off. She shivers and I can't tell if it's because she's cold or excited.

"Touch me," I tell her as I kneel in front of her.

She doesn't hesitate. She sits up slowly, eyes locked on mine as her hand reaches out, fingers wrapping around my thickness. I shudder as she strokes me, slow and purposefully, like she wants to feel every inch.

Without a word, she shifts forward on her hands and knees. The sight steals the breath straight from my lungs. Her eyes are hungry, her movements smooth like she's about to take what's already hers.

My shoulders pull back and I lean slightly as her lips wrap around my dick. A shiver runs through me as I watch her stroking the base of my cock, her tongue swirling my head like she's licking a lollipop.

"Jesus, Little Devil," I rasp as I fist a handful of her hair. I guide her rhythm, slow at first then deeper to match the heat building in my gut. "You look so pretty with your mouth wrapped around me."

Her eyes flick up to mine, sultry and heavy with desire. Fuck if that look alone doesn't undo me.

I watch, completely wrecked, as she takes every inch of me into her mouth. Her throat tightens on reflex, but she doesn't stop. Her lips stretch, jaw flexing as she pushes through it.

She hums sinfully, like she knows exactly what she's doing, and that revelation both thrills and infuriates me. The vibration shoots through me, hitting my balls first, and before I can brace myself, my orgasm threatens to break free.

I yank her head back, her hair still tangled in my fist.

"I need to be inside you," I rasp.

As much as I love her mouth on me, I need to fuck her. I need to feel her wrapped around me, skin to skin, nothing in the way.

Like the good little devil she is, she nods, even as spit slides down her face. Her cheeks are flushed, eyes watery, but I've never seen anything more beautiful. I help her off the floor, and once we're standing, I pull her into another bruising kiss. She comes to me willingly, like we both needed this moment more than anything else in the world.

Guiding her to the bed, I ease her onto her back, and she parts her legs as I crawl on top of her.

There's no need to ask if she's sure, I see it in the way she looks at me, feel it in the way her body pulls me closer.

She wants this just as badly as I do.

I lean in, mouth brushing her ear. "Are you on the pill?" I whisper before catching her earlobe between my teeth.

She gasps. "Yes."

With that, I press forward, sliding into her inch by inch. Her heat swallows me, stretching around the head of my cock like she was made to take me.

"Fuck," I breathe, the word torn from somewhere deep.

My eyes stay locked on hers as I push into her, filling her, pulling back, then sliding in again. Over and over. Euphoria consumes us, and we lose ourselves in the rhythm of each other's bodies.

The way she takes me, the way she looks at me, it undoes me.

I reach down and hook her leg beneath my forearm, lifting it to my side and opening her up just right.

"Damn, Callan." The sound of my name on her lips is pure sin. I can't help but smirk as I go a little deeper, watching her eyes roll back in absolute bliss.

"That feel good, baby?" I murmur.

She nods. "God, yes. Don't fucking stop, Callan."

"Not a chance, baby girl."

I drive into her...*hard*. Once. Twice.

Her body jolts with each push, back arching and her nails digging into my back. A few more thrusts and her head is flush against the headboard.

Her breath catches on a gasp, and I slide a hand beneath her neck, guiding her face to mine. Then I kiss her hard because I can't get enough of her mouth. Her lips part for me instantly, like she needs this as badly as I do. It's deep and messy and full of heat.

She tastes so damn good. Feels so damn good.

Dragging her nails down my back, her moans echo around us. I feel her walls contract around me, squeezing like they never want to let me go. She comes again, her body trembling beneath mine.

Fuck. Watching her come is like Christmas morning. The way her body tenses, then melts into bliss is a goddamn gift.

"Callan," she cries out.

That's all it takes.

A surge of electricity shoots through me. My muscles lock, every nerve lit as I come completely undone by the sound of my name on her lips.

"Fuck!" The word rips from my chest as my unstoppable orgasm crashes into me.

I freeze, buried deep, as I pulse inside her.

Then I thrust once more, riding out my release and making sure she takes every last drop of my cum. Our eyes meet and something I don't expect happens. Avery reaches up, her fingers brushing along the side of my face, wearing a smile that makes me want to go to war for her. Every cell in my body pledges its allegiance to her at this moment.

"I missed this," she whispers. "I think I missed you more than I ever realized."

Relief crashes over me, knowing she's not going to run this time. "I missed you too," I murmur, pressing a gentle kiss to her cheek. With an exaggerated sigh, I collapse on top of her, both of us breathless and spent. Her arms wrap around me like she never wants to let go, and I hold her just as tightly. Our skin is slick with sweat, the stickiness of our release clinging between us.

I shift, sliding off her carefully before rolling onto my back and pulling her into my side. She rests her cheek against my chest and takes a deep, steadying breath. We lie there in silence, letting our hearts sync. Avery doesn't move to get up, and neither do I.

"That was...nice," she says with a small giggle.

I tilt her head to look at me, eyebrows raised as I stare at her curled into my side. "Nice? It was fucking amazing."

"It was pretty amazing," she admits, her cheeks turning red.

A few more minutes pass before she stirs, her fingers brushing across my chest as she shifts. "I should go get cleaned up."

I nod, watching as she rolls off the bed and walks to the dresser. She pulls out a worn t-shirt and a pair of light pink sweatpants.

If we were in my room, I'd be slipping one of my shirts on her, looking like sin and mine all at once.

After grabbing a bag, which I assume holds her toiletries, she pauses at the door. Her hand ghosting the knob, eyes flicking back to me.

"I don't want to go out there alone," she says quietly. "What if whoever left that box is still out there?"

I sit up, jaw tightening. One of the many things I hate about these damn dorms is that the bathrooms are all the way down the hall and shared with complete strangers.

I'm on my feet in seconds, grabbing my boxers and yanking them on. "I'll go with you."

She lifts a brow. "In your boxers?"

"Sure. Why not?" I shrug.

Instead of arguing, she just opens the door and lets me follow. The hallway is quiet, too quiet. The kind that makes you glance over your shoulder more than once. Not for my safety, but for hers.

We slip into the bathroom and go into separate stalls to clean up.

When we get back to her room, we collapse onto the bed like the night wrung us out. The adrenaline is gone, and the weight of everything settles in.

Avery's head rests on my chest and I curl an arm around her, running my fingers up and down her arm.

"Tell me about Julian," she whispers, her fingers trailing lightly over my chest.

This is what I was afraid of. She knows too much now. I guess after she was branded, it was bound to happen. I could refuse, try to keep her in the dark so she might have a chance at freedom one day. But I know that's not possible. Once you're in, you're in. There's no going back.

"He was one of us," I say quietly. "An Ice Lord. Held my position before I did. Before he betrayed us."

I stop there because she doesn't need the weight of the rest. Doesn't need to know what came with that betrayal.

I don't tell her I was given the task of ending him and returning with his tongue.

I don't tell her how I drove four hours north with Julian barely conscious in my back seat, blood crusted on his shirt, bones shattered, and how I spent most of the drive praying to a God I wasn't even sure existed.

I wasn't begging for guidance, though. I was asking for forgiveness. Because I was gonna do it. I was ready.

Then I failed.

My hands were shaking violently, the knife pressed against the thin skin of his throat. Then his slitted eyes stared up at me as he muttered, "Please."

I broke.

I dropped to my knees screaming because I didn't know what the hell I was doing anymore. I couldn't kill him, but I couldn't walk away empty-handed either. As much as I believe in dedicating my life to this society, I didn't realize that meant signing up for murder. Sure we hurt people, but murder feels a little too far for college hockey.

As soon as I stood back up, I knew what I needed to do. Julian seemed to understand that if he wanted to walk away with his life, he'd have to make a sacrifice. Aidric's words echoed in my ears as an idea took shape: *"He used his dirty mouth to tell our secrets. Now it's your turn to silence him."*

And I did.

I went back to the car and grabbed a lighter, spending three solid minutes heating the blade of my knife until it glowed hot enough to do the job. When I told Julian to open his mouth, he didn't hesitate. He knew I was sparing him, and this was the only way either of us walked away from it—the only way he lived.

The slice was clean, even through his screams. And when I pressed the heated blade to the stump where his tongue had been, he passed out cold. That made it easier to get him to a hospital. By the time we arrived, he was conscious enough to walk himself inside.

He looked like complete shit, but it was that or leave him on the curb and hope someone found him. Hospitals have cameras, and we couldn't afford witnesses.

Avery's head lifts. "Is he alive?"

I look away. I hate her seeing this version of me, the one who hesitates, the one who fails.

"I don't know," I tell her truthfully.

I watched him walk in, but that doesn't mean he didn't die from complications. I don't think he did, though. I've been scouring the internet ever since, constantly checking for any reported deaths in the town where I left him. So far, nothing.

Aidric and Seb think he's dead. Hell, maybe he is. But I can't be sure.

"Then his name stays on the list," she replies. "We can't take any chances."

And just like that, her head lowers again, like we didn't just discuss a man having his tongue cut out. Like this is just another chapter in whatever twisted bedtime story we've fallen into.

A few minutes later, her eyes drift closed, but mine don't.

They stay wide open as the memory of Julian's broken voice bleeds back in, mixing with the haunting nightmare of the night Evan fell.

Two ghosts, two failures—both haunting me.

CHAPTER 28

AVERY

THE MINUTE MY EYES OPEN, Callan is shoving sweet tea and donuts into my hands, pressing a kiss to my forehead, and telling me to get my ass dressed. Says he has a surprise and wants to take me somewhere.

I don't even question it because when Callan gets demanding, there's no point in fighting. Besides, I'm pretty excited to spend the day with him. I just hope it's a normal day. We could really use one of those.

I can't even begin to guess where we're going, though. With Callan, it could be anywhere from a morgue to Sunday morning church. He's both a sinner and a saint in that way.

I stare out the window of his SUV, curiosity thrumming in my chest as my eyes track each building and street sign waiting for a clue.

But it's all familiar. We just passed The Effin Bar on Seventh Street, heading in the direction of the NRU campus.

We take a sharp right on Third Street, and I turn to look at him. "Are we going to the arena?"

He smirks, eyes still on the road. "Close. But no."

I growl under my breath, arms crossed tight over my chest. I love surprises. But I hate surprises. I'm weird in that way.

Callan reaches across the center console and gives my thigh a squeeze. "Almost there."

He's loving every second of watching me squirm, wonder, and overthink every scenario. And of course, he's not giving me a damn clue.

A minute later, I straighten in my seat, eyes going wide as the sign comes into view.

Callan just drives right past it like it's nothing, but my heart's going wild. My hands actually start to shake as I take in the scene unfolding around me.

"What are we doing here?" I ask, barely able to keep the smile off my face.

He doesn't answer right away. Just flashes me that knowing smirk that drives me mad and turns his eyes back to the road.

"Callan Cromwell!" I blurt out. "Why are we at NRU's archery field?"

He squeezes my thigh again, that cocky grin stretching from ear to ear. "I owe you, remember?"

I think back to the day he showed up to my dorm and we told a little lie to Avery that I was helping him and his team study. In return he was getting me access to his university's award-winning archery field.

I stare at him, stunned. "You're joking?" Then it hits me. "I don't even have my gear."

He tips his chin toward the back seat. "I got you covered."

When we pull into the parking lot, I look around, noticing it's oddly empty, aside from a few stray vehicles and two men talking in the distance.

At this time of day it should be packed. Not only is it Sunday, but mornings and evenings are prime for archers, when the light's just right and the air is still calm. Exactly how it is right now. It's a beautiful day for shooting. Not a single cloud in sight. Yet, the field looks empty.

"Where is everyone?" I ask.

"There is no one else," he says casually. "Just us. I rented the field for an hour."

"You what?" I gasp. "Callan! That had to cost a fortune."

He lifts a shoulder, completely unbothered. "It's worth it to see that look on your face."

I'm speechless. I can't believe he did this for me. I follow him as he pulls open the back door, prepared to give him hell and tell him this is too much and I can't accept it. But when he pulls out my case, my heart swells.

He put thought into this. He planned it. *Just for me.*

"Shall we?" he says as he closes the car door.

I roll my shoulders, my smile never fading. "I guess we shall." I bounce on the balls of my feet, barely restraining myself from leaping into the air and taking off in a run. This is, hands down, one of the coolest things anyone has ever done for me.

Callan exchanges a few words with a guy in a collared shirt and slacks, then he shakes his hand.

I trail close behind as he leads me onto the most stunning archery field I've ever laid eyes on.

A crystal-clear lake curls around it on three sides, with a meadow of wildflowers bordering the shore. The sky is flawless blue, and the sun is shining brightly, with snow-capped mountains resting in the distance. It looks like I could reach out and touch them, even though they're miles away.

The grass is pressed flat and crisp green. It literally looks like it was manicured by hand.

If it weren't already amazing enough, that's when I notice the lanes. Each one has stone borders and lanterns on wooden posts for after-dark sessions.

Even the targets are next level. All perched on a stainless steel tripod and marked with numbers for each lane. This isn't just a field, it's a stage.

"Pinch me," I say as I take it all in.

Callan laughs as he crouches down to open my case.

"I'll pinch you later," he says with a smirk, handing me my bow. "Right now, you shoot because we've only got an hour."

My shoulders drop and I press a hand to my heart, the bow cradled in the other. "You have no idea how much this means to me, Callan. It's probably...no." I pause, correcting myself. "It's without a doubt, the nicest thing anyone's ever done for me."

His hand drags through the air. "It's nothing."

The way he stands there so confident, so effortlessly sexy, it does something to me. Something I wasn't expecting. Something I'm not even sure I want. But it's there, and I can't shake it.

"It is," I say softly. "It's definitely something."

I like Callan. A lot more than I planned to. Over the past few days, he's gotten under my skin in the best and worst way. He's grown on me, and I'm starting to think he's not going anywhere anytime soon.

Our eyes linger for a moment before Callan breaks it, handing me my quiver clip.

A minute later, I'm in my lane, bow to my shoulder, drawing back the string. The world shrinks to this single point in time. Steady hands. Taut line. Just me and the target.

I center myself, breathe in, then release on the exhale.

The arrow lands dead center in the bullseye and I'm not sure who's more excited, me or Callan. But the way he's sweeping me into his arms and spinning me around, I'd say it's definitely him.

"Damn, Little Devil. That was fucking awesome."

I'm not sure when, or if, he'll ever stop calling me that. But as long as it's just him and not Aidric, I can deal. Honestly, I'll take it over Sebastian's *Little Lamb* any day.

Innocent and meek? Please. I'm a damn warrior. And after three more arrows sink into the bullseyes, I'm pretty sure Callan would agree.

As the hour closes in on us, I lower my bow from my shoulder and turn to face Callan with a wide grin.

"Your turn," I say.

"Me?" He presses a hand to his chest, then shakes his head. "Nah. I'll pass."

"Oh, come on," I taunt. "Just once. You never know, you might be a natural."

He drags a hand down his cheek, sighs dramatically, then strolls over.

"Fine," he mutters. "But if this thing flies past the target or ends up in someone's head, I'm blaming you."

I laugh, picturing it happening. "I'll take full responsibility."

He takes the bow from me, and I step aside, giving him my spot in front of the target. When he presses it to his shoulder, I reach in to adjust it so it sits just right. I could part his legs farther, but I'm not training him for the Olympics, so his stance is fine.

"Lucky for you, my strings aren't super tight," I say. "So you shouldn't have a problem pulling them back."

He scoffs. "Was that a jab?"

"Maybe a little."

"Well, in that case," he says, taking the arrow from my hand, "I'll let you know if it's tighter than what I had last night." He winks.

"Ohhhh," I drawl. "Smooth."

He lines up the arrow, and I catch the slight shake in his hand. It's cute seeing him nervous like this.

"How the hell do I do this?" he asks shamelessly.

I don't even ask if he's ever shot a bow, because it's obvious he hasn't.

"Draw the string back smoothly," I say, keeping my voice calm. "Use your back muscles, not just your arm. When it's anchored under your chin, close one eye and find your target. Focus on it."

He follows each instruction as I speak, and I won't lie, it feels kind of good having him follow my commands for once.

"Now, don't pluck the string. Just relax your—"

Before I can finish, the arrow sails through the air and sticks in the second outer ring.

"Not bad," I say, giving him a swift pat on the back.

He shrugs, totally unfazed. "I'll take it. At least I didn't kill anyone." He glances at his watch. "We should head out before they kick us off the field, though."

Callan tosses me the keys and tells me he needs to run in and thank the manager. While he's inside, I load my case into the SUV, then turn the radio on to "Risk" by Gracie Abrams. I crank the volume up and roll the front windows all the way down to let the cool breeze spill in.

When Callan returns, he pulls open the door and grins. "Loud enough for you?" He laughs.

I just shake my head, reach over, and turn it up even more, then I shout out the lyrics like I'm singing to save my life.

This was the best day I've had in a very long time and it's only ten in the morning. We've still got hours ahead of us, and there's no doubt in my mind who I want to spend them with.

CHAPTER 29

CALLAN

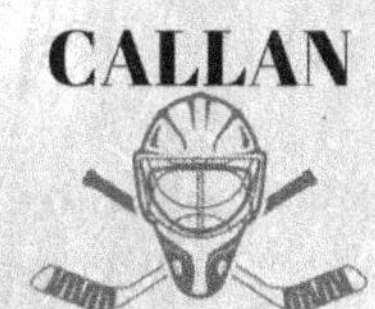

I PULL the mask over my face, the cool edge pressing against my skin as I round the curtain and step onto the altar beside Sebastian. Aidric falls in behind me, silent as ever.

It's the third Wednesday of the month, which means it's time for our monthly meeting in The Chamber.

"Decades ago, a man named Edison Einhorn stood in this very spot," Sebastian says as he looks down at the hem of his sleek black robe settling at his ankles. It's as if he's having an out-of-body experience.

"He held this very branding iron as the first Ice Lord took his pledge." He raises the iron in the air, the same iron we've all been branded with. Also the same one Avery was branded with.

She's not here, though. Just because she's marked by an Ice Lord, doesn't make her one. Which I recently learned.

Sebastian's voice grows louder, booming off the brick walls. "You shall have no mercy on the enemy. Where there is an Ice Lord, there is power," he howls. "And we are Ice Lords."

The seated members chant along with him, fists raised in the air as they repeat our motto. "Where there is an Ice Lord, there is power. And we are Ice Lords."

A moment later, Sebastian raises a hand, settling the crowd, and the room falls silent. His posture shifts, voice taking a serious edge.

"There's been talk," he begins, tone even. "Word going around about exclusivity."

He's referencing the conversation I had earlier with him and Aidric after I relayed Slade's concerns. Slade felt like we were keeping secrets, like he and the others were being kept in the dark.

Sebastian continues, voice cool but commanding. "We want to address those concerns. Myself, your Lord speaker, alongside your leader and your council advisor."

A pause stretches.

"You may have noticed a girl around lately," he says. "More than once. More than most. And I know how it usually goes. None of you keep women around longer than necessary. They don't linger. They don't last."

A few whispers and laughs rake over the crowd.

"But this one has," he continues. "Her name is Avery Castle."

He lets the name hang in the air for a moment.

"And while I won't get into the specifics of why she's still here, I will make one thing absolutely clear. Avery is off-limits." He eyes me, because that was my demand. "No one in this room will lay a hand on her. No one will harm her. If anything, you'll protect her like one of your own."

His gaze sweeps the crowd.

"Avery has become one of the few females to be branded into The Ice Society. She may not be an Ice Lord by title, but she *is* one of us. And she will be treated accordingly. Watch her. Protect her. Accept her." He pauses. "She's not going anywhere anytime soon."

After Aidric spoke with his father, who is a veteran in The Ice Society, we found out the truth. Avery wasn't the first. There have been other branded women. Some through marriage. others by initiation, and a few through force—like Avery.

We still don't know exactly what that means for her future.

But I plan to do everything in my power to keep her safe. Avery isn't just some girl to me—never was. I may have shelved the love I had for her in the past, but not anymore.

I can now say with certainty, Avery's future is with the Ice Lords.

With *me*.

CHAPTER 30

AVERY

"Oh no!" I laugh into the speaker of my phone as I twist the key in my dorm room door. "Did he chase him down and try to exchange him for a ten?"

I pause, hand still wrapped around the doorknob, as Brogan finishes her story about Hayes accidentally tipping their food delivery guy a hundred bucks instead of a ten.

Her voice bubbles through the speaker. "Yes! He tried, but he was on foot and the guy was in a fucking car. Needless to say, he didn't catch him."

Still laughing, I push open the door. But the second I look inside, the sound dies in my throat.

My smile vanishes because lodged straight through the comforter, in the dead center of my bed, is an arrow. The echo of Brogan's voice lingers in my ear, but I don't hear anything she's saying.

Frozen in the doorway, I choke out, "I…I have to go, Brogan. I'll call you later."

I end the call without waiting for a reply, the phone slipping to my side.

My heart is in my throat as I step forward, every breath shallow, eyes locked on the arrow like it might move.

As I get closer, something else catches my eye.

Tucked just beneath the arrow, partially obstructed by the shaft, is a piece of paper with a handwritten note.

I lean in slowly, heart pounding against my ribs, and squint to make out the words scrawled across the page.

Never trust a Lord who doesn't pray, and a Devil who doesn't sin.

My breath hitches, caught somewhere between my throat and my tongue, like I want to scream but know it wouldn't come out anyway.

The room suddenly feels like it's closing in on me. Like someone is out there, pushing the walls and pulling the strings.

My skin prickles, and for a moment, I swear I can feel breath on the back of my neck.

This wasn't just a warning. It was a message.

Someone knows something. But why me? None of this makes any sense. Why come after me when I haven't done anything except help cover up evidence, and even that wasn't by choice.

A full-blown panic attack slams into me like a freight train. My knees buckle under my own weight, and I slide down the edge of the bed, limbs useless as I land hard against the floor.

Why would someone do this? *Who* would do this?

The questions spiral, looping through my mind. My body trembles uncontrollably, fingers numb, mind swimming in a sea of terror. I lift my head for a second, eyes locking on the arrow sticking up from my bed like a twisted flag.

Then, second by second, something shifts inside me.

"No!" I shout, my voice raw and my eyes on the shaft. The panic is still there, but now it's mixed with fire. Callan was right, nothing gets done if I sit here and cry. And I refuse to let whoever this is have a single one of my tears.

"You won't win!" I scream, pushing myself to my feet as I

hear Callan shouting in my head, telling me to anchor myself. "You don't get to control me!"

This is real. *I'm real.*

In one swift motion, I reach forward and rip the arrow out of the mattress.

A sharp gasp escapes me. A smear of blood stains the shaft, like the arrow had been pulled from the heart of a deer and not a mattress.

I stumble back, my heart hammering against my ribs. When I toss the arrow down, I notice something new. The arrow has black-tipped steel with barbs that curve backward, designed to cause more damage if pulled out. I got a set of these after winning a tournament. They're my favorite because of the way they whistle slightly when I shoot them. The ones I won had my initials inscribed just above the metal.

This isn't just any arrow. *It's mine.*

I kick it away like it's on fire, then immediately pull out my phone. My hands are shaking uncontrollably, but somehow I manage to tap on the video icon next to Callan's name.

It rings, and rings, and rings, then he finally answers.

He's driving, one arm raised on the wheel, that gorgeous face lighting up my screen.

"Callan," I cry, breath hitching. "Please come over."

His smile vanishes, eyes snapping from me to the road. "Avery? What the hell is going on?"

"Can you come to my dorm?" I sniffle. "I need you."

He doesn't hesitate. The wheel jerks, tires squeal, and I watch him spin into a full U-turn.

"I'm on my way."

"Stay on the call with me," I whisper, "I'm scared."

"I'm here, baby. I'm not going anywhere." His voice shakes, terror written all over his face. "I wasn't far from you. I'm almost there."

The sound of him flooring the gas echoes through the speaker. "Be careful," I tell him.

My back presses against the door, and I find comfort in knowing it's there if I need to escape. Not that there's anything in here that can hurt me. Nothing except the splatter of blood on the floor and the deranged note beside it.

"Can you tell me what happened, Avery? Are you hurt?" His voice is laced with fear—real, raw fear.

There's no doubt he cares, and it's comforting to know I don't have to go through this alone. Not anymore.

"I'm not hurt," I tell him truthfully. "Not physically, anyways. But someone was in my room again."

"Who?" he stammers. "Do you know?"

I shake my head. "No," I say quietly. "But they left a note."

"Fuck!" Callan screeches. "Fuck, Avery. I can't stop."

My heart jumps, every nerve in my body prickling. "What? What do you mean you can't stop?"

His back slams against the seat, legs kicking like he's trying to outrun the panic.

"My brakes won't work!" He stares through the camera, through me, his eyes lit with panic.

"Callan!" I scream, the painful sound ripping out of my throat.

Suddenly, the screen jolts. His world tips sideways, metal screeches, and the phone seems to levitate for a moment as the car flips.

Then the call drops.

"No!" I scream, collapsing to my knees. "Callan!"

This is my fault.

All of it.

EPILOGUE

CALLAN

"AVERY," I call out, but my voice splinters, breaking apart in the thick haze. Smoke curls around me, swallowing every sound.

I try to move, but I can't.

I'm pinned.

My head's twisted sideways, jammed against the crushed roof. I'm hanging upside down, blood fucking everywhere.

Gazing around, I search for my phone, but I don't see it. I don't hear her beautiful voice anymore.

Swallowing hard, I worry when it feels like glass is scraping down my throat.

The visor snaps open and the map dangles above me, clinging to the clip like it knows one wrong move means the end.

Then I see a small corner of the picture behind it. I move my arm, shrieking through the pain as I stretch up.

"Fuccccck," I howl as I pluck the picture down.

It flutters into my hand and I hold it like it'll somehow get me through this. It's Avery and her mom—the one she had in her music box.

After I grabbed the box from her room, I stole the photo. Told myself I'd get it back to her someday without her knowing it was me.

But that was before. Things are different now.

She was just a wide-eyed kid in this photo, untouched by the world. No idea her future would be swallowed by the Ice Lords.

My body might be a wreck, bruised, crushed, and screaming in pain, but it's nothing compared to the weight sinking into my chest.

She needs me and I'm not there.

I shift my shoulders, fighting the cage of twisted metal around me. Something's gotta give. Blood drips down my face, hitting my lips. I drag my tongue across them, spit, then keep pushing to free myself.

Just then, I hear the shuffle of footsteps outside the door. About damn time someone came to fucking help me.

"Hello," I call out. "I'm here. I'm stuck."

A pair of black boots steps up to the shattered window. They're so close I could reach out and grab them if my left hand weren't stuck.

"Hey!" I shout louder. "A little fucking help, please!"

But I hear no response.

The figure crouches down in front of the window frame, and that's when I see the robe and mask.

One of *our* masks.

My breath catches. "Who the hell are you?"

He doesn't say anything, just reaches inside the car like he knows exactly what he wants. Then he rips the photo from my hand.

"Give that back!" I shout as loud as my compressed lungs will let me.

I look into the eyes of the mask, but all I see are hollow black holes.

He isn't one of us. He isn't an Ice Lord.

"I'll fucking kill you," I seethe.

Still clutching the photo, he stands and disappears from sight.

The ear-splitting screech of metal grinding against concrete rips through the air.

"Help me, dammit!" I shout, heart hammering, gut twisting with unease. Something's wrong. *Something is really fucking wrong.*

The sound of sirens rings out. I exhale, relief rushing in.

Then, flames roar to life around me. In less than a minute, heat licks my skin, smoke choking the air. I have to heave for breath but I do it, pushing through as much as I can because she needs me.

My eyes grow heavy, despite my fight to stay awake.

Flickering black spots consume my vision.

Without my permission, the world fades away.

"Avery," I whisper, barely more than a breath as I hang onto her name.

Then, darkness swallows me whole.

The End. For Now.

I hope you enjoyed the first book in the Ice Lords series.
I promise this isn't truly the end.
Ready for more?
Preorder Bend The Pucking Rules now! http://mybook.to/btpr

ALSO BY RACHEL LEIGH

Ice Lords

Book One: Break Your Pucking Heart

Book Two: Bend The Pucking Rules

Bastards of Boulder Cove

Book One: <u>Savage Games</u>

Book Two: <u>Vicious Lies</u>

Book Three: <u>Twisted Secrets</u>

Wicked Boys of BCU (Coming March 2023)

Book One: <u>We Will Reign</u>

Book Two: <u>You Will Bow</u>

Book Three: <u>They Will Fall</u>

Misfits

Heartless Monster

Wicked Scandal

Beautiful Devil

Redwood Rebels Series

Book One: <u>Striker</u>

Book Two: <u>Heathen</u>

Book Three: <u>Vandal</u>

Book Four: <u>Reaper</u>

Redwood High Series

Book One: <u>Like Gravity</u>

Book Two: <u>Like You</u>

Book Three: <u>Like Hate</u>

Fallen Kingdom Duet

<u>His Hollow Heart</u> & <u>Her Broken Pieces</u>

Black Heart Duet

<u>Four</u> & <u>Five</u>

Standalones

<u>Forget Me Not</u>

<u>Ruthless Rookie</u>

<u>Devil Heir</u>

<u>All The Little Things</u>

<u>Claim your FREE copy of Her Undoing!</u>

ACKNOWLEDGMENTS

Thank you so much for reading Break Your Pucking Heart. I'll apologize now for that ending, but I hope you enjoyed the rest!

A special thanks to my wonderful team for all the hard work you put into helping me create this book: My dedicated PA, Carolina Leon. All my girls for your support, friendship, and advice. My Rebel Readers VIP team for your help in getting the word out.

A an extra special thanks to…

My amazing alpha reader, Taylor you are a true gem! Not just as an author and reader, but as a friend. Thank you for everything!

Tease Designs for the stunning covers!

Fairest Reviews Editing Service for the beautiful edit!

Rumi Khan for proofreading and being so flexible!.

Valentine PR for spectacular PR Services.

XOXO Rachel

ABOUT THE AUTHOR

Rachel Leigh is a USA Today and International bestselling author of new adult and contemporary romances. She loves to write—and read—flawed bad-boys and strong heroines. You can expect dark elements, a dash of suspense, and a lot of steam.

Her goal is to take readers on an adventure with her words, while showing them that even on the darkest days, love conquers all.

Rachel lives in Michigan with her husband, three little monsters (who aren't so little anymore) and a couple fur babies. When she's not writing or reading, she's likely lounging in leggings, with coffee in her hand, while binge watching her favorite reality tv shows.

Join My Reader's Group: Rachel's Ramblers

facebook.com/rachelleighauthor

instagram.com/rachelleighauthor

bookbub.com/profile/rachel-leigh

goodreads.com/rachelleigh

amazon.com/author/rachelleighauthor

pinterest.com/rachelleighauthor